THE LONG SEARCH

BY ISABELLE HOLLAND

The Long Search
A Fatal Advent
Bump in the Night
A Lover Scorned
Flight of the Archangel
A Death at St. Anselm's
The Lost Madonna
Counterpoint
Marchington Inheritance
Tower Abbey
The Demaury Papers
Grenelle
Darcourt
Moncrieff
Trelawny
Kilgaren

THE
LONG
SEARCH

ISABELLE
HOLLAND

DOUBLEDAY
New York   London   Toronto   Sydney   Auckland

PUBLISHED BY DOUBLEDAY
a division of Bantam Doubleday Dell Publishing
Group, Inc.
666 Fifth Avenue, New York, New York 10103

DOUBLEDAY and the portrayal of an anchor with a dolphin
are
trademarks of Doubleday, a division of Bantam Doubleday
Dell Publishing Group, Inc.

BOOK DESIGN BY CLAIRE NAYLON VACCARO

Library of Congress Cataloging-in-Publication Data

Holland, Isabelle.
    The long search / by Isabelle Holland. — 1st ed.
        p.   cm.
    I. Title.
PS3558.O3485L58   1990
813'.54—dc20   90-34993
                                                  CIP

ISBN 0-385-26545-X
Copyright © 1990 by Isabelle Holland
All Rights Reserved
Printed in the United States of America
November 1990

First Edition
BVG

For Carolyn Anthony
with thanks

Somebody once said the past is another country.

She had made it not only another country, but another continent. The iron curtain that had once been so impregnable was no more so than the wall she raised, brick by brick, between the girl she once was and the woman she became. Conscientiously, with great care, she had obliterated every possible trace of that girl with her terrible secret. . . . So that no one, ever again, could know or could find her.

But she had forgotten about one person, someone she had once loved.

Now his moment, the moment he had built his whole life towards, had come. Nothing stood in the way except the girl who was now buried. To find her, and eliminate her, became the one necessary step he must take before he could drop his mask and come out and change the world.

If it involved a few deaths, he reasoned, so be it.

1.

I suppose, on some level, I had been looking for her for the past eighteen years. But if so, that level was not where I could reach it or even be aware of it. To me the matter was closed, beyond reach, put out of my life forever. And then, suddenly, it was back, and the embers of an old hatred blazed into flame.

It's terrible to hate your father, a violation of the old commandment: "Honor thy father and thy mother, that thy days may be long in the land the Lord thy God giveth thee." As with several of the commandments and other great principles, extenuating circumstances don't count. The fact that my father was dead and I hadn't seen him for a year before his death hadn't alleviated my loathing. I simply thought it no longer mattered. . . .

■ ■ ■ My office at Braddock and Terhune, publishers, was small, inconvenient and did not overlook Fifth Avenue. The larger offices that did were reserved for the president of the corporation, the editor in chief and their highly placed, highly paid flunkeys. But I didn't envy them. I had a glimpse of Central Park, several blocks north, and, by craning around my twenty-sixth-floor window, could see a small patch of Hudson River. To be a newly promoted senior editor of one of the leading publishing houses at the age of thirty-seven was not a bad accomplishment. Considering everything.

And then came the day that Patti Strong of the Human Resources Department—a new and fancy name for Personnel—passed by with a sheaf of papers in her hand and wandered in, putting a couple of them on my desk.

"What are those for?" I asked, eyeing them. In the course of my life I had come to mistrust forms of all kind.

"New insurance rules," she said blithely. "There's going to be better and more health coverage, all explained in the first sheet, and everybody has to have a complete physical before the beginning of the month."

I picked up the first sheet. "Why?"

"Like I said, it's a new insurance outfit. They're going to cover more medical expenses, but they want us to have physicals at the beginning. After all, it's only reasonable."

Along with mistrusting forms, I don't like rules that are touted as being for my own good. "I had one."

"When?"

I evaded the issue. "A while ago."

"How big a while?"

"I can't give you hour and date, Patti. But I don't see why I have to be weighed and measured and thumped and invaded just because we have new insurance."

"You're always so difficult," Patti said.

"Since you only got here three months ago, what's with this 'always'?"

She sighed. "It's in your file. Everybody else goes along and sticks out its tongue and says 'ah' but you practically have to have a court order before you'll do it. What's the matter with you? It's all for your own—"

"Don't say it!" I almost yelled. And then, when her round young face started showing genuine alarm, I said, "I'm just an anarchist."

After she left, I looked at the huge form, designed to track every stray health issue, however wispy, turned up by every physical examination and blood profile however general or even inaccurate that I'd ever had. Remembering some of those examinations, and where I'd had them, and under what conditions, I let out a crack of laughter. The slightest hint of any of them would send a shudder through the distinguished company I worked for and the even older insurer who was now promising to do so much for my own good.

Thinking of this I contemplated with relief the fact that I lived in a country where it is easier to disappear—and then reappear—than in most western nations, where identity papers are part of everyday life. Quietly I slid the form in the waste basket. I knew it was only postponing the day. Sooner or later, Patti, or someone, would come around and inquire when I would have the form made out. I would pretend that it was done and already handed in by my secretary. After that it would take another while for them to find out they couldn't locate it. Who knew what postponing action I could take after that? But I had become a master at small, unimportant delays. When the last delay was finally thrust aside, then—but that was in the future. I grinned to myself as I remembered a story I had once heard on a television program. It went something like this: In the days of old, a jester at a royal court did or said something that angered the king. The king ordered him to be arrested and beheaded. The jester fell to his knees and pleaded for his life, saying, "If you will just be merciful, Sire, then, within a year I'll—I'll teach your horse to talk."

The king said, "Very well, but if, at the year's end, my horse doesn't talk, your head falls." And he walked away. The jester's friend said, "Are you crazy? What were you thinking of? You can't teach a horse to talk!"

The jester shrugged. "Who knows what will happen in a year? In a year I might die, or the king might die, or the horse might die—or the horse might talk!"

Where had I been when I saw that television program? I remembered, then, where. And how many years had I spent counting on the fact that, ultimately, the horse might talk?

■ ■ ■ At three that afternoon my telephone rang and the receptionist announced William Macrae, author of a book I'd been assigned. His previous editor had left for another house and he, along with the departing editor's other authors, had been reassigned. There were others of the books I'd have preferred to have, but Macrae's was considered by everyone else to be the plum. Written in a down to earth, "just the facts, Ma'am," style, the book, titled *Exposé*, chronicled the tracking down of two men and a woman employed in sensitive areas of government, who had first fed classified secrets to the Russians and then defected. It was considered by the other editors and the marketing staff certain to be a blockbuster best-seller, and I was thought lucky to be given it.

Actually, I was not too happy about it, but there wasn't anything I could do, and made an appointment to meet the author this afternoon.

So, when the receptionist said Macrae was waiting, I got up, glanced in a small mirror tacked to the wall and gave a slight push to my dirty blonde hair. Slowly, over the years, I'd let it go back to its natural undistinguished color, and found a certain satisfaction in seeing once more a part of my old self. I knew I looked less than my thirty-seven years and that the suit I had on was flattering to my taller than average and rather spare figure. As I stepped out of the door of my office an old, accustomed dread of meeting someone I didn't know and had never seen before slowed my feet for a moment. Then, as always, I shook it off and went out to the waiting room.

■ ■ ■ William Macrae was tall and thinnish with a big frame, blue eyes and gray-black hair. A proper Irishman, I thought, or a cop. Then I reminded myself he was simply a journalist who had gone after a story and written it down. Nothing but that.

I walked forward and held out my hand. "Janet Covington," I said.

"How do you do?" His hand, long in the fingers but broad across the palm, clasped mine.

"Come on back into the office," I said. "We can talk there. I must tell you," I said as we sat down, "how much I enjoyed reading your book." It was a lie, but a necessary one. "It was extremely well done." That much was the truth.

A faint color touched his cheeks. "Thanks." Then, abruptly, "Haven't we met before?"

I was aware of the sick thunk of my heart, but managed to say in a normal voice, "I don't think so. At least I have no memory of it. Are you sure?"

He shook his head and smiled, relaxing his rather austere face. "No, not really. I just thought—for a minute—that you looked familiar."

"I think I must look like everybody's girl next door," I said lightly, "I've been told that before."

He shook his head. "No, you don't. I must have been wrong."

We went over the galleys and I made a few minor suggestions of my own, indicating a cut here and there that would speed the action.

To my vast relief he agreed to everything. Apparently he was not overly burdened with author's ego, although if his book were to become a best-seller, I wondered how long that pleasant state of affairs would last.

It was after about an hour of work and conversation that I finally identified something in his voice. "Are you English?"

"I grew up there," he said. "But I'm an American and have been back over here quite a few years."

"Of course," I said. "I remember now. I read it in your bio sheet."

I waited for him to go on. Most people are chatty enough about their lives. But he did not explain or offer any further comment. "Well," I said, "why don't you let me know when you finish these small revisions and we can have lunch." It was an offer I should have made when I wrote to him, telling him that I was now his editor and looked forward to meeting him. I had inherited two more of the departed editor's authors, and I had taken them both to lunch. Why hadn't I done the same with Macrae? There were plenty of acceptable excuses: my calendar for the next week or two was filled; the other authors were relative unknowns who would probably be flattered and thrilled at being taken to a fancy lunch; one was an elderly woman, the other a boy, barely out of college, who had pasted together some amusing sports anecdotes; I had not enjoyed reading Macrae's book (although I had to admit it was well written) and didn't like lying about it. None of those was the real reason for not inviting him to lunch, of course, but I decided not to dwell on it. Paranoia could get out of hand, I told myself.

He stood up. "All right. I'm a fairly fast worker, so I should be calling you in a day or two. Thanks for your suggestions, I think they'll improve the book. Good-bye," and he was out the door before I knew it.

■ ■ ■ There was a promotion meeting that afternoon, and I doodled as I listened to Linda Barry, the house's publicity director who seemed to operate perpetually in fast forward, describe all the goodies she had lined up for *Exposé*.

"The 'Today Show,' 'Live at Five' and '60 Minutes' are all interested," she said, "and that's only a beginning. Janet, when are we going to see copies of the final proofs?"

"As soon as he's finished the revisions."

"I thought he'd finished the editing."

Suddenly I remembered a waft of gossip that had come my way: Linda had lately been showing more than a professional interest in one of our authors. Somehow I had figured it was an author whose book was already published. But with something of the publicity potential of *Exposé* it was more than likely that Cecy Summers, Macrae's previous editor, would have brought publicity into her planning at an early stage. There was also more than a possibility—in fact, just about a certainty—that Cecy, in her new job, would do her best to re-attach Macrae for his next book.

I woke out of my musings to realize Linda was staring at me intently, waiting for an answer. The trouble was, because my mind was on something else, I'd only been half listening and now couldn't remember what her question was. Not smart, I told myself. I might have been recently promoted, but Linda had been a power at Braddock's for several years and to everyone's certain knowledge more than one publishing house had tried to woo her away.

"Sorry, Linda," I said, and then suddenly remembered what she had asked. "I asked Macrae to do some minor revisions which he seemed to agree with. As soon as I get the changes, advance proofs will take only a week or two." At that I also remembered that Linda and Cecy were good friends. Which did not mean for one moment that Linda wouldn't be loyal to Braddock's interests, but friends gossip, and publishing, even today, is small enough to be like a village. I saw that my own enthusiasm should not seem to be lagging. "Cecy did a super job of editing —and Macrae is, of course, a terrific writer—but a couple of recent events made it necessary to cut the last chapters."

"Okay," Linda said. "Let me have the copy as soon as you can. By the way when do I get to meet him?"

So Macrae was not her current romantic interest. I smiled. "Soon."

"Good," she said, and went on to a different book. Maybe, I thought, at that fancy lunch I would have to take Macrae to, I should also invite Linda. The thought gave me both pleasure and an odd disappointment.

■ ■ ■ By the time I got back to the apartment on Charles Street in the Village, Paul was already there, half reading the New York *Times,* half pretending to read what looked like somebody's dissertation and wholly listening to some angry politician on television.

"Do you think you're going to do justice to whatever student has toiled over that thesis or dissertation?" I asked, as I went in and dumped my things on a chair.

"He doesn't deserve justice," Paul said. "He's been reading my book, *Campaign Fraud,* and had the nerve to dispute everything it proves."

I didn't say anything, having just seen the drink in Paul's hand. Since on Wednesday his classes end at about three o'clock, this could be his first, second or even third drink, and if it were the last, that would mean his contentiousness level would be high.

"Well, isn't that a kind of compliment? Instead of any sociology text, he decides to take on your famous denunciation of the American political system?"

"Po-faced little squirt!"

"Watch it! Your raisings are beginning to show. If you're not careful, somebody'll take you for a down-home good ol' boy."

There was a short silence. "I never denied being a Southerner."

I almost spoke what was on my tongue, which was, No, not if you could make some mileage out of it. Because if Sinclair Lewis had achieved fame by stripping the American small town of any rag of the illusion in which it was once held by the American public, Paul had done the same for American politics. "We excoriate Soviet Russia, call it the Evil Empire," was one of the more ringing quotes from *Fraud,* "but oh how we love those lying speeches about how this is the land of opportunity for everyone."

I went to the kitchen to make my own drink, which consisted of a diet soda poured over ice.

When I returned, glass in hand, Paul, without removing his attention from the politician, still declaiming and still angry, asked, "And how was the great creative world of publishing?"

"Okay." After a moment I added, "I met a new author today."

"What's so special about that?"

I sat down and swallowed a large mouthful of soda. "This one wrote *Exposé*—you know, the book I told you about."

"You mean the umpteenth one about Communists in our midst?"

"Yes."

"What's he like? Some sort of redneck conservative?"

There was one thing about Paul, I thought. His prejudices were as dependable, predictable and immune from argument as those of radicals, fundamentalists, yuppies or, for that matter, the KGB itself.

"Right on," I said.

Paul Davenport and I had been living together for the past

three years. We'd met at a party given by the National Institute of Arts and Letters to which I'd been taken by the editor in chief, Dirk Bowman. "It'll be dull and boring," Dirk had said, "but the drinks will be superlative and the company fascinating —filled with potential authors!"

Paul turned out to fill all of those happy portents. His book was a modest success, especially in academic circles, and a year later he moved into my apartment. His old apartment, on Riverside Drive, was still occupied by his former wife and three children. Ours had been a fairly happy relationship, but I knew Paul had found it less than totally fulfilling. More than once he had said to me, bitterly, "If you'd ever come from behind those defenses, I might get to know whoever it is you're shielding back there."

And I had tried, really tried. But I—the real I—had spent too many years in hiding for me to be able to do this. We loved and battled and had a passionate sexual relationship, but as Paul commented bitterly one night, "With you, it's thus far and no farther." Then he got up out of bed, dressed and went out and got drunk. I didn't see him until the following evening.

"Well," Paul said now. "Is he?"

"Is he what?"

"A redneck Southerner?"

"No, neither redneck nor southern. As a matter of fact—" I stopped.

"As a matter of fact what?"

"He was brought up in England."

"Redneckness is a state of soul, not body."

"He's not a reactionary. At least, I don't think so. His book just logs what happened, day by day, step by step. No editorializing." I thought for a minute. "Historical analysis but no rhetoric."

"Sounds dull."

"I profoundly hope you're wrong, or our large advance will have been wasted."

"Talk about heart-rending tragedy!"

I decided greater wisdom lay in changing the subject. "You want me to fix something, or should we go out to dinner tonight?"

"Where are you suggesting"

"Maybe Foo's?"

"I'm tired of Chinese. I want something . . . something French."

"All right. Leblanc's. I'll make a reservation."

■ ■ ■ On the following Monday Macrae had his changes ready.

"You're quick," I said approvingly. "That's wonderful! Did my ideas work out?"

"Always," he said. "Now how about that lunch?"

I was aware of two impulses, one to try to postpone it, or better still, get out of it altogether. The other a thrust of pleasure. I glanced at my desk calendar. "Are you free tomorrow or the next day?"

"Tomorrow."

"Good. How about the Four Seasons at twelve-thirty?"

He smiled. "You mean that expensive, ritzy place?"

"I do. Any objections?"

"Absolutely none." He got up. "See you there."

I spent the rest of the day reading his revisions and mentally congratulating him. At least two of them were rather subtle, and it would have been easy by cutting and revising to make them stick out, even be strident. But he had avoided that. Then my eyes stopped as they read a new paragraph in the middle of the book. I reread the sentence I had just read: "My early years as a federal agent stood me in good stead here . . ."

I read it again, and then pulled Macrae's bio sheet from his file in my drawer. As I remembered, there was no mention of it in his bio.

2.

I sat at my desk staring at the bio file for I don't know how long. At the end of that time, I could have recited the bare facts: William Christian Macrae, born San Francisco, California, 1947. When father entered U.S. Foreign Service, moved with family to Switzerland, Guatemala, England. Private schools, England. Oxford, M.A., Columbia School of Journalism, reporter on Washington *Post, Time.* Divorced, two children.

Nary a mention of being a federal agent at any time. If he knew he was going to mention it in the course of the book, why not say so in his bio? Was he ashamed of it? Surely if he were doing undercover work even now, he wouldn't have spilled the beans in the book. If he was, what kind of work? Investigating what? Whom? On the other hand, maybe he just forgot. Remembering his face, I couldn't make myself believe he forgot.

I started to pick up the phone, then put it down again. You can't see the face of the person you're talking to on the phone. Holding the bio file, I walked out to the bank of elevators and pushed the down button. When I was delivered to the floor below I followed one of the labyrinthine hallways to Linda's office. I could see her through the glass partition, on the phone, as always. Knocking lightly on the doorpost, I went in, and when she turned and indicated the chair beside her desk, sat down.

"Okay, then," she said into the receiver. "We'll have him there at four and I'll pick him up an hour later." She put down the phone.

"I ought to go with Joe," she said to me. "He's sweet, but tiresome. And anyway, after ten books he ought to know the ropes."

"True. How about a luscious and expensive lunch tomorrow at the Four Seasons with Macrae and me?"

"Don't you want to be alone with him?"

It was so on target it almost took my breath away. I glanced quickly at her, but her penetrating dark eyes were no more piercing than usual. In fact, if you made allowance for the fact that she resembled nothing so much as an avid bird dog, she didn't look anymore than normally predatory.

"I wouldn't put it like that. His first, last and middle name is publicity, so I think your presence would add considerably to his pleasure." I told myself if it were not true now then it probably would be very shortly. Else why did he write the book?

"Okay. I'll have to cancel a lunch with Esther Martin—you know, our tender novelist of relationships and sensibility. But first things first. If she sells out her first printing it's going to be a marvel."

A spurt of anger went through me. First novelists of any kind were—or should be—what publishing was about. Suddenly I remembered a small bookstore in Boston where I used to drop in after school and an old man, the owner, his hand lovingly stroking the spine of a long out-of-print novel, discoursing on books that had barely sold out their first printing and were now classics.

"Yes, I know what you probably think about that," Linda said.

"How do you know?" I asked coolly. Once I had been told by

a lover that everything I thought and felt showed instantly on my face and in my eyes.

She shrugged. "Maybe I was guessing."

I smiled. "I'm as fond of profits as anyone. After all, they pay for the less-profitable, literary books."

"Indeed yes. Well, I'll be happy to join you. What time? Twelve-thirty?"

I nodded and got up. "By the way, his bio file here does not say anywhere that he was a federal agent."

"Was he?"

"According to a comment he made in one of his revisions that he just delivered. It wasn't there before."

Linda got a faraway look in her eye. "Strange. But good. We can get a lot of mileage out of that."

The next day Linda and I shared a cab to the restaurant, deliberately getting there about ten minutes early. A good table in a corner was reserved for us and the waiter hovered, waiting for drink orders.

"Scotch and water," Linda said.

"A diet coke," I added.

Linda glanced at me. "You never drink, do you?"

"It doesn't agree with me. I'm inclined to go to sleep."

"I'm glad it doesn't have that effect on me. Here comes our author."

I had been watching the door and was aware when he appeared there. Was that disappointment flickering over his face when the waiter started leading him towards us? The room wasn't lit brightly enough for me to see. And anyway, what was that? Wishful thinking?

"You've met Linda Barry?" I said. "Our publicity director?"

"No. I haven't had that pleasure. Hello."

"Well," Linda said, as he slid between us and sat on the banquette. "You're one of the few authors whose publicity photos don't do justice to. After seeing the pictures, most authors are a severe disappointment."

I'd heard Linda deliver that line more than once, but this time she was right.

Macrae smiled. "I'll have to pass that remark on to my friend, Andy, who took the pictures. Maybe he can charge me more in future." He looked at me. "Were the revisions okay?"

"Terrific. You really did a good job."

He nodded.

Linda cleared her throat. "As I told the promotion meeting the other day, we're in the happy position of being able to pick and choose among the top shows for you, because they all want to have you. Believe me, that's a publicist's prayer. We spend most of our time begging and pleading to get our authors on anything!"

"That's gratifying," he said, not sounding particularly gratified. He looked me. "Don't you think so?"

"Absolutely. I know they're working on a cross-country tour to coincide with publication in early September."

"To say nothing of the bookstores that want you for signing," Linda put in. "And speaking of which"—she glanced at me—"you have an editor who's had her own publicity."

"Come off it, Linda," I said, uneasy.

"Oh, what?" Macrae asked.

"It was in a *Newsweek* story on changes in the publishing world and new rising stars." Linda indicated me. "Your editor among them."

"Linda exaggerates," I said. "As usual. The rising star they were talking about was Jack Lederer, our new managing editor. I just happened to be talking to him at some publishing gathering when the camera shot us."

"Yes, but the caption mentioned you," Linda said stubbornly.

I pushed away the unworthy thought that Linda wished she

had been the one talking to Jack. I did, too, however. I was never happy to have my photograph, however casual, appear in public.

"Maybe that was why I thought I'd seen you," Macrae said.

"Probably," I agreed with relief.

Macrae dropped his bomb. "I don't mean to seem ungrateful. Any publicity here in the New York area—within reason, of course—is fine, but I don't want to travel."

"Why not?" Linda's words came out like shots.

"Drink, sir?" the headwaiter, hovering, asked.

"Scotch and water."

"Yes, why not?" I asked, when the headwaiter went away.

"My children will be staying with me from mid-August to the middle of September. I don't want to be away then."

"Fatherhood has its prices," I said drily. "It's a pity, though, a coast-to-coast tour right after Labor Day could send your sales up mightily."

"We'll just have to push them up without that."

"For the sake of the book—and my job—" Linda said, "I have to ask you if you couldn't forgo this vacation with them? Even in as big a house as ours, with as many best-sellers, missing publicity opportunities for a book like yours is a shame—a . . . a real shame."

Knowing Linda, I was aware that she was on the point of calling it more than a real shame—something more like a bloody outrage. Her face, with its permanent tan, had grown darker, which meant she was angry. To have a glittering publicity prize like this snatched from her was almost more than she could bear.

"I'm wondering if we could postpone publication till October when your children will have left," I said. "It's usually better not to postpone a book. All the hoopla put off and then off again inevitably takes some of the icing off the cake, but if it meant you could take a tour then—"

"Yes," Linda said. "That might be a way out."

"Sorry," Macrae said. "I don't mean to mess up your plans, but I have things I have to do in the later fall."

Silence.

Then Linda, in a different, light voice said, "Well, we'll just have to do the best we can now, won't we? Let me go over some of the plans that are shaping up for New York."

I knew Linda, and I knew she had by no means given up on putting Macrae on talk and news shows from New York to L.A. She had simply regrouped and decided to try another tactic. Well, I thought, as I listened to her chatting about this talk-show host and that, good luck to her. This promised to be a case of the immovable object and the irresistible force and it would be interesting to see who won. I wanted Linda to win. I wanted Macrae occupied with his book and occupied elsewhere. I was surprised at the strength of my feeling.

■ ■ ■ It was a small item in a California newspaper, one I would normally never see, but one of my authors, exhilarated by hometown publicity, had sent me a clipping. There's an old rule in book publicity: the smaller the hometown, the bigger the hoopla can be, and, according to this paper, the whole town, including the one bank, three churches and all the stores had turned themselves inside out to pay homage to their native son, tying their ads and announcements in the town's weekly paper into the publication of his book.

"Wow!" the happy author had written on the top of the full page he'd sent. I smiled, glanced at the other side and was putting it in my Out box for filing when the name at the bottom of the page caught my eye.

Blair is not that unusual a name. Theodosius Blair is. I couldn't make myself believe that there was more than one. When we were all growing up together outside Boston we called him Ted. Anybody who called him Theodosius was liable to get a punch in the nose. He was in my class at school and, before the terrible shoals of adolescence came upon us, we were good friends. After that, I referred to him as the "dumb jock" and he called me Wacko. Our relationship went downhill from there. And then, some years after I had started on my own fearful journey, he married my younger sister, Julia. I only knew that because I read it in one of the Boston papers. By that time I had severed all ties with my family. Or perhaps it was Father who did the severing. As he said the last time we spoke, "I never want to see you or talk to you again as long as I live. None of us does. Ever."

It was the kind of thing, particularly in the late sixties and early seventies, that enraged parents were saying to their dropped-out children or the children were saying back to the parents, with unspoken reservations on both sides. Or, if there were no reservations, Time, the great healer, did its job, the children eventually passed the high-water mark of thirty and diplomatic relations were resumed. Or common sense, or normal affection or familial need finally surfaced. Or something.

But not in our case. I had gone too far. The wounds had been too savage. And forgiveness had never been our strong suit.

So what had happened to Ted Blair, my brother-in-law? And for that matter, my sister? What were they doing in California? My eyes went back to the news sheet. Ted Blair had made the paper because he had been killed in a car accident. What was much more of a shock was the statement at the end of the article that Julie had died two years after the marriage, giving birth to their only child, a boy, named Anthony, after his maternal grandfather.

So Julie was dead. I was surprised at the sadness that flooded me. Julie and I had not only not been close. We hadn't even liked one another. My father, who hated me, adored her. She had always been exactly what he wanted: small, delicate, shy, the dream child, the perfect girl, the ideal daughter. Instead, as his first girl, he got me, dubbed The Lump at school, because in those days I was not only tall and gawky, I was fat. And my father, who was fat, detested it. Every time he looked at me it was like looking in a mirror, a humiliation he could not endure. Eventually, I got thin—not healthily thin. Anorexically thin. And how I loved it. . . .

Back to Julie. She had been dead now for more than eleven years. I found my throat aching, the first herald of tears. Why should I cry? It had been so long, and even the memories were bad. Yet I got out some tissue and blew my nose and prepared again to toss the paper into the box. I could have found out anything I wanted to about all this years ago. Surely I was not, at this stage, suffering an impulse to bring back together the severed pieces? I had never regretted the complete split with my family. It had been as much my choice as my father's. Why now this strange ache? I started once more to put the news sheet in the Out box.

This time it was the last sentence in the small news item that stopped me. Anthony, the son, had died at the age of four as a result of complications stemming from hemophilia.

I stared at the word and then threw the page into the box. That was the end of our family. Julia and I were the only children. Both parents were dead. Even thinking the word "our" was a betrayal of my old self. I had repudiated them. They had repudiated me. Now they were all dead. Rest In Peace, I thought. *Requiescat in pace.* All of you.

■ ■ ■ Like most other people I knew about the most famous hemophiliac of all—Alexis, the Tzarevitch, son of the last Tzar of Russia, Nicholas II. Russia, locked into its mediaeval social system, was due for a volcanic eruption. But the illness of the heir to the throne and the royal family's dependence on the mad monk, Rasputin, who seemed to be the only person who could bring temporary healing to the child, contributed to the ferocity of the Revolution when it did come, and to the exile and execution of the entire royal family. Books had been written on the subject and more than one film made. I also knew that the disease is hereditary. Beyond this, what was there to know? I decided to see what the house library might offer on the subject.

At the end of an hour's reading of various standard medical references, I had learned that hemophilia is almost always manifest in males, but that the immediate carrier of the gene is female. It is thus through their mothers that sons get it.

Surely I had heard that before! So why was this relatively common piece of knowledge bringing such a chill with it?

Because if Anthony, my sister's child, had had hemophilia, that meant it had come to him through Julie. It was a recessive gene, according to the learned document I had just read, so the fact that there had been no instance of hemophilia for at least one generation before us was normal. But before that? My mother's parents were born in Europe. That's all she knew about them, because she had been adopted. But that wasn't important. Anthony had been a hemophiliac; he had inherited it from my sister. Did that mean that I, too, could be a carrier? To find out whether I was or not was not difficult. All I needed was a blood test. If I were not, fine.

If I were—

I pushed the haunting old pain out of my head. That was gone, gone, forever. How many years had I spent hammering that into my consciousness, so that I could hang onto my sanity —once so fragile and threatened?

I got up and pushed the books away for the librarian to see to. I won't think of that, I thought.

3.

But, of course, I did.

That night, as Paul and I were eating our tortellini and salad I heard myself ask casually, "Do you know anything about hemophilia?"

"No, why?" Paul asked. "Has somebody submitted yet another book on the Tzarevitch?"

"More or less." Already I regretted bringing up the topic. But with my dislike of all institutions, which included foundations and organizations, I had shrunk from taking the obvious path of directing my questions to anybody in the medical or related fields. "It's a proposal for a book on famous people who've had it," I improvised. "I thought if you knew anything I could pick up some information the easy way and be better able to make a judgment." It was a poor explanation, but the best I could come up with at short notice.

"Any book today would have to have a big section on hemophiliacs who get AIDS and or hepatitis from the blood transfusions most of them have to have. Largely because the incompetent medical establishment's too lazy or too stingy or both to have the blood checked properly. In a decently run government agency—"

My heart leapt up. "You mean you can catch hemophilia? Surely not—"

"Don't be a dummy! It's hemophiliacs who catch AIDS from blood donors."

"Yes," I murmured. "Stupid of me."

"As I was saying—"

I tuned Paul out and went back to trying not to think about

the nephew I never knew I had who had died from a genetic disease which he could only have gotten from my sister. And from everything I had read in the office library, that meant that I had a fifty-fifty chance of being a carrier myself. A blood test would make it certain. If the test determined I was not a carrier, I had nothing to worry about. If I was—

"Hello, hello out there. Janet, it's me, Paul. Come back, little Sheba . . ."

I snapped out of my ponderings to see Paul waving his fork in front of my face.

"Do you do this often?" he asked.

"You've lived with me for three years," I replied. "What do you think?"

"I think it's come over you more lately. Are my charms fading?" There was a bite to his voice.

"Sorry," I said. I put my hand out and brushed his arm.

"Touching," he said. "Literally and otherwise. I'm sure you'd much prefer to be spending time with your new author than with me, anyway."

I was astonished. "What a weird statement!"

"Is it?"

"Yes. It is. Is that why you've been so . . . so cross lately?"

"I hadn't realized I'd been cross."

"Maybe not. But anybody who knows you couldn't miss it." I smiled. "Your argumentativeness reaches a higher level. You don't say 'Why haven't you paid more attention to me lately?' You say something like 'The political system is beginning to collapse of its own weight,' or 'The political establishment is showing itself for the institutional hypocrisy it always was,'— words along that line."

"Are you suggesting it isn't true? That the phoniness of—" he stopped. His mouth lifted in a half smile. "Am I really that much of a bore?"

"No, Paul." As I said it I knew that it had become true. I

had once loved what I took to be Paul's idealistic intensity even though I was convinced it was useless. When had it—for me—become hollow, an out of date posturing? "I just mean for you it's an all-purpose sort of grumbling when what you're really mad about is something else, maybe something more personal. Is there something else?"

"I just told you. You've seemed somewhere else these past few days." He looked at me. "Are you?"

All my carefully assembled defenses told me to lie. But I decided to tell the truth. "Yes. But it's nothing to do with Macrae—or any other man."

"Something out of that past of yours that you never talk about."

"Yes."

Inquisitive though he could be, Paul had a rigid sense of honor when it came to poking into affairs that people he cared for wanted to keep secret. It came, I suppose, from his youth as a fiery radical in the early seventies: burning his draft card, protests, demonstrations, confrontations with the police, running off to Canada. Friends of his had gone underground, others had been jailed. He was middle-aged now and a member of the sober middle class, supporting a divorced wife and children, teaching in a distinguished university . . . but the old codes held. Of all people he would be sympathetic to what I could tell him. But my jaw seemed locked in place. "Yes," I repeated finally, knowing how inadequate it sounded.

There was a moment's silence. Then he got up. "I have papers to correct," he said.

"Paul." I got up too and went over to him and put my hands on his arms. Because of my height, his face was on a level with mine. It was a handsome face, with blue eyes and blond hair in which the gray hardly showed. But there was something in his eyes that made me—for the moment—forget the tired rhetoric and familiar bluster. I put my arms around him and kissed him. "I'm sorry," I said, though I wasn't sure for what. I had once loved him as much as I could love anyone.

■ ■ ■ I could, of course, wait for the free examination promised by our super new insurance. At that point I remembered that I had thrown the form away, so I made a point of strolling past the medical office.

"Hi," I said to Patti. "I seem to have lost that form you left. You'd better give me another one."

"Well, that's an improvement!" She opened her desk drawer and took out the form. "Usually I have to come after you."

"I know. I'm allergic to forms."

"So are a lot of other people. You'd think we were trying to spy on them or something, instead of giving them new wonderful coverage."

"You sound as though it was you they were rejecting—no, you don't have to explain," I said hastily as she opened her mouth, and I remembered how full of enthusiasm and lacking in humor she was. "I understand. By the way, I have a question. Just how fearless and searching is this test? I mean, if you have some . . . well some weird disease in your family background, would they find it out in the blood tests and so on?"

"What weird disease?"

"Nothing in particular. Just curious." And I got out, kicking myself once again. I could just hear her comment to the head of her department. "What genetic horror do you suppose Janet Covington is trying to hide?"

Well, I'd have to deal with that when it came my way. There wouldn't be anything automatically threatening in my saying my nephew died of complications resulting from hemophilia and can you test me to see if I'm a carrier—if it weren't for the fact that embedded in the rest of the fiction I supplied the personnel department when I was hired was the statement that I was an only child.

A long time ago, in that other country called the past, my mother had once said to me, "The trouble with telling a lie, Felix, is that you'll have to tell at least seven more to cover it."

That was in the days when my name was Felicity and my mother and sister called me Felix. Not my father, of course. Like everything else about me, he disliked my name and used it as little as possible. It had been my mother's choice and he had grudgingly gone along. Consequently, as the relationship between us, never good, got worse, he compromised by calling me "Daughter"—like something out of a dour nineteenth-century novel. I grew to loathe the word.

But all this was not getting me any further.

When I got back to my office I resorted to the telephone directory, and when that yielded nothing, to calling various hospitals to see if any of them had any genetic expert I could talk to. When they asked me why, I told them about my nephew. And when I finally discovered a genetic counseling department in one of the bigger hospitals, I even told them my name. After all, it was not my real name, and they assured me everything would be kept confidential. So I made an appointment. I found, when I hung up the phone, that my heart was beating frantically and told myself that I did not have to show up for the appointment —I had not given them my address or phone number and I was not in the telephone book.

I looked up from the telephone and saw Macrae standing there. "How did you get past the receptionist?" I asked more sharply than was entirely suitable for such a potentially big author.

"I didn't sneak past, if that's what you mean. There wasn't anybody at the desk. Do you want me to leave?" He spoke with the same chill I felt.

"No, sorry. It's just—never mind. What can I do for you?"

"I thought you might have lunch with me, if you weren't busy. Or is that a foolish assumption?"

"No, of course it isn't." At that point I meant to explain that I was busy. But as a matter of fact, I didn't have a date. Or I did, but I could easily change it. Rather to my astonishment, I said, "Fine," and wondered if I'd gone out of my gourd. I didn't hobnob with federal agents, either past or present.

"All right. How about The Bazaar on West Fifty-sixth Street?" He paused. "Why are you surprised?"

"Because I thought you'd pick some place like . . . well, like—"

"O'Leary's Bar and Grill?"

I grinned. "Is there such a place?"

"As a matter of fact, yes. Do you want to go there?"

"No. But The Bazaar caters to people who go in for quiche, veggies and salads."

"And you thought I didn't look the type. You shouldn't indulge in such stereotype thinking!"

"You sound like Paul."

"A sensible man, I'm sure. Who is he?"

I hesitated, then said, "The man I live with."

"A man of good taste, too. As well as wisdom. What time shall I meet you there?"

"How about one?" My appointment at the genetic offices was at three-thirty. That would give me just about the right amount of time to get across town.

"One it is. See you there."

■ ■ ■ I tried to work on a manuscript, calling on all my experience in blotting out everything except what I was doing at the moment. It was a talent I was proud of and usually didn't have much difficulty in exercising. But this morning I found myself reading sentences and whole paragraphs not twice but three and four times. By the time twelve-thirty came along I was heartily wishing I had made the appointment earlier and decided to walk there instead of taking a taxi. At least that would absorb some of the time.

Macrae was sitting at one of the wooden tables frowning at the menu when I walked in.

"Are you sure you didn't make a mistake?" I said, sliding into the chair across from him. I looked around, salads of all kinds abounded on every table. "It's very green."

"No, as a matter of fact, I rather like salads and vegetables. They made a pleasant change from army food when I came out, and I kept on with them."

I decided on one of the numerous salads and was ready when the waiter came up. "A diet coke and a Mexican salad," I said.

"A beer and a chef's salad," Macrae said.

"You didn't say you were in the army in your bio."

"I didn't think it was particularly relevant."

"When were you in?"

"During Vietnam."

The word itself was once an offense. "Were you drafted or did you volunteer?"

"I volunteered."

"Why?"

"I felt guilty about getting deferred simply by being in college when those who weren't were being drafted."

"So no protest or an escape to Canada?"

"It didn't strike me as an acceptable way out."

I once could have said a lot to that. Once I would have got up and walked out. Once I wouldn't have even sat down unless I checked out his basic assumptions. Like Paul. Now I went on eating my salad.

He drank some of his beer. "Why does that upset you? Were you on the other side of the barricades during that disastrous episode?"

"At least you say it was disastrous."

"Yes, but my reasons might be different from yours."

If I went on with this conversation it might lead me down roads I had avoided now for nearly twenty years. "Yes," I was surprised to hear myself saying. "Like a lot of other college kids, I was on the other side of the barricades."

I waited for him to say something, but he didn't. So I said, "Another thing that wasn't in your bio file was that you were a federal agent. Did you leave that out because you thought it was irrelevant?"

"Yes. Does it make you angry?"

"I'm not angry," I said and realized I was.

"In that case when you are angry you must indeed be formidable!"

I laughed. "Why did you become an agent?"

"I did some investigative work in the army and when I got out the job was offered to me. I took it, spent a few years working at it, then decided I wanted to be a journalist. So I quit and went to the Columbia School of Journalism."

"I bet you found plenty of people in journalism who weren't a bit enthusiastic about your background."

"You can say that again. Prejudice abounds on all sides. I'm convinced I missed out on two jobs I wanted very much when that detail was discovered."

"Is that why you wrote this book about the three who gave secrets to the Russians?"

"No. At least not directly. I was given the assignment when the whole business started unraveling—probably because my editor thought my background would help in rooting out all the information. The book came out of that."

I knew I could ask more questions along the line of "What kind of investigative job did you do for the army? For the FBI? Tracking kids who were being rebellious?" But I didn't dare.

"Tell me about your background," he said. "What brought you into publishing?"

It was an ordinary question often asked. Why then did I tighten up?

"Or let's talk about something else, if you'd rather," he said.

Macrae was neither stupid nor insensitive. "No, I don't mind," I said, and proceeded to trot out the story that had been mine since I had first painfully put it together. "I was brought up in New York. My father was an accountant with yearnings towards the literary life. I went to school here and got my first job on a small magazine that subsequently went out of business. Then there was another magazine that went under—no connection, I hope—and finally got a job as an assistant to an assistant at Braddock's."

"No college?"

"Night school from time to time."

"Funny, I'd have said you come from New England, around Boston."

"Who are you? Professor Higgins?"

He smiled. "If you grow up abroad you become very good at accents."

"Why?"

"Well, in my case, I talked English English at school to keep myself from getting into a fight at the first jibe about a Yank accent, and American at home, to keep from being blasted by my father who looked upon broad A's as the first signs of subversion."

"Did you like going to school there?"

"Yes and no. I was the only American in every school I went to until Oxford, so I had a permanent exile complex. On the other hand, there are qualities I like about the English and I got an excellent education."

Suddenly my eyes fastened on a clock set into a high partition. "My God—I have an appointment in twenty minutes. I have to go. Here, let me pay my share!"

He pushed his hands against mine rooting in my handbag. "Not this time. Run or you'll be late."

■ ■ ■   When I got to the genetic counseling place I told my tale and waited while they took my blood. "How long before you can tell me?" I asked.

"A few days, maybe a week. We'll call you."

4.

It was a bad week. Paul got drunk every night and we had stupid, silly fights over nothing. Macrae's book had gone into production with RUSH written all over it, and I got a call from the copy chief. "Jan, if you want this rush-rush, then you're going to have to accept the fact that there are some facts we won't have time to check."

"Such as?"

"Such as the author's statement that Senator Bates got his son out of a drunk-driving charge in Virginia through pulling wires and a little genteel blackmail, and the deputy head of the Justice Department was mixed up with a doozie from the local call girl circuit. Your author was pretty good about giving references on practically all his assertions, but a few, like those, don't have any. Have you checked with the legal department?"

"Not yet."

"Well, see if he can back up his statements."

I called Macrae and got his answering tape. So I left a message to phone me as soon as he could.

I called the copy chief back. "I left a message on Macrae's tape, but don't wait. Flag what you need to check and go on. We're pushing to get the book into the bookstores by Labor Day."

■ ■ ■ That night Paul and I went to a friend's house for dinner. Jason and Alison Hovik were both colleagues of Paul's at the university, Jason in the history department and Alison in chemistry.

Things started out poorly before we even got there, beginning with a swift exchange when I asked Paul if he liked my dress.

"New?"

"Yes. I ran into a shop on Madison when I was coming back from lunch one day." I swirled around. The skirt was long and full and I thought the green color looked well with my rather tawny hair.

"Must be nice to have money enough for Madison Avenue."

"For Pete's sake, Paul. It was on sale."

"Hundreds—no, thousands of homeless in the streets, and you drop what—four hundred dollars?—on a dress when you have a closet full?"

I recognized the signs. Paul had had a drink in his hand when I got home. I didn't know how many he had while I was showering and dressing. But it was fairly obvious he was getting drunk and picking a fight.

I turned. "What are you mad about tonight, Paul? No, I'm not talking about my fall from grace by joining the middle class. I mean, what are you really mad about?"

He glared at me, then put his drink down. "Let's go. It's time we got started."

The evening went downhill from there.

■ ■ ■ Jason and Alison Hovik lived on Morningside Heights in an old rambling apartment overlooking Morningside Park and south Harlem.

"Every time I come here I go through spasms of envy," I said, as we got out of the cab.

"Why?" Paul asked, paying off the cabbie. "It's no longer exactly a refined neighborhood. The Third World is closing in and even you with your upscale salary would find it difficult to pay for cabs both ways going to and from work. When, that is, you couldn't put it on your expense account."

"I suggested coming by bus," I said.

"We'd have had to start an hour earlier, which would have meant your getting home from the office earlier," Paul said. "An unthinkable contingency."

I turned to him. "You've been spoiling for a fight all evening. If you want one, that's fine with me. But we'll have it here or go back home and have it. I'm not having you make an ass of yourself and me in front of other people. Or you can go on in by yourself."

There was a tense, unpleasant silence. Then Paul defiantly marched up the four steps to the apartment house door and rang the bell. I followed slowly enough so that by the time I got there the front door was being buzzed open. We went up in the elevator, standing side by side, facing the door, silent. When we got to the eleventh floor the Hoviks' door was open and Jason was standing in the doorway.

"It's been much too long," he said, smiling. He shook Paul's hand and kissed me on the cheek.

The other guests were already there. One couple I knew: the

husband was in the Romance Languages Department at the university, the wife, I believe, taught art history. I'd never met the other couple, an attractive woman with red hair and her husband, a tall, good-looking man with graying black hair and a falcon's profile. Their name seemed to be Cunningham. I wondered which of them taught up the hill at the college. The conversation before dinner turned on various tidbits of university gossip. Drinks were poured. I took a soda and lime. Paul accepted two of Jason's powerful martinis in fairly rapid succession. When I saw how tightly my hand gripped my glass, I realized how tense I was. I made myself relax my hold and tried to calm down. The Cunninghams seemed an intelligent, amusing couple, though I still couldn't figure out their connection to the university.

We were in the middle of dinner when the conversation took a political turn. I glanced at Paul. His face was flushed and his eyes had a shine to them. Alison said something about an item that had been in the news—a protest of some sort that had taken place on the steps of the Capitol in Washington. I was trying frantically to think of a way to wrench the subject matter onto a less incendiary topic (as far as Paul was concerned) when I heard his voice. "You should ask Janet about that. She seems to be joining the right wing with her new FBI author."

There was a dead silence. I said, "He's not in the FBI any longer. He's a journalist. Anyway, I can't choose the authors that are assigned to me when another editor leaves."

"What's the book about, Janet?" Jason asked.

"It's a fairly low key account of the three people who recently defected to Russia—you know, the two men who worked in some supersecret agency, and the girl friend of one of them who was in another department involving national security. The book isn't accusatory. It is a 'just the facts, Ma'am' kind of account, but it is fascinating to know what kind of people they were and how they came to do what they did."

By now Paul had pretty much abandoned the food on his plate and was drinking the white wine that went with the meal. "But isn't it interesting that it's an ex-agent who's chosen to do that? Not the kind of reporter that anyone would trust, not here, at this table, anyway, except, of course, for Janet."

Silence.

Brett Cunningham said, "Well, in England they've had quite a few books about Philby, Burgess, McLean and Blunt."

"At least they had some class!" Paul exploded.

"If you mean in the social sense, yes. But does that make it better?"

"The point is Janet's own defection—"

I got up. "Excuse me," I said, and went into the bedroom where we'd put our coats. Then I shut the door, because I didn't want to hear whatever Paul was saying. I knew now that I had to do something about our three-year relationship. I was not surprised when the door opened and Alison came in.

"I'm terribly sorry, Janet. But I'm not sure what we can do to calm him down. I'd suggest that he leave, but God knows what he might do to you on the way home." She sat down on the bed. "Why don't we stay in here a while. Maybe Jason can calm him down."

It suddenly struck me that she was not very surprised. "You don't seem, well, astonished, at the way he's behaving," I said.

"It was just a matter of time, wasn't it? Given what's happened in his department."

I turned towards her. "Why? What's happened?"

"You don't know?"

"No."

There was a pause. Then, "Oh."

"What did happen?"

She said slowly, "There was a full professorship coming vacant. Everybody expected Paul to get it—most of all Paul. But he's not going to. He's being passed over."

The anger and drinking that had shot up lately suddenly made sense. But which was the chicken and which the egg?

"Why, Alison?" I asked. "Whatever his faults, he's always been a good teacher."

"One obvious reason is that he got drunk too often at the wrong parties and insulted the wrong people. You were at one of those yourself."

Yes, I had been. My efforts to point out, after the fact, that that wasn't the best way to treat the people who had the power to promote or not promote him brought on one of our worst fights. After that, I went as little to his parties as I could.

"Somehow," she said. "Somehow I thought he would have told you."

"Things—things haven't been going so well between us lately."

There was an awkward pause. "What's all this about your ex-FBI type?"

I squashed down a feeling of impatience. "Like I said, he's an author I inherited. The book was contracted for and written before Cecy, his former editor, left. I don't know why Paul's made a federal case out of this." I paused. "If you'll forgive the word."

"Well, we both know he's a sixties radical who gloried in being against almost everything you can think of—especially anything to do with the government and all its investigating agencies."

"But isn't he doing exactly what he accuses the government of doing—giving somebody a bad name on an out-of-date charge, and never letting up on him."

"Maybe he feels a little sauce for the gander is in order."

At that point the red-haired Mrs. Cunningham came in. "Sorry to intrude but nature calls."

"I'll get back," Alison said.

I knew I ought to do something—leave altogether or go back

with Alison to the others. But I didn't move. In a few minutes Mrs. Cunningham—I hadn't caught her first name—came out of the bathroom. Since I'd never met her before I expected to feel some embarrassment at the scene she'd witnessed. Curiously, I didn't. She hadn't said much during the drinks and dinner, but there was a quality about her—a kindness and warmth that was somehow also detached—that I found reassuring. So instead I asked, "How are things in there, now?"

"After a while Jason managed to get Paul off the subject of the FBI. For how long, I'm not sure. He showed signs of being a homing pigeon on the topic." She smiled a little and started running a comb through her hair.

"You're not by any chance a doctor, are you?" I don't know what made me ask that question, except for the anxiety that now underlay everything else in my life.

"No. Why?" She hesitated. Then, "I'm a priest and a psychotherapist. I don't know if either of those categories would be of help, but if they are—"

I found the fact that she was a priest astonishing. I looked up. "Apart from the fact that you're Mrs. Cunningham I don't even know your name."

"My professional name is Claire Aldington. I'm an assistant rector at St. Anselm's Church down on Lexington and Sixty-second Street."

It seemed far away from the university world. "How do you know Alison and Jason?"

"Alison and I went to undergraduate school together and have remained friends." She paused again. "Did you ask about my being a doctor because of Paul?"

I shook my head. I had known everyone who was at this ill-fated dinner for much longer than I had Claire Aldington and her husband. Yet it was to Claire that I could finally tell some version of the truth.

I was startled to hear myself say, "I've just found out that a

nephew of mine—one I didn't know I had—died as a complication of hemophilia. I've also learned just enough to know that his
mother, my sister, must have been a carrier, and there's a fifty-
fifty chance of my being one, too. I had a blood test a day or so
ago, and am waiting for the results."

"I seem to remember that you don't have any children, so is
this with the future in view?"

"No. No one, and I mean no one alive today—at least to my
knowledge—knows this. But I do have a daughter. She was born
when I was eighteen. I never even saw her. It was a bad birth. By
the time I came out of the anesthetic she'd been taken for adoption. If I am a carrier, she may be, too. I have to find out if she's
still alive, and if so, who and where she is. And I have to do it
before she has a child of her own." And I started to cry.

5.

Claire had been kind and wise, letting me cry, occasionally pat-
ting my shoulder and handing me tissues. When I finally
stopped she said, "I take it Paul doesn't know."

I shook my head. "No."

By the time I got back with the others Paul had passed out in
the spare bedroom. I was more relieved to go back home alone
than I wanted to admit.

That night I lay in bed, wide-awake, thinking about my conversation with Claire. For all her professional credentials I was
still surprised that I had confided in her. The burden of the

secret I had carried for so long must have become far heavier than I'd realized. It had burst out of me like a lanced boil. And, of course, it was only part of the truth. Now all I could do was to wait for the report from the blood test.

Paul was back home when I returned from work that day. Neither of us said anything. He looked bad, his face sallow and the lines deep. I was fairly sure that he had not been drinking when I walked into the apartment, but a while later he asked me politely if I wanted one.

"Not right now, thanks," I said, hoping it would inspire him to abstain. Of course it didn't. "Suit yourself," he said, and poured himself a martini. He took it back to his chair with him and retreated behind his copy of the *Times*.

Feeling stupid, I started to pour myself a soda. When I sat down I said, "I'm sorry about . . . about the professorship."

"Yeah." He folded back a fresh page of the paper.

"Is there anything—"

"Look," he said, and lowered the paper. "I don't need your sympathy. It's all the usual politics. I've had feelers out, and it looks as though I might get an offer from another place." He took a large swallow from his drink. "I think you and I have about had our run. I'll stay here until the offer comes through, and then I'll make other arrangements."

"But that won't be until next fall, will it?"

"Maybe sooner. Why? Because you can't wait for me to go?"

"It's not that—"

"Don't lie!"

"All right. When you're like this, now is not too soon. Is that what you wanted to hear?"

We stared angrily at one another. I no longer loved him. Living with him had become like living with a time bomb. Yet I knew he wasn't well, and I worried about what would happen to him.

He got up suddenly. "I'm going out." He snatched his coat

from where he had thrown it when he came in and left the apartment, slamming the door behind him.

I sat there, staring at my drink. I had a manuscript to read, another to finish making notes for for the next editorial meeting. There was plenty for me to do, yet the thought of sitting by myself going doggedly through a book, page after page, was almost worse than I could bear.

But it had to be done.

It was late when I got to bed. Even so, Paul hadn't come in yet. And he wasn't there when I woke up the next morning. There was nothing I could do about it.

The phone call came in two days later. My blood test showed that I was a carrier of hemophilia, that any daughter of mine had a fifty-fifty chance of being a carrier. Any son of mine had a fifty-fifty chance of having the disease. Would I please come in so they could counsel me on what to do?

"I can't come in right now," I said, "and there's no urgency in my finding out what to do now. I'll call later and make a date." And I got off the phone.

■ ■ ■   The trouble was, I had no idea how on earth to go about finding my daughter. I had spent eighteen years trying desperately not to think about her, but she was always within me, a layer of pain and anger beneath everything else. When I finally accepted the fact that my initial frantic and terror-stricken efforts to find her proved useless, I flung myself into a self-destructive chaos that lasted seven years and almost cost me my reason.

My father knew, of course. He was the one who took her. When I came out of the illness that followed her birth, my daughter was gone. Father had taken her and given her to somebody somewhere. I begged and stormed and pleaded and promised anything if he would just tell me. But he sat there in his chair, his eyes like blue marbles, his face and bulky frame a heavier male version of my own, spouting idiocies about his duty and the child's own good and, most of all, my total incapacity for bringing up anyone.

"After all, look at you!" he said.

"I thought you wanted me thin."

"I wanted you to look like a girl—a pretty girl—not like a bag woman."

Despite everything, I grinned. From being pudgy I had become anorexic. My bones stood out—and not just the interesting ones. "I thought you liked me skinny," I said. "You certainly talked enough about it when I was growing up."

He just stared. He had the clout and the power because he alone knew where my daughter, Laura—in my mind I had named her Laura—was.

I abandoned trying to find out from my father. I went to the hospital, but their records revealed only that they had sent Laura home in the care of my father and a baby-nurse.

"Who was the nurse?" I asked.

They had no idea.

I went back home. "I'll be a good daughter," I promised. "I'll live at home and go to college and graduate with a good degree. No more drugs or rock bands or wild friends. I'll be exactly what you want me to be, if you'll just let me have Laura."

"You know how much your promises have been worth in the past."

"I'll do all this for a year. I promise. If you will tell me where she is after that."

"You couldn't keep it up for a month, let alone a year. Remember the promise to study? Not to sneak out at night? You were fourteen then. The next thing I knew you were being brought home by the police—stoned out of your mind."

"This is different."

"No, I want my granddaughter to have a chance." He

paused and then dropped his heavy weapon. "You won't even tell me who the father is."

As I was silent, he added with heavy sarcasm, "If you know."

I knew all right, and I was desperately afraid he knew—or suspected. As I debated how to answer so as to infuriate him least, he veered. "One of your radical friends, no doubt."

I welcomed the diversion. "We have a right to our own opinions."

"Including tearing down the school? Sitting in professors' offices? Destroying their research work? That's a right?"

My father, also a teacher, had lost ten years' worth of research from a student sit-in in his office. The kids had grown bored. Boredom had led to anger. They decided my father hadn't been sufficiently sympathetic to their cause so they would punish him. They went through his files and systematically destroyed his notes and research on what was to be his major book. That was before I knew I was pregnant. When I learned about it, I can't remember whether I was stoned or drunk, but I told him it was the most liberating piece of information I'd ever had.

Looking at him as I pleaded to learn where he had put Laura I knew we both remembered it. "All right. I shouldn't have said what I did. I'm sorry you lost your research. I'm sorry for all the other things. I'll be everything you want me to be."

"We'll see."

At that moment I wanted to kill him more than I had ever wanted anything—except to find Laura. But my father didn't matter. What mattered was getting Laura back, and if it meant cleaning up my act, sanitizing myself, then so be it. I'd promise anything to have her again. And once I had succeeded and she was with me? Ah, that would be another story. My father wasn't the only one who knew how to make something disappear.

So we stood there, he and I, in the middle of our lace-curtain dining room, with the pictures of Dublin and Donegal and Galway on the walls, and the coat-of-arms of some Hibernian society over the mantelpiece. Both of us were lying, I came to think. I knew I was, and I was almost as sure he was. Because I knew his sordid little secret. What really gave him pleasure was tormenting me and since Mother, who tried to stand between us, had died, he'd had a free run on that.

But I was younger than he was, I assured myself, and therefore stronger. I'd be everything he'd wanted, even if it made me throw up every night in the bathroom.

My resolution held for three months. I left the university and transferred to a college near my home. I attended Mass every Sunday with my father and sister, and went out with nice Catholic boys who held my hand and then brought me home. At the end of three months I bumped into a boy I'd known before in the wild days. He told me about a rock concert that was going to take place that night. We went and while I was there he offered me a joint. I took it. As I breathed in the drug the anger and tension and fury of the past months lifted. When the boy told me he was on the run from the police and asked me to go with him I went. I stayed more or less stoned for three months. Being stoned kept all unpleasant memories at a distance. At the end of the three months the boy I was with was arrested. I went back home. That was when my father told me he never wanted to see or talk to me again. I knew then he would never tell me where my daughter was, and somehow convinced myself that even if I had stayed home he wouldn't have told me. So I informed him that his feeling towards me was entirely mutual and took off. I never saw him again.

■ ■ ■   I read about his death from a heart attack a year later in the newspaper and went back to Boston to see if I could find out anything about my daughter. But my father's lawyer was dead. When I demanded to see all my father's papers I was shown by a new associate what I was assured was all of them. There was nothing in them concerning Laura. I had missed the funeral, of course, and missed seeing Julie, a fact that did not grieve me. By the time I got there she had returned to her own prestigious college. I went to see her to ask if she knew anything about Laura. With my revolutionary outfit and deliberately abrasive manner I cut quite a swath as I swaggered through the dormitory. The fact that Julie, Daddy's golden girl, was embarrassed and visibly ashamed of me added to my pleasure. I did not tell her I had had a child; I didn't trust her with that information. But I was fairly sure if Father had told her, she'd be unable to resist taunting me about it.

But she never brought it up.

I went to California—as far away from Boston as I could get —and took up with some of my transplanted buddies, now on the West Coast. One of those was Jeff Dysart, a student at Berkeley whom I had known in Boston. At one time I had been in love with him, and I fell in love again with his slate-blue eyes, thin, intense features and sudden warm smile. He was, in every way, unlike anything my father had ever been or represented. Under his guidance I drifted into radical politics. This meant cutting down on my drugs, which I did. Fortunately, I had not gone so far with them that it was an impossible task. After a while the elation of sit-ins, marches, protests and underground activities were a good substitute and I became more and more embroiled with the less lawful aspects of protest.

"Come on," Jeff said one day, "enroll at Berkeley, we need you." I still had a little money from my mother that my father hadn't been able to tie up, so I enrolled and, at Jeff's additional suggestion, did so under a phony name and with a phony background. "No use giving the pigs more than they need to know," he said casually.

So we made up another name, Liz Porter, and a new and fictitious place of birth, Los Angeles. He grinned suddenly. "If somebody comments on your New England accent, you can tell them you moved there for a while when you were a child."

"Is Jeff your real name?" I asked. It had never occurred to me before it wasn't, but lately I'd begun to realize I knew little about him, and what I did know seemed to shift from time to time. For a second, there was something in his eyes that made me sorry I asked. Then he smiled. "You know the rules. At least you should by now. Never give your real name, not when you mean to light a few fires."

I didn't ask him again what his name had been. And he never told me, not then, and certainly not when we were running from the police. Jeff said we would light fires, and for the next four years that's what we did.

■ ■ ■ The week after I had received the news from the genetic counseling clinic Macrae called me. "Sorry," he said. "I've been away, or I'd have returned your call sooner. What's up?"

I told him about the copy editor's queries.

"Yes, I meant to document those when I did the revision. I'll stick them in the mail to you right away. Sorry about that."

"That'll be fine."

There was a pause. Then he said, "Or better yet. Let's have dinner and I can hand them to you. Or lunch, if that's easier for you."

I was about to refuse when I suddenly thought of his background as a federal agent. Maybe, just maybe, if I went about it carefully I could get some helpful information on how to find someone when I had nothing to go on, except, of course, for the date and place of her birth.

"Fine," I said. "When would you like?"

"Tonight?"

"All right. Where and at what time?"

He named a West Side restaurant noted for its seafood. "Seven o'clock?"

"See you then."

I decided to work that evening until it was time to meet him. Certainly Paul had made it clear that he had no further interest in defending his rights or his turf as far as they concerned me. In fact we had barely talked since he announced that we were through and, as far as a small apartment would allow, had circled cautiously around one another. He slept in the study on the sofa, which, however, was not that much of a difference from the previous weeks. It was a long time since we had made love. If it had not been for my preoccupation about my blood test and what I was going to do about finding my daughter I would probably have been more aware of the situation. Whatever else had been wrong in our relationship, sex had been right. Now that was gone. But logic and consistency had not lately been Paul's strong point. If I went home before meeting Macrae Paul might very well ask where I was going and with whom. And I wanted to have a clear mind before my dinner with Macrae so I could extract as much information from the former gumshoe as I could.

When I got to the restaurant I noticed that lobsters no longer adorned the window.

Macrae was waiting at a table, and stood as the waiter led me up.

"I thought this place went in for lobsters and crabs and other sea creatures," I said as I sat down.

"It changed about two months ago. I'm surprised you didn't know."

"Why should I, particularly?"

"Because my impression of successful editors is that they're well up on such things."

"I suppose Cecy was. Yes, I remember. She loved to keep up with what eateries were newly in or newly out."

As the talk drifted on, I tried, without being too obvious, to lead it gently in the direction of Macrae's experiences as a federal agent. With that on my mind I said, carelessly and without thinking, "You must have had a lot of experience in tapping phones and following people."

"I, personally, have never tapped a phone, and only once or twice actually tailed anybody."

"Is it a hard technique to acquire?"

"Not especially, although there are tricks to it as there are to any trade."

"It's the kind of thing you always read about in spy books."

"I was a federal agent, not with the CIA."

"But didn't you have to hunt subversives here?" I was pleased with the neutrality of both the tone and the question. Even so, I added, "I mean, when people bomb places and . . . and so on."

He didn't answer right away. Then, "One of the cases I worked on was that of a man whose wife and child had been kidnapped. Eventually we found them, still alive, but not in very good shape. They'd been tied up in a house in the desert, without food, but especially without water. If it had been twenty-four hours later, they'd have been dead. We could have found them sooner if the older brother of the child, who was at college, had given us some clues we needed. But he felt it was against his principles to help us." Macrae put down his fork and reached for a roll. "That's about the way you would have felt, isn't it?"

I made myself respond casually, ignoring the sudden beating of my heart and the emotion that went through me, whether of panic or rage, I didn't know.

"Why do you say that?"

"You sounded angry when you asked that question about spies."

"I suppose so. The FBI weren't heroes to my generation."

"But I can't help feeling that it's something about that—to you—discreditable episode in my life that you wanted to talk about. Isn't that why you said you'd come to dinner?"

6.

My first thought was my dinner companion was not dumb. Having read his book I should have remembered that.

"Am I right?" Macrae asked.

"You must have been a good agent," I said, and smiled a little.

"Well? What is it you want to know?"

"Just tell me first how you arrived at this—er—realization."

"That you wanted to talk to me about my being a federal agent?"

"Yes."

"Your interest in my book—its subject matter—was polite but not overwhelming until I stuck that reference to being a federal agent into my revision. Certainly that's the way Linda seems to see it."

"Our publicity director?"

"Yes."

"I'm glad you've been in touch."

"Let's say she's been in touch."

There was another short silence. Most people, I've found, including me, rush to fill such gaps. Obviously Macrae didn't. His question, "What is it you want to know?" just lay there. Just as I was about to take a breath I remembered again what he'd said when we first met: "Haven't we met before?" A harmless enough question if one didn't consider the details of my stormy history and the fact that Macrae had served as a federal agent. And how happy I'd been at our Four Seasons lunch to let him attribute it to the *Newsweek* story. Now—for a few seconds—I considered abandoning the idea of asking him how to find a lost daughter. But after what I'd learned about the genetic curse I was carrying, I knew I couldn't, however risky it might be for me.

"Yes?" He was sitting back, his plate clean, his hands in his lap. "You almost said something. What stopped you?"

"Nothing. What I wanted to ask was, how do you find a missing person?"

"How missing, and for how long?"

"Eighteen years." I took a breath. Here goes, I thought. As a child in Catholic school I would have crossed myself. "Eighteen years ago I had a baby, a daughter. I was ill for some time . . . it had been a difficult birth. Anyway, when I came to, she'd been taken for adoption."

"If I'm to help you in this, I'm going to have to know a lot more. Ask a lot of questions you may not want to answer."

"How . . . how do you know that I'd hate to answer them?"

"Because there's something about you that makes me think of a sealed and locked package—" he smiled a little. "A safe, maybe."

"All right."

"Who, in your words, took the baby?"

"My father. He's dead now, and I can't ask him."

"It seems an extreme thing for a father to do. Why?"

"Because I was not married, the baby was therefore a bastard and, anyway, he hated me. He kept talking about the child's own good."

"Perhaps he meant it. Did he have reason?"

Father'd been dead so long I'd forgotten the particular kind of rage that surged through me when I had to have anything to do with him. "I suppose he thought he did."

"Did he leave no record of with whom he'd left the child?"

"None. I got the lawyer's office to show me all his papers."

"And your father's lawyer himself?"

"He died a year before my father did. And with his death the old law firm that handled my father's affairs all but dissolved. The man I saw was new to the family concerns."

"Well, try again. Tell him—or his office—who you want to find and why. At least you should be able to discover whether your father even told the original lawyer, or, if he told him, had also left strict instructions that the lawyer was not to let on that your father'd discussed it with him."

"If the lawyer I saw stonewalled then, wouldn't he do it now?"

"The laws are a little easier now towards adopted children who want to find their natural mother, and—I guess—towards mothers who want to find their children, although I'm not sure about that. Probably because of well-known cases where adopted children are abused—that kind of thing." He added quickly, "I didn't mean to imply that your daughter had any such experience. I'm sorry."

"It's all right. I've thought of it—often."

"Why—why do you want to get in touch with her now?"

"Because I found out by accident that my sister and my brother-in-law were both dead. What I didn't know was that they had a son and that he had died at the age of four from a complication of hemophilia. I got in touch here with people—medical and counseling people—connected with the disease. I learned that hemophilia hits the male, but he inherits it from his mother, who is a carrier. That meant that my nephew almost certainly got it from my sister. I had tests to see if I, too, am a carrier and found out I was. If . . . if my child had been a boy whoever adopted him would certainly know almost instantly that he had it. But since it was a girl, she has a fifty-fifty chance of being a carrier, like me. She's old enough now to marry and have children and she has to know it."

"Yes. I see. It's the lack of a blood clotting factor, isn't it?" He got out a pencil and some paper. "Is Covington a married name?"

Talking about my daughter hadn't been as hard as I thought it would be. After all, I'd broken the ice with Claire. But if I gave Macrae my father's name—which I would have to do—that would unlock the next layer.

Macrae was watching me. "Do you have some objection to giving me your maiden name? I can't get very far without it."

"Graham. My father's name was Anthony Graham. He . . . he lived and worked in Boston."

"That accounts for your slight Boston accent."

I'd tried to lose that identifiable way of pronouncing words and take on the West Coast manner of speaking, but in moments of stress, and this was certainly one, Boston crept back.

"Yes."

"So your name is Janet Graham?"

"I . . . I changed my name, all of it, for a variety of reasons. I was . . . it was . . . Felicity Ann Graham."

"Very pretty. Why did you change it? Or is that one of the questions you'd rather not answer?"

"Unless . . . unless it becomes necessary to find Laura—" The name slipped out. I hadn't intended to use it, since it meant nothing.

Macrae frowned. "You know her name?"

"No. It's just my name for her—in my own mind."

There was a pause. "You have no idea, no hint, as to where your father would have placed her?"

"No. Nothing would make him tell me."

"He sounds somewhat implacable."

"Yes."

Another pause, then Macrae said, "Is there anything else I would have to know to try to locate her for you, or at least to tell you how to go about it?"

I shook my head. "I don't think so. If it turns out that—that you need more, then I'll tell you."

He looked at me for a moment, then down at the paper. "All right. If she was adopted through one of the regular agencies it shouldn't be too hard. But you realize that a lot of children—particularly children who come from middle-class families—are adopted through family friends, doctors, lawyers and so on. And there are few documents around to record the transactions."

"Please . . . please don't spread the information around about me, what I've given you, more than you absolutely have to. It's—it's important." How important would mean opening up another layer of the sealed package. I wanted desperately not to do that. It could mean my safety, my freedom. Even my life. But, of course, armed with my real name, Macrae could probably find out the rest, anyway.

"You haven't finished your dinner. Didn't you like it?"

I had no memory of eating anything. But I had disposed of about half a steak, a small amount of potato and left the salad untouched. I forced a smile. "I guess I got distracted."

"Do you want to finish it?"

I shook my head.

"Dessert?"

"No. No thanks."

"Coffee?"

I nodded. Then said, "It's not the fault of the dinner."

"No, I think it was the subject under discussion."

There was no answer to that, except yes, and I wanted to get off of it now as soon as I could. The trouble was, any questions I might ask about him were laid out in the bio. Finally I said, "How old are your children?"

"Fourteen—that's my daughter—and my son twelve."

"What are their names?"

"Annette and William Christian—like me."

"What do you call him? Bill?"

"Yes."

"Is that what people call you?"

"No, Mac."

"Do you have pictures of them?"

He hesitated, then took a billfold out of his pocket, extracted two photographs and handed them to me. "They were taken about a year ago."

The boy looked like him—an extraordinarily handsome child, with wide-apart gray eyes. "But your eyes are blue," I said without thinking.

"Yes. He got them from my own father."

"He's very handsome."

"Yes."

Why I said the next statement, I don't know, but afterwards, when I went back over the evening I realized I was quoting somebody, maybe Jeff—something to the effect of all FBI men being oily accountants or dumb jocks. "Good at sports?"

"Moderately." He paused and added wryly, "He has two main enthusiasms, animals and computers. The two cats I have are basically his. His mother is allergic to them so I keep them."

"Animals?"

"Yes, he wants to be a vet, that is, when he isn't wanting to be a computer programmer."

I looked at the picture of the girl. She had red hair and her father's blue eyes. "She has lovely hair."

"She doesn't think so. It's the great trial of her life."

"Red hair is very attractive. Also very chic. I hope you've told her that."

"Often. It doesn't seem to do any good. And her mother—her mother seems to have a low opinion of it, too."

"That doesn't help, I guess." I found I was seized with a desire to ask impolite questions, such as, what kind of a woman is your ex-wife? Down, Rover, I said to my inner self, then jumped when Macrae said, "My wife's a pianist. She's teaching in one of the conservatories, but she used to do concert work."

"Does she concertize when you have the children?"

"As much as she can."

"Do you play at all?"

"Some."

"You're as tight with personal information as I can be. What does 'some' mean? Chop sticks? An album of favorites from musical comedies? Chopin?"

He smiled. "A little of each, maybe. My former wife was the serious musician. She was making strides in her concert career when she got pregnant with our daughter. So she stayed home for that, and when she was thinking of getting a permanent nurse, Bill was on the way. And anyway, we couldn't afford a really good nurse. And she wouldn't think of any other."

"You must miss them."

"I do."

I looked down at my empty coffee cup. "I should be getting back now. It's been . . . it's been a good evening. And I don't just mean, getting your help about . . . about Laura."

He put his napkin down. "It has been good. I'll let you know when I have something to tell you."

"You don't have to take me home," I said, when we got out.

"No. But I will." And he hailed a cab.

Sitting in the dark back of the cab with him, I expected to feel his hand reaching for mine. But he stayed on his side. When we arrived at my apartment he got out with me and stood while I groped for my key. Theoretically, I was grateful for his physical distance. Actually, it annoyed me.

"Good night," I said.

He held out his hand. I thought, but could not be sure, there was a satiric look in his eyes. "Good night."

▪ ▪ ▪ It was only about ten when I let myself into the apartment, not sure what I would find. What I did find was Paul sitting in his usual chair reading a journal of some kind. The television was on, but it was an old set and an occasional fit hit the picture tube which was liable from time to time to collapse what was on the screen into erratic patterns resembling nothing so much as nonobjective art. But the audio was fine and a soothing voice was discussing how to plant and take care of tulips.

"They don't look like tulips to me," I said, and went over and wiggled a button at the back of the set. A stout man in front of a parade of tulips appeared.

"I liked it better the other way," Paul said.

I turned it off.

"How was your date?"

"Fine."

"Did you learn all about the inner workings of our own KGB?"

"No, we didn't discuss those." I wondered how he had found out that I had gone out with Macrae, but I was damned if I was going to ask him.

"Well, what did you talk about?"

"His book, among other subjects."

"I haven't noticed that you dine out with the elderly Mr. Bernardin." Alex Bernardin is a Braddock regular. A new book of his cooking appears every year.

I turned and faced Paul. "What difference does it make to you at this point?"

Paul stood. I thought for a moment he was going to hit me. But he shrugged and turned away. I saw him march to the bedroom door and wondered what he was going to do there. But as his hand hit the knob he said, "I entirely forgot. I've been banished to the study, haven't I?"

"Paul, you've slept in the study of your own accord before, and it was you who said whatever we had was over. Remember?"

"You're trying to pin it on me, I can see that. It must be because of your new boyfriend, mustn't it?"

As he walked he swayed a little.

"Go to bed, Paul, you're drunk!"

And then I was afraid. He turned and came towards me swiftly and without a quiver in his gait, and stood eighteen inches from me, his head thrust forward. "Don't judge me, Janet. I know too much about you. Much more than you think I do. So don't sit in judgment. You understand?"

7.

I waited in the living room for the count of ten, breathing slowly to calm myself, reminding myself of the way Paul had been these past months. As his drinking had increased, so had his attacks of contentiousness and hostility. It meant nothing, I told myself, except that his drinking was reaching a new level.

But I remained unreassured, so I went to the study door, opened it and walked in. Paul was standing by the window, drinking.

"Don't you believe in knocking?" he asked.

"Since when did you go in for such bourgeois customs?"

"Oh stop being such a smart ass! And don't confuse me with all your old radical buddies!"

"At least they believed what they were spouting! They didn't live in splendid apartments, teach in rich private universities and enjoy their investments all the while talking about the liberation of the people!"

"Sounds like something your reactionary author might have said."

I was about to answer in kind when I recognized the exchange for the diversionary tactic it probably was. "What did you exactly mean by that crack about knowing too much about me? It sounded like a threat—almost like blackmail."

He shrugged. "Nothing special."

"Either you were telling the truth and you know something about my life before I . . . I came to New York. Or you're bragging."

He didn't reply, just kept his back to me, staring out the window.

"Or are you remembering the time you finked out on your friend Professor Henry—they never would have caught up with him, if it hadn't been for your help."

That was nothing but speculation and guesswork on my part. A jab in the dark. Professor Josiah Henry, actually the Reverend Josiah Henry who taught at a well-known Catholic University, had, during the late sixties and seventies, carried his pacifist beliefs to messing up as many government funded labs as he could empty a hose over, or toss some Molotov cocktails into. He became a highly visible and much photographed symbol, successfully keeping one step ahead of the law. Then one day the FBI caught up with him and took him off to a federal prison. No one seemed to have the full story, but the generally accepted version was that Henry, hiding out in what he thought was a safe place, was betrayed by someone in his own group. I knew that Paul had also started out his teaching career at the same distinguished institution as had Professor Henry because when he first moved into my apartment I had seen some snapshots in an old album of Paul's of the two of them together, looking very much like buddies.

"I didn't know you knew Josiah Henry," I said at the time.

"Oh well, that was some years ago," Paul had muttered, and swiftly turned the pages of the album.

"You looked pretty buddy-buddy," I said. "What's the professor doing now? He must be out of jail."

"Who knows?" Paul picked up the album. "How about going out and getting some Chinese food?"

One Saturday when Paul was up at the university attending some function, I looked everywhere for that album, but could never find it. I found myself worrying about it, thinking about it at night sometimes when I woke up. A hundred times I had started to bring the subject up to Paul. But I never did. Somehow, still knowing nothing, I did at least know he didn't want me to. And I was in love—or as much in love as I could be—so I told myself not to borrow trouble; that Paul didn't want to be queried about his onetime friend. Yet, unconsciously, I had put together the little plot I now flung at Paul's head.

He whirled around. "That's a goddamned lie!" He started towards me. "If you open your mouth to a living soul about that garbage, you'll be sorry you ever thought of it."

Once again, suddenly and unexpectedly, I was afraid. He had never struck me, not in his most drunken moments. But I knew now he could, and probably would. I turned and walked out of the room. When I got to my bedroom I closed the door, and after a moment, turned the bolt. I stood there, near the door, for a few minutes, waiting to hear if there was any sound on the other side, such as footsteps on the polished wood floor. But there were none. After a while I opened my own door, walked a few feet into the living room and stood there, listening. What I heard were snores, reverberating from inside Paul's study. He must, I decided, have passed out shortly after I left.

I stood there, irresolute. I could go spend the night with a friend from the office who lived on Waverly Place. On the other hand there was no way I could do that without some kind of explanation. Paul had never before appeared on the point of physical violence. He was now obviously passed out. I decided to stay in my bedroom, with the door locked.

I didn't sleep much that night. I thought about Paul's words, "Don't judge me, Janet. I know too much about you. Much more than you think I do."

I thought about the words. I also thought about what they possibly referred to.

■ ■ ■   I'd never felt about anyone the way I did about Jeff Dysart. Never mind that as well as protests, marches, petitions, confrontations, all of which I found even more elating than I had the drugs I now seldom used, he taught me to steal and cheat.

"Look, Liz," he said once, when I was showing what he described as chickenheartedness, "when the world is put back together in decent shape, then we can care about middle-class taboos like don't steal, don't cheat and so on. Those are the rules of the rulers. To beat them, we have to do it by our rules, not theirs!"

It wasn't hard to convince me. All I had to do was to summon up a picture of my father, discoursing, as he often did at meal time, on the fruits of centuries of civilized behavior, the lessons of Greece, Rome and Jerusalem, the general superiority of us and the general inferiority of all who wanted to take the country away from us. The trouble was, these fine, high-minded thoughts would often be abruptly interrupted as he caught sight of my hand snaking out for another roll or another cookie, "For

God's sake, haven't you had enough to eat? Aren't you fat enough?"—a public slap of contempt that would send a jet of rage and burning shame through me as my little sister tried to muffle appreciative giggles.

While Mother lived, I would hear her afterwards, pleading with him. "Don't humiliate the child! Do you think that will help her to . . . to become what you want her to be?"

And when I would sob my misery out in her arms, and wail, "Why does he hate me so much?" she'd say, more often than not, "Oh, Felix, he hates himself, the way he looks, where he comes from, everything. And since you look like him, he takes it out on you. He wants the best for you. Really he does! He wants to save you from the humiliation he's always felt about himself. He just doesn't know how to go about it."

I knew she wasn't consciously lying to me, because she didn't lie. But I also knew she was wrong.

And then, of course, a few years later, there was my child, which he had taken from me. It was more than enough after that to attach myself passionately to Jeff, and everything he stood for.

As the decade slid on through the seventies our activities became less purely political protest and more violent. We needed money, money for gas, for arms and for food. As did most universities in that time, ours periodically closed down. The faculty joined us in refusing to cross lines outside occupied buildings. That was when we joined forces with one of the more violent radical groups and I had my first experience of seeing the terror in the eyes of ordinary people as we faced them with our guns. They were bankers and their customers, shopkeepers and little merchants—the greedy bourgeoisie, as I had learned to look at them, caring nothing for the truly starving who were also the truly deserving. When, in the middle of an operation some forgotten scruple would pop up as I looked into the terrified eyes of a middle-aged woman, I would superimpose on her face the image of my father. After that, whatever I had to do would become easy—a pleasure.

■ ■ ■ To my surprise, Claire Aldington called me at the office the next morning. "Just wanted to be sure you're all right," she said. I was touched. "Thank you. Yes—more or less. Paul isn't in too great shape."

"I was afraid he might not be."

Of all the people we knew she was the only one who had commented on Paul's drinking—at least to me. "You sound like you might know something about it."

"I've worked a fair amount with alcoholics. And the other night he was showing some of the classic signs of his disease being fairly far advanced."

I decided, once again, to tell her the truth. "Claire, he and I have officially broken up. His suggestion, by the way. But the apartment's mine and he doesn't really have any place to go right now. He's already supporting one establishment—his former wife and children's place, and of course he's not been invited back for next year at the university. He says he has some irons in the fire, jobwise." I hesitated. "I wish to God he had another place to go, but I feel it would be sort of brutal to shove him out at this point."

"Heartless as it may sound, it would be better if you did. Better for you, and also better for him. It might make him do something about his drinking sooner. If he can stay indefinitely at your place with no particular responsibilities, then he has immediate security. In my experience, nobody ever stops drinking until the cost of drinking becomes higher than the cost of not drinking. The AA people call it hitting bottom. You'd be doing him a favor forcing him to do that sooner."

"He doesn't have any money—I mean he's going to get his

salary for the next few months, but I don't think he's saved anything."

"Probably drunk it up."

"You sound tough."

"On that subject, I am. Softness doesn't help. It really doesn't. Has he become violent?"

"Not . . . not yet. But . . . but I had a feeling he was on the verge of it last night when I walked out of the room. You know I can't believe this! He's always been belligerent about his opinions, and once—well once I found them more . . . more congenial than I do now. But in his personal relationships, he's been a truly gentle person."

"And when did it start to change?"

"He started having personality changes about a year ago. It went on from there."

"If you don't get out, he will become violent. And how would that help either one of you?"

I didn't say anything.

"Sorry to be such a downer. Don't answer the following question if you don't want to, but how are you progressing in your search for the . . . the girl?"

"I've asked somebody—the author who was mentioned so unflatteringly at dinner—to help. He was once a federal agent, and I went on the theory that he'd have entrées left over that I certainly wouldn't."

"Sounds like a good idea. I hope it works out."

Something made me say suddenly, "Are you ever free for lunch?"

"Yes, sometimes, if there isn't an emergency or I don't have to take the noon service. Where are you?"

I told her and we made a date for the following week at a restaurant halfway between us.

As I hung up the phone I sat there for a minute and thought.

For the past eighteen years I had confided in no one. I had too much to lose. Yet within a few days I had talked (relatively) freely to this priest-therapist and to my ex-federal agent author. Was I being dangerously stupid? Perhaps. Yet what I felt now was an overwhelming sense of relief. Somewhere I had heard someone—I didn't know who—say, "You're as sick as your secrets." Maybe one manifestation of that was my inability to love beyond a certain point. In fact, if love is giving of the self, at all. I'd never been good at it. With Jeff, what I felt was a combination of violent attraction, gratitude and the heightening that comes with either drugs or danger, and we had both, although Jeff was sparing in the use of drugs. He had a mission, and he wasn't about to let anything—or anyone—deflect him from it. With Paul, I now realized, it was a combination of sex and loneliness. There was nothing wrong with sex, but when that went, in our case, it didn't leave much.

■ ■ ■   Macrae called me that afternoon. "I don't have much to report yet," he said, "but I wanted you to know I've put a couple of lines out and will be in touch the moment I hear anything." He paused. "I'd like to ask you to dinner again, but I also want to make it clear that my going on with the search for Laura is not contingent on your having dinner with me."

"I didn't really think it was," I said, and was interested to learn that that was the truth.

"So, how about dinner?"

"All right. Where and when?"

"Tomorrow night? Geraldo's on West Fifty-third? Eight o'clock? I know that's late, but I am flying down to Washington tonight and won't get back until around six tomorrow."

"No, that's fine." I'd plan to stay at the office, I decided. I had enough work to keep me more than busy.

■ ■ ■ That night I had a dream I'd never had before, or at least not that I remembered the next morning. I dreamed I was back in the boarding school where I had gone for two unhappy years. I was sick and in the infirmary. Suddenly my father appeared. He was smiling and patted my hand. "I'll soon have you out of here and home," he said.

"Oh, please take me home," I cried. I hated being there.

Then he picked me up, put me over his shoulder and marched downstairs with me, with the nurse and the headmistress protesting in the background.

When I woke up my face was wet. Curiously, something not unlike that had actually happened when I was about eleven. But I had forgotten all about it.

8.

"I'm sorry I haven't been able to find out much yet," Macrae said.

We were sitting across from one another in the half light of the restaurant, which I had vaguely thought would be Spanish as in Central or South American, but which turned out to be Spanish as in Barcelona. Geraldo himself, a Castilian with a profile like a Roman coin, greeted us. It was obvious Macrae was a favored customer.

"Thanks for trying, anyway." I was unprepared for the intensity of my disappointment. Somehow I had convinced myself that Macrae, with all his old Bureau contacts, would be able to dig out right away where Father had placed Laura. Where do I go from here? I wondered despondently.

The evening slid down from there. I felt as though a door had been slammed in my face, but I brought all my training in hiding my feelings and my thoughts to keeping Macrae moderately entertained. Mechanically I smiled, mechanically I replied as various topics came up. When dinner was over, pleading overwork, I said I had to go home.

Macrae looked at me for a moment. "Is that what you want to do?"

"It's not—it's not to do with you," I said.

"It's to do with the fact that I wasn't able to turn up any information about your daughter." He said it matter-of-factly.

"Yes."

He hesitated. Then, "Can you think of anything else you can —or are willing to—tell me that could give me further leads?"

I shook my head. "No."

"All right. Let me tell you what I did find out. I found out your father was a university professor, teaching classics and classical history; that his older colleagues and some of his students from the fifties thought he was a good classicist and teacher. But that as the late sixties came along and rebelliousness became the order of the day he grew more rigid, opposing every change instigated by student radicals and by their sympathetic faculty. The climax came when a bunch of students occupied his offices one day and destroyed the research of years for a book he was writing. When confronted by the dean and the newspapers about this, the student leader justified it on the grounds that Professor Graham opposed everything they stood for."

It came back, that scene with my father when he told me about it. I could see his eyes, as blue and as hard as two marbles.

"You really hated him, didn't you?" Macrae said.

And then, out of nothing, came the memory of my dream. I

nodded. It was only when I saw Macrae's hand, holding a hand-kerchief, did I realize my cheeks were wet and my nose was about to run.

I grabbed the handkerchief. "Thanks."

"You're welcome. Shall I go on?"

I nodded.

"I found that he was married to a woman who had been adopted and who died when Graham was about forty-five, leaving him with two daughters, one, Felicity Ann, aged fifteen, and Julie, aged eight. He never married again, and as far as records show, he lived an abstemious life both as to sex and to drugs or alcohol."

I burst out, "He was a bloody puritan! Mother once told me that he told her he was a virgin when he married. He'd been brought up by a strict and religious family and for all his learning, he didn't change in that. He could talk admiringly about the Romans and their art and their lives and then come over to us like Cotton Mather!"

After a pause Macrae said, "Shall I go on?"

I nodded.

"I learned his older daughter, Felicity Ann, did everything she could to defy him—got into the drug scene shortly after the mother died, left Boston when she was nineteen, and then disappeared. After that, he refused to discuss her with anyone. As far as Graham was concerned, his daughter was dead."

"He didn't . . . did he find out anything about her when she went back to California?" Or tell anyone about it? I didn't say the words, but they were there. On Macrae's answer hung a great deal. I wondered if he knew.

"No. Or if he did, he left no record of it."

We sat there for a minute or two. Finally I said, "You found out a lot very fast. How did you do that?"

"I phoned a couple of people at the university who remembered him, talked to the priest of the church he used to go to—St. Malachi's, looked up some old news accounts."

"So now you know, I was a druggie and an unwed mother."

"That could be said of a lot of young women at that time. Anything else?" He smiled.

I thought to myself, if you but knew . . .

"Did you say you wanted to leave?"

"Yes."

At my door he bade me a formal good night.

Paul wasn't home, but he must have come in sometime during the night. The next morning when I unlocked my door and came into the living room, I saw his door was open. He was sprawled, fully clothed, on his bed. His face was red, his mouth open. It was impossible now to see in him the witty, sarcastic teacher whose comments on the passing scene were entertaining and provocative, whose intelligence was always several jumps ahead of mine, whose quirky good looks I'd found devastatingly attractive the first time I saw him.

■ ■ ■ Working was a relief. I could think about the manuscripts I was editing, the books I was involved with that were about to come out, and the authors whose needs and egos I had to cope with. But I didn't dwell too much on the latter. It inevitably led to thoughts about Macrae and I wanted to avoid that at all costs.

There was, I told myself, also a fifty-fifty chance that my daughter, if she were still alive—my heart stopped at the thought she might not be—would not be a hemophilia carrier.

I concentrated on that. The glass as half-full, not half-empty.

Then three days later I picked up the New York *Times* and found in its science section an article on hemophilia, and on those who had contracted other diseases—hepatitis, the dreaded

AIDS—because of their dependence on transfusions. That was probably what had happened to my nephew, it could happen to my grandson.

That afternoon Gil Mayer strolled into my office. Gil sometimes acted as my assistant. He was a pleasant young man who hid all the persistent drive of a workaholic under a pleasantly mild manner. He and I always got along, partly because I liked him and also because I once rescued him from the managing editor who had taken a dislike to him by saying that I needed his expertise and help on a certain book. By the time we'd finished that particular book, the managing editor had gone on to another house. But ever since, Gil had been an ally.

"Can I close the door and sit down?" he asked.

"Sure. Do you have some disgraceful confession to make?"

"No. But I think I ought to tell you that someone is trying to get information about you."

I sat very still for a moment. "Who?"

"I don't know. But a guy's called me at home. Said he's an old school chum trying to write a piece about you for the alumni rag in honor of you."

The only school of which I was an alumni—other than the night school I'd taken courses at here in New York—was the rigid convent which I attended in Boston. It was true I'd been—briefly—at Berkeley, but I didn't stay a year, let alone graduate. It was a fairly transparent lie.

"Alumni of where—what school?"

"I asked that. In some very clever way he managed not to answer."

"What did you tell him?"

Gil shrugged. "What there was that I knew, all of which was perfectly innocent and right there for anybody to see. You'd been working here for eleven years, had risen from skivvy to senior editor, had some top authors and were on your way up. He asked some background questions about your past. I told him he'd know more about you than I, because I knew nothing about you till I went to work for you."

"Do you know anybody else he's called?"

"No—at least not for sure."

My mind froze. Macrae was behind this. After all, this was his technique, the one he carried out over the phone to Boston. If he could find out something for me, he could also find out things about me. A faint voice in the back of my head proposed the question: Why should he? But old mental habits died hard. Maybe a onetime federal agent couldn't or wouldn't change his spots that much. Maybe his inquiries in Boston had elicited some information about my activities in California that had aroused his (formerly) professional interests. I took a breath. "Sorry you were bothered, Gil. And thanks for telling me. I think I know what it's all about, and it's nothing to get upset over. Do you know if anybody else was approached by our Mickey Spillane?"

"I tried to find that out, but couldn't. Sorry." He stood up.

"Thanks, Gil, for letting me know. I owe you one."

"It's still the other way around." He smiled and left the room.

■ ■ ■ My concentration that had been operating so beautifully now vanished. I tried to go back to the manuscript I'd been working on, but found myself reading sentences over and over again. After a futile effort I gave up on that. I tried reading a new one that one of the editors had asked me to glance over and report on the following day. At the end of half an hour I had no idea whether it was fiction or nonfiction. It could even have been a cookbook for all the impression it made.

"This isn't any good," I said aloud and stood up and went to the window. Far in the distance was the green rectangle of Central Park. Between me and it were several streets, a church, a museum and a new office building that shot straight up like a slab of black marble.

I could not shake the conviction that I was responsible for all this by asking Macrae's help in finding Laura. My faint inner voice that counseled reason was now drowned out. I should have remembered his past with fear, not tried to use it. And I should have known the chances of his not going beyond what I asked him to find out were not very great. Given all of that, by this time, how much did he know?

I stood there, clutching the sides of the window, calculating. Not everything, anyway. Or he wouldn't have sicced one of his buddies or former colleagues onto making inquiries about me. Or maybe his helpful friend was simply checking to make sure there wasn't anything left to know. In which case, what would happen now?

"I do hope you're not contemplating leaping out the window," Linda's voice said from the doorway.

I turned.

"What's the matter?" she asked abruptly. "You look like you've seen—to coin a phrase—a ghost."

"No, no ghosts." I made myself smile. "Have a seat."

"All right." She sat down. "Just a few points that should have an answer before next week's promotion meeting." She went rapidly and efficiently over invitations various authors had received to appear on this or that show or be interviewed by this or that book page or program. We talked about them. Then she said, "I've been on the phone trying to persuade Macrae to be a little flexible about traveling when his book appears. It's one of the supreme ironies, not to say tragedies, that the talk shows I'd give my soul—not to mention my body—to get an author on, want him, with no prodding from me."

"Has he relented?"

"Of course not! Don't be an idiot! I wouldn't be here weeping all over your desk if he let me talk him into one or two, or even one show say in Chicago, and one in L.A. But stubborn doesn't even begin to describe him." She paused. "I thought maybe you might have better luck getting him to change his mind."

"What made you think that?" I asked sharply.

"No offense. If there was any emotion in my voice it was envy. I had the impression that he had a distinct tendresse for you. In fact, when we were at dinner—"

"He seems to have one for you, too," I said, before I could stop myself.

"That would be nice, but not true."

"He asked you to dinner."

"If you want to know, I asked him."

"You can have him," I said and was shocked at the feeling in my voice.

"Wow! What happened between you two? When I called him an hour or two ago and suggested the two of you might join me for drinks he said with a chill that almost froze the phone that he didn't think you'd like that."

"He was right. Sorry!"

"Would it be any good if I pointed out that if he helped out with publicity the sales on his books would go up—and that affects you, too."

"No. It wouldn't. I'll talk to him if you like, Linda, and point out all the things you've pointed out to me. But I think he takes his time with his children very seriously."

"I've always wondered why I got on better with the lowbrow, commercial types. Maybe it's because they're usually not as bloody-minded as the ones with high principles." She got up. "If you see a crack in the defenses let me know."

■ ■ ■ It was a long time since I'd felt this trapped. I knew I couldn't sit in my small office any longer. On the other hand, I also couldn't go home. I grabbed my handbag and my tote bag, stuffed a couple of manuscripts into the latter, called my secretary and, after telling her I was going out on an appointment and wouldn't be back for the rest of the afternoon, left the office. With both my handbag and tote slung around my shoulder by straps, I wasn't too burdened as I walked swiftly up Fifth Avenue, then strolled up the East Drive of Central Park. After a while, I abandoned the drive, walked up a hill and sat down on the grass. Central Park is notoriously dangerous at night, but during the day it was dotted with people doing what I was doing on this June day. The city was not as hot as it was capable of being, but it was warm. I lay down and stared at the sky, most of which was an intense blue, with the merest puff of a cloud here and there.

Back in California, even after we went underground, Jeff and I and a few others would head into the Sierras and take picnic lunches, just like ordinary middle-class people instead of dangerous revolutionaries wanted by the police. I used to love the country then, loved the smell of wet grass, of the pines and redwoods that dotted the coast up towards Oregon. Later, I came to fear open places. City streets were safer, as were alleys with doorways into which you could disappear . . .

I must have been drifting off to sleep, lying there in Central Park, with the famous skyline only slightly visible through the network of the trees. Then, quite suddenly, I was awake and sat up. There had been a family group of three about twenty yards down the slope and a young couple tumbling with jeaned legs and groping hands around in the shrubbery, and on the shallow slope opposite, a single male, his shirt white on his back as he read his book. The family and the couple were still there. The slope across from me was empty.

But there had been someone—someone quite near me. Why did I think that? I had been half asleep, mooning over lost days and lost loves in California. But I knew I had drifted off and had also been dreaming. What had I dreamed about? Something about a man bending over me—I drew in my breath. In my dream he had on a white shirt—a shirt like the man who had been sitting on the slope across from me. Only he wasn't there anymore. The slope was empty. I glanced down. Not far from where my head had been was the faint mark in the grass, an imprint really, of a shoe. Some of the grass blades were slowly rising back into place. He must have been within a foot or two of my head. A shiver went through me. There in the warm sun I felt cold.

9.

I walked home, going down Seventh Avenue, down through the prostitutes and pimps near Times Square, weaving my way among panhandlers, hustlers with small tables playing three-card monte and other nimble devices for parting the hopeful and naive from their money. Every now and then I stopped at the window of a bar or little store and pretended to look at the sleazy wares and watched the street behind me.

Whether it was truth or paranoia that somebody might be following me I didn't know. But while it was turning into a cool day for June, I had my rage at Macrae to keep me warm. So he had sicced his Bureau buddies on to me! Was it because he now knew more about me than he had let on, or because old habits were hard to break. It didn't matter. I knew I couldn't trust my instincts at this point, but I was at least partly sure that somebody was following. And I couldn't forget either my dream or the man in the white shirt.

When I got back to the apartment it was nearly three hours after I had left the office, but it was still only five o'clock. For some reason, after his almost continual absence, I was surprised to see Paul sitting in his chair, reading.

"Hi," I said.

He put down his book. "Hi."

I sat down and picked up a newspaper. "I forgot to look at a paper today."

"The big world goes on."

I looked at Paul. He had obviously been drinking again; there was a half-filled glass on the table near him. But he seemed relatively sober. "How do you feel?"

"Considering everything, not too bad." He made a business of smoothing his book. "I'm well aware that owing . . . owing to recent lapses, I owe you a large apology. I'm sorry. Truly."

Twenty-four hours ago I would have told him what he could do with his apology. Now, by contrast to Macrae, he seemed indeed a *parfait* gentle knight. Where had I heard that alcoholism was a disease, not a moral weakness, certainly not a moral weakness like betraying a trust and spying on people who had confided in you?

I smiled at Paul. "Accepted."

And for the rest of the evening, it was as though the quarrels, rages and hurled insults of recent weeks had never occurred. It was, in fact, very like the first year we had been together in the apartment. That it was not completely like was a thought that kept presenting itself and that kept being pushed back. I wanted desperately for it to be the way it had been once between us, before I knew my nephew had died of hemophilia-related complications, before I knew I was a carrier, when the past was safely dead and buried.

Suddenly, on impulse, I said to Paul, "You asked if what was bothering me came from the past . . . the past I'm so uncommunicative about." I paused.

"Well," he said after a minute.

I took a breath. "The other day, on the back of a clipping an author had sent me from California, I saw something that led me to have a blood test to see if I was a carrier for hemophilia."

Paul's astonished eyes met mine. "That must have been quite a clipping!"

"The details aren't important. I learned . . . I learned of the death of a nephew I didn't even know I had. You know, because I've told you, that I broke completely with my family. Anyway, the test came through, and I am a carrier of the hemophilia gene."

"I didn't know you were planning to have children."

"For God's sake, Paul! I'm not. I've already had a daughter, eighteen years ago, given up for adoption, I have no idea with whom. But she, too, could be a carrier."

There was a long silence.

"I'm sorry," Paul said. "But there's not much you can do about it now. Maybe by the time she has a child, if it's a son, science and the health care establishment will be able to do a better job." His tone was sympathetic, but also dismissive.

I told myself I should have remembered Paul's first concern was principle—political and/or scientific—not the individual— except, of course when his jealousy was aroused.

"I hope so," I said. I had even, I realized with amazement, been going to tell him that I had asked Macrae's help. Fortunately I didn't. He seemed to have developed a phobia about Macrae.

And then two nights later I woke up suddenly overwhelmed by a sense of urgency and lay there, my heart beating heavily.

Beside me Paul stirred. Our relationship had resumed. It had certainly been at Paul's suggestion, but I had made it easy for him.

Slowly, gently, I slid out of bed, threw on my robe and went to the living room, silently shutting the door behind me. There I sat until the first light appeared over the roofs of the houses to the east.

How much did Macrae know about me by now? If he knew everything, what did that mean for my future? True, he was not in the FBI now, but I brushed that aside. Once a cop, always a cop, and the bureau was made up of supercops. It meant, or could mean, two things: one was, I could go to jail. I had been formally charged by the prosecuting attorney in Los Angeles. I was therefore still a fugitive and could still be put in jail if caught. The other was, I would never find my daughter.

■ ■ ■ It seemed I had always run. How many times had I changed my name? I couldn't now even remember. Jeff and I and some of the others became expert at that. We learned how to print up identifications, how to dye our hair, how to talk with different accents, how to talk as little as possible to any other than ourselves, how to live in tents, how to live without bathrooms.

"Listen, Liz," Jeff had said once, rubbing my cheek. "One day you'll be able to live like a nice middle-class person again, with plumbing and a decent diet, but before you start feeling sorry for yourself, remember the people in this rich, rich country who live the way we are now, only for them it's all the time, because they don't have any choice."

Maybe it was because I had just been violently sick and was suffering from an insidious diarrhea which left me weak and sweating. Whatever the reason, I repeated something that with my father had been a religion. "Everybody has a choice, Jeff.

Maybe it isn't a very wide one. But everybody has one, even if it's only how to react to things that happen."

It wasn't a statement calculated to win much sympathy from Jeff. "Jesus! You sound like your old man, the old capitalist himself. All that land of opportunity crap. What's the matter with you?"

The thought that I could in any way be like the hated enemy, my father, was unendurable.

"I'm sorry. Jeff, I didn't mean it!" And I had tried to take his arm as another paroxysm shook me. Loyalty to everything Jeff and his friends stood for was the most direct way I could harm my father, and that was the main object of my life. I had thought it was love for Jeff. Much, much later, I realized he was simply an instrument.

In our next foray to assist in what Jeff called the redistribution of wealth he decided I should do the driving—something I was never good at. And the whole operation was a fiasco. We never got the money we were after, and a teller at the bank and one of our own group were both killed. Three weeks later Jeff and two of the others planted an explosive in a government building, damaging one wall and wounding a clerk who was there doing overtime and killing a security guard. I was furious that he hadn't even let me go along.

"Yeah? Look what happened the last time you got involved! The whole thing fell apart. You're better off staying out of action."

I was humiliated, and our relationship slid. Nevertheless, when the feds issued their Wanted posters, my name (the name I had then, Liz Porter) was on it along with all the rest.

When I first saw it I was in a mall post office after doing some grocery shopping for the group. Waiting until I thought no one was watching, I tore it off the wall to take back to Jeff as proof that even if he didn't think I was effective as a revolutionary, at least the feds did. At that time we were living in a shack just outside of L.A. But when I got back with the groceries the place was empty. Jeff never returned. Nor did the others. I was left there by myself. I never saw him or them again. But I did hear from Jeff. Through one of his contacts he saw to it that I got a note from him. The note said simply, "If you ever let on that you know any of us, you'll have the same fate as that security guard. And so will Jock. J.D."

Jock was my dog. He had been a stray when I adopted him and I had managed to cling to him through all the moves and all the hasty leavings in the face of angry opposition from Jeff and most of the others.

"All we need is a spotted dog hanging around to identify us," Jeff had pointed out. "What's this crazy thing about animals you have?"

I couldn't explain. It seemed childish to say, "Father didn't like dogs." He claimed he did, but he wouldn't let them in the house, which was one of the many things I held against him. So instead I said, "They're nicer than people," which, on the whole, Jeff excepted, I thought was true.

Two years later in San Francisco where I was living under yet another name, I finally had to part with Jock. Stoned, anorexic and half out of my mind, I threw in the towel and went to a rehab. Before I entered I gave Jock to a girl who had other animals of her own. I knew she would be good to him.

■ ■ ■ I sat there, watching the light broaden in the garden below my apartment. Even if Jock had lived out in health and happiness his full span of life, it would be highly unlikely that he would be still alive. I had not had another pet. Why? I wasn't sure. Partly perhaps out of loyalty to Jock. Partly because on some level I felt I had betrayed him. I had contracted with him to give him a home after what must have been a miserable life. Giving him away wasn't part of that contract. I couldn't forget his face and eyes as I drove off from the girl's house. Before I could shut the window I heard him start to cry and saw him strain against his collar as she held him. I had deserted Jock. I had, in effect, deserted my daughter. The one final thing I could do for her now would be to let her know that she might give birth to a child that could break her heart.

Which brought me back to Macrae. I could, of course, ask him how much his snoop had learned. Other than show my fear and confirm whatever suspicions he might have beyond what he already knew, I wasn't sure how much this would yield. I couldn't see that iron man telling me anything he didn't want to. If he had found out as much as I was afraid he had, then I might be done for. I could be taken into custody on an old offense. I could go to jail. That was the rock. The hard place was, if I didn't do everything I could to warn Laura about the genetic curse she might be carrying, she could have a hemophiliac child.

"Your choice, my dear," I could hear the voice of the counselor back at the rehab fourteen years before. "Always remember you have a choice."

The fact that I was able to accept this favorite dictum of my father without spitting in her face was probably to me the single greatest indication that I was going to make it.

And now I had another choice.

I got up, and as I did the door opened.

"My God! What hour is it?" Paul asked. In the morning light he looked gray.

"Just past six."

"Why the dawn patrol?"

"I couldn't sleep."

"Got any coffee made?"

"I'll put it on now."

Once, I thought, we would have gone back to bed again. But once was not now.

After I had drunk my coffee and showered, I left for the

office. I needed to be alone, and at eight-thirty I figured not too many people would be there.

I brought some more coffee with me into the office and stood there at the window, drinking it, looking out at the patch of Central Park. Somewhere, probably at the rehab, I had learned that I couldn't think my way out of a problem or a dilemma. The reasons for taking either way could be summoned, added up—and meant nothing. If I put the matter in the back of my mind, and left it there for a while, not thinking about it, then I would, before too long, know what I had to do. The trouble was, sometimes the "while" was longer than I felt I had now. But there wasn't much I could about that. So I stared out at the park and tried to think of nothing, except how pretty it was.

I don't know how long I had been doing that when, seemingly out of nowhere, the name Mahaffey presented itself in my mind.

Martha Mahaffey, I thought. How long had it been since I had thought about my father's secretary—short, stocky, very Irish, very Catholic, very pigheaded? In the fashion of the old country from which her parents came, she was inclined to call Father "himself." "Himself was on the phone and would like to speak to you." "Himself was not at all pleased with the report card from school."

I used to wonder what she felt about transmitting such messages. Once, when in fury I shouted, "Himself can go and stuff himself!" I expected the phone to blow up or the sky to fall in. But all she said was, "Now, Miss Felicity, what would your mother think of your speaking of him like that?"

"And so can you!" I had screamed back, because in invoking my mother she had used an unfair weapon. After that, I stayed off the phone and out of the office because I was convinced she had, of course, told my father about my disgraceful language. The fact that he hadn't mentioned it to me was simply part of his craftiness, I told myself. But when Christmas came there was a card and a present from Martha, a pretty cardigan of exactly the right size in a soft red. On a day when I knew my father would be out of town, I went to his office, wearing it to show her. All she said was, "Himself is not here, Miss Felicity."

"How do you like my new sweater?"

"Very nice. Do you have any message for Mr. Graham?"

"No." It was a flat, angry word. "Thank you for the sweater."

She said nothing. But her cheeks got a little pink.

"I'm sorry . . ." I took a breath. "I'm sorry I said what I did to you. But I'm not sorry about the message to Father." And I got out before she could say anything.

Martha Mahaffey, I thought. She had retired before I'd even had Laura. Father had a new secretary then, a very up-to-date young woman who'd have been as likely to converse in Gaelic as she would to refer to my father as himself. After Father's death I had queried her about the adoption, but she claimed to know nothing and somehow I believed her. I hadn't even thought of Martha then. Nor since. But there she was in my mind now. If she were alive she'd have to be in her eighties. When my secretary came in I said, "Helen, I'm going to have to go to Boston for a day or two. Is there anything I have to cancel?"

"No, but Macrae called yesterday. He wants you to call him."

"I'll do that when I get back. And Helen, if he should call again, please don't tell him where I am. In fact, don't tell anyone outside or inside the office. I'll tell Jack myself." Jack Lederer was the managing editor, so I'd have to check in with him. I'd have to ask him not to drop the information to his various flunkeys. Jack was fairly laid back, but I wondered if he would accept my request without comment.

Then I discovered he, too, was away. "Would you tell him I'm taking a couple of days' vacation and will be back Monday,"

I asked his secretary, and left before she could inquire as to where.

When I got home I was relieved to find Paul not there. Strictly speaking, he shouldn't have been there, but that hadn't meant too much in the past weeks. I left a note about having to meet an author up in Boston and that I would be back Sunday night. With the new peace between us, I hoped he would accept the letter without too much suspicion. Then I put a few things in a bag and took a taxi to the shuttle at La Guardia. Staring at the various passengers who got on the plane with me, I wondered if any of them was Macrae's stooge who queried Gil Mayer. Well, I thought, mentally shrugging, there wasn't much I could do about it. First things first, and Laura came first.

10.

I hadn't expected an easy time when I got to Boston, and I didn't have one. I didn't really think Martha'd be in the phone book, or in any of the suburbs circling the city, and she wasn't. But I had expected the personnel office at the university to have some address or phone number. Or, if she were dead, for them to know it. At the college few even remembered my father who had taught there for so long. And they certainly didn't remember Martha.

Finally one moderately sympathetic person said, "You know, it's almost an impossible thing you're trying to do, particularly if she never married, had no children." She paused. "Mahaffey is a common enough name in Boston. God knows how many there are in the phone book. Did she have any brothers or sisters?"

I had no idea, I was always far too self-centered to do anything as uninspiring as ask about her family. And my father, also self-centered, never mentioned it.

I sighed. "I could always just go through the phone book and ask every Mahaffey who answers if they know or are related to the Martha Mahaffey who worked at the college."

"Lotsa luck."

I had hired a car when I got to Boston, and was busy unlocking its door outside the college when I saw a man strolling on the opposite side of the street. There were plenty of people around, students and older men and women. But they had the "look" of college about them somehow. He didn't. I was more than aware that the fact that I was so instantly suspicious had at least as much to do with my own jumpiness and paranoia as anything particularly odd about him. Still, I did notice him and suddenly I was frightened.

I stood there, my hand on the handle of my car door, watching him. If he were watching me, then he would certainly notice me watching him. Would that force him to move out of my range? Probably. But if he did, and if he had been hired, then he would get in touch with whoever had hired him and he/they would send somebody else, someone whom I had not noticed. Better the devil I knew than someone I wouldn't recognize.

I opened the car door and got in. The man was several yards up the street, going away from me, the suit of his jacket square across his shoulders. I pulled the car away from the curb, made an illegal U-turn, and then went down a side street going away from the man. I had no sooner executed that maneuver than I could have kicked myself. I would, most likely, recognize his back again, provided if he was wearing the same sports suit. But I had not seen his face. It would have been a lot smarter to speed up and go past him and then look back.

Well, it was done now. What with one-way streets there was no way I could get the car around to coming towards him. Why was it that in my life, the moment I took action I became almost immediately convinced that I should have done something else? Just natural klutziness? A depressing thought!

■ ■ ■ I went back to the hotel to start making phone calls to the apparently numberless Mahaffeys.

Half an hour later, sitting on my bed with the phone on the night table, I had lost count of how many numbers I'd dialed and had pretty much decided it was a futile exercise when a male, very Boston Irish voice said, "Aye, I think you're talking about my aunt. She used to work for a professor at the university."

My heart fluttered and jumped. "Where is she now?"

"If the Church hasn't been putting us on all these years, with the blessed saints."

"She's dead," I said.

"She is that."

The disappointment was overwhelming. Somehow I pinned a lot of hopes to this. Finally I said, "When did she die?"

"Not six months ago."

"Was she—did she live alone?"

"No. She was in St. Jude's Home—it's a nursing home outside the city. She died there."

"Oh."

"What would you be wanting her for, if you don't mind me asking?"

I hesitated.

"Not that it's any of my business, I'm sure." There was a faint sound of huff in the Irish tone.

I thought then of Laura and plunged on. "Martha worked for my father at the university. She was his secretary and was very good to me all the years I was growing up, especially after my mother died. My father . . . he had occasion to place a child for adoption. For . . . for various legal reasons it is essential for me now to find Martha. Did she ever mention anything about it to you or, to your knowledge, any other member of the family?"

"Legal reasons, you say."

"Yes."

"I remember Martha mentioning your father. But she never said anything about his placing a baby for adoption. Surely it'd be his lawyer you'd be wanting to talk to."

"He's no longer alive."

"Whose baby would it be?"

The words stuck in my throat. Why couldn't I say simply, she was mine? "The daughter of a close friend."

"Couldn't you ask her?"

As Mother said, tell one lie and you have to back it up with seven others. "Unfortunately, she's dead, too."

"Someone in her family then?"

"I'll try that," I said, and hung up. I sat there thinking.

It was obvious I had to drive out to the nursing home. Maybe Martha Mahaffey talked to one of the aides or nurses out there. It was a long chance, but all chances at this point were long.

■ ■ ■ St. Jude's was grander than I had thought it would be. The patients were housed on two floors, the very handicapped on the first floor and those who were less so on the second. Everything was so spick-and-span I wondered if the home were private, and if so, how expensive it was. The woman in charge of St. Jude's, Sister Mary Joseph explained, "Yes, it's private, though a few of the patients are on Medicaid alone. There is an endowment that makes up the difference for them. The rest

either have the money to pay the extra or have more insurance."
She sighed. "I wish it could be like this for everyone. But under
present conditions, that's impossible. But you came to talk about
Martha Mahaffey, didn't you?"

"Yes. I hadn't realized she was dead and was hoping to talk
to her, but her nephew told me she died six months ago." I took
a breath. "As I explained to you, she was secretary to my father
for years and years. He . . . he placed a child for adoption eighteen years ago. I was wondering if she mentioned it to anyone—
as to the parents he gave it to and where they'd be."

The nun's wide-apart very blue eyes regarded me for a moment. "I don't know. Some of the nurses here would certainly
have known Martha. Is it important?"

I could feel the blood in my face. "Yes."

"All right. Let me see if I can find out for you. I think it
would be better that way than for you simply to question the
women. There are about three nurses who might fit the bill. I'll
talk to them. Where can I reach you?"

"I'll be at the hotel until tomorrow noon. After that, you can
reach me at Braddock's in New York." I scribbled both numbers
on a piece of paper and handed it to her. "But I would rather
talk to you about it while I'm here if it's at all possible."

The nun nodded. She strongly reminded me of some of the
older nuns who still dressed in the traditional way when I was at
school. Yet her skirt was short and her veil did not conceal her
hair. It must, I decided, after thanking her and leaving, be something in her manner that gave me such confidence in her, which,
considering the enthusiasm with which I had kicked over the
Church and all its teachings, was strange.

■ ■ ■ Being back in Boston was having its effect on me. I had
not been in the city since I had left it, shaking its dust from my
feet, following my father's death. And I now found its streets

filled with my own much younger ghost. As I drove back from the nursing home I took various detours, visiting first the suburb in which I had spent my early childhood, then, crossing the river, I went back to the street we lived in when my father got his job on the university faculty, the section I had been in that morning. This time, instead of a single, separate house on a suburban street, our home had been one of a row of old houses. I knew Father took particular pleasure in it. Being a snob, he had taken on the biases of his colleagues on the faculty and had nothing but scorn for the typical suburban split level or fake Cape Cod house.

But Mother was still alive when we were in our simple white frame house and Father was still teaching in his Catholic college, before he got promoted to the big time. That was the only part of my childhood I could bear to think about, because those were the years when Mother stood between me and the tyrannical man whose mirror image I was.

With relief I turned the car towards the Common and the hotel. Being in Boston, I decided, was like being in a cell. In New York I was free—free of my own past. But in Boston it crowded back, threatening to strangle me.

I parked the car and walked through the lobby. By tomorrow, I told myself, I would, for better or worse, have talked to Sister Mary Joseph again and could return to New York.

■ ■ ■ I decided to have dinner in the coffee shop attached to the hotel rather than in my room as I had originally planned, whether because of an attack of frugality or a hovering claustrophobia I wasn't entirely sure. But in case Sister Mary Joseph called, I told the front desk where I could be found. I was in the middle of a spinach omelet when the headwaiter in the coffee shop came over. "Are you Miss Covington?" When I nodded he said, "There's a phone call for you. You can take it at the desk there, or you can use one of the house phones outside."

I decided to use the house phone, one of several just outside the coffee shop. I was expecting to hear Sister Mary Joseph. But when I said, "This is Janet Covington," a male voice said, "Why don't you leave well enough alone. Let the past stay past, or you might be sorry." And hung up before I could reply.

11.

Although I knew it was useless, I jiggled the receiver and, when the hotel operator came on, asked if the man I had just talked to had identified himself in any way.

"No, he simply asked for you and said you were in the coffee shop."

"You mean he told you I was in the coffee shop? You didn't transfer the call from my room as I told the front desk to do?"

"No, I didn't know you had left those instructions. I just came on. Is anything wrong?"

"It was an unpleasant anonymous phone call," I said.

"I'm very sorry. But how could I know?" She sounded vaguely aggrieved.

"You couldn't. I didn't mean to reproach you about it."

"Do you want me to transfer you to the hotel manager?"

I thought for a moment. Other than to repeat that the phone call was anonymous and threatening, what could I tell him? "No. That's all right."

The spinach omelet was cold and unappetizing when I got back. "Just coffee," I said when the waitress cleared it away. After she left I stared out the window to the darkening street outside. The street lights were on, of course, and though the boutiques were closed at this hour, there were plenty of people walking about, many of them, no doubt, on their way to one of the numerous nearby restaurants. One man staring into the lighted coffee shop window and then putting his quarter into a public phone would know exactly where I could be located. "She's in the coffee shop," the anonymous caller had told the hotel operator, because he could see me there.

Flinging down a tip, I snatched up my bill, paid it and left. In my room, I took a long, soaking bath, washed my hair in the shower and put on my nightgown. It was still early for anyone of my late habits, but I went to bed anyway, hoping I could stall off thinking by going to sleep. I should have known better. Two hours later, still wide awake, I got up and turned on the television. However brainless, it would absorb the hours until morning when I could call Sister Mary Joseph.

And though I knew it was useless, while I watched the characters on the screen in front of me chatter and interact my brain worked at trying to figure out who called me and why. I did not recognize his voice. To my knowledge I had never heard it before. Why would somebody try to threaten me into stopping the search for Laura? Making up reasons was not impossible. In my role as editor I often had to imagine arcane motives for bizarre acts, especially in cases where the plot demanded it and the writer's inventiveness had given out.

Laura, wherever she was now, whoever were her adoptive parents, was due to come into money and my inquiries might screw it up.

Why? Who would care?

Her adoptive parents? A child born to them after adopting her?

Someone who planned to become her husband?

People who threatened were usually frightened. Frightened of what? How could my knowing where Laura was now endanger anyone?

Except Laura herself. But again, how?

Why would an anonymous caller threaten me?

Back to square one.

The only thing of which I was moderately sure was that Macrae, ex-cop, was mixed up in all this. Until he walked into my life—even more, until I decided, idiotically, to confide in him—my life had been running smoothly. A small voice whispered inside me that Macrae's arrival in my office had nothing to do with my discoveries concerning my hemophiliac nephew, but I pushed that aside as irrelevent, dwelling instead on the fact that until Macrae appeared I had left the past far behind me, had been living happily with Paul and, most important, no one had come around the office asking questions about me. I stayed with that thought until the first dim light started pushing its way past the venetian blinds. Then I got up and threw my few things into a bag. I wanted to be ready to move fast, if I had to.

I ordered breakfast as soon as Room Service opened and asked one of the bellhops to bring me a newspaper. Somehow the hours until I could decently call Sister Mary Joseph passed. At nine I dialed the nursing home. "Sister Mary Joseph," I said.

There was a gasp and something that sounded like a sob at the other end. Then I heard the phone being put down. The next voice was a man's. "Who is this?" he asked.

Fear, hovering around since the evening before, now gripped me in earnest. "What's happened?"

"Is this Sister Mary Joseph's sister?"

"No. What's happened," I repeated.

"Sister Mary Joseph has had a bad accident," the man's voice said.

"What kind of accident?" I asked.

"She was knocked down by a car early this morning when she was on her way to Mass at St. Michael's."

"Is she . . . will she be all right?" Please God, I thought, Holy Mother, let her be all right!

"I don't know," the man said. And then again, "Who is this?"

But I had put the phone down. I had to think, I decided rather frantically.

Had her accident had anything to do with me, with my questions to her? It seemed farfetched. People, even nuns, were knocked down by cars all the time.

But over the next few minutes and despite my reminder to myself that accidents in a busy city thoroughfare were a constant, the questions persisted:

Had Sister Mary Joseph talked the previous evening to any of the nurses about Martha Mahaffey, as she said she was going to?

If she had, did she hear from any of them whether or not Martha had said anything about her former employer—my father—placing a child for adoption?

And if Martha had said something to one of them and whatever nurse it was had passed it on to Sister Mary Joseph, did that fact have anything to do with her accident. And if it did, then how? Had someone overheard her? Someone who might have followed me there and might have overheard her conversation with me? If so, who could it have been?

I tried to recall every moment after I arrived at St. Jude's. Certainly no one had followed me there or, to be more accurate, no one came up behind me while I was standing at the front door ringing the bell. Sister Mary Joseph had taken me to a small reception area off the lobby and we had talked there. But there was no door, in fact the reception area was simply a sort of L, not a room at all, and a stream of people—women, priests, some men in civilian clothes, to say nothing of various nuns—walked past going in or out or stood in the lobby and conversed or stood in the lobby and waited.

The thought that my request of Sister Mary Joseph might have been responsible for her accident sent fear and self-reproach through me.

Should I now go out to St. Jude's and try myself to question any of the nurses who had known Martha?

Before the thought was even half-formed I knew it would be pointless and dangerous. I remembered the man who had called me in the coffee shop the previous evening. If he were connected to what happened to Sister Mary Joseph in any way, then he wouldn't hesitate to stop me as he had stopped Sister Mary Joseph. If he were the one danger, then for Laura's sake I'd risk it. But there was an older and greater danger to me involved. I didn't know whether the man who talked to me on the phone and told me about Sister Mary Joseph's accident was a policeman. He could have been a doctor or a helpful bystander. But I didn't think so. His repeated question "Who is this?" and the sharp way he asked it almost certainly in my mind made him a policeman. If the police were there I wouldn't be allowed to question anyone without their cooperation and/or supervision. I had spent nearly twenty years fearing and running from the police. I was, legally, a fugitive. How long before they checked the FBI files? It was true, they most likely wouldn't find me there under the name of Janet Covington, but I did not share Jeff's arrogant and gratifying assurance that all cops everywhere were basically stupid. And if Macrae had, as I now was pretty convinced he had, shared with them all the incriminating details I had confided in him, then they didn't even have to use what minds they had. It was laid out for them.

All of which made me think of Macrae. As the name went through my mind it was accompanied by a surge of rage. I couldn't believe I had been such a fool as to make the mistake of trusting him. Did I find him that attractive? The answer was one

I didn't want to contemplate at this moment. I shoved it to the back of my mind.

I felt desperately sorry for Sister Mary Joseph, but, if I was to continue my search for Laura, the only thing I could do now was to get myself to Logan Airport and safety as fast as I could.

■ ■ ■ Everyone in the hotel seemed to be trying to check out when I got to the lobby. I waited in line, not too patiently, and when the clerk seemed to favor getting his papers in order before coming back to me, said rather snappily that I was already late for my flight to New York. Grudgingly he came back to the counter, took my credit card and completed the formalities.

"Have a nice trip," he said, handing me the receipt with a forced smile on his face.

"Thank you," I said, not even bothering with the smile.

Crossing the lobby I saw two people I knew. One was the man I had suspected the day before of following me. For a moment I froze, but I had to concede my identification would not have satisfied a court or a police report. It was the man's back, not his face, that looked familiar. I stopped. Then I moved as quietly as I could close up behind him. Just as I was about to veer out and step in front of him where I could see his face, he turned.

He didn't look remotely the way I thought he would. I had somehow envisaged a thin, narrow face with shifty eyes set close together and a sallow expression. Whether all this came from my imagination or not I didn't know. Had I seen, at least, his profile? Now, with his full face turned towards me and not more than six feet away, I felt a considerable fool. This man's face was middle-aged, full and florid. He stared at me. I stared at him. Then he said, "Excuse me," stepped around me, and approached the desk.

Shaken, I continued across the lobby to the swinging doors at the front. The man who followed me the day before could have been middle-aged, full faced and florid, but everything in me screamed that it was not the same man. Was that simply the stubborn, tenacious power of a preconceived notion, with no basis in reality? It was possible—theoretically—but I couldn't make myself believe that the man I had just seen was the man outside the college yesterday.

I stalked to the doors, full of self-doubt, afraid, angry and therefore not looking where I was going. Vaguely I was aware that a man was coming towards me on the other side of the glass doors, but since I was looking out into the light, he was just a shape.

"Excuse me," I said, as the man came through the doors almost on top of me.

"Janet," Macrae said.

We both stopped. I stared at the man who, I was convinced, was the author of all the instructions, the snooping and the anxieties of the past few days. "Well, Mr. FBI man," I said furiously. "Aren't your spics doing a good enough job? Are you here to give it your personal attention?"

"What the hell are you talking about?" Macrae said.

"Would you mind?" An irritated man, his path blocked by the two of us, was trying to get past.

"You know perfectly well what I'm talking about," I said, moving a few paces. "And your air of innocence doesn't say much for your early gumshoe training." I turned to push the door open when I felt a hand around my arm.

"Just a minute," Macrae said.

"Take your hand from my arm. If you don't, you'll hear one almighty bloody yell."

He removed his hand. "Hit and run, right? Spew your poisonous accusation and then leave quickly before you have to explain it. All in the best female tradition. Yes, that's right," he said, as I opened my mouth, "I'm also a male chauvinist pig. Be sure to put that in my publicity material." And he stalked towards the desk. I watched for a moment. He was, after all, a prominent author. Then I shrugged. Let him request another editor.

I got my car and drove out to Logan.

Leaving the car with the car rental agency, I was hurrying across the terminal floor to catch the shuttle due to leave in about seven minutes when a man stepped in front of me, a shield in his hand. "Miss Covington? I'm Lieutenant Farrell." He indicated the tall black man standing beside him. "This is Sergeant Jones. I wonder if we could speak to you."

Because there was nothing else to do, I stopped. "I'll miss my plane."

"There'll be another in an hour."

I took a breath and glanced at him and the man with him. "All right. What do you want to talk about?"

"Why don't we step into the room here just off the lobby?"

"I'm not stepping anywhere with you until I know what it's about."

"It's about Sister Mary Joseph's—er—accident."

My heart seemed to stop beating for a moment. "Are you implying it wasn't an accident?"

"That's what we're trying to establish—"

"How is she now?"

"She died a few minutes ago," the policeman said.

"Oh! Oh, God, I'm sorry!"

"Shall we go into this room. Somehow it seems a better place to talk."

"Why don't we just step over here to the side. I can keep an eye on the departure board that way."

"All right. I thought we would, for your sake, have more privacy in the room there and we could sit down. However—"

"By the way," I interrupted, "just out of curiosity, how did you recognize me?"

"The hotel clerk said you'd be driving a rented car. He knew because you used the hotel garage. Also the nuns at St. Jude as well as the clerk gave me a description of you." The lieutenant paused. "What did you see Sister Mary Joseph about? According to the reception sister, she was with you for an hour or more. Is that right?"

"Yes." My mind scurried around all possible answers I could make to this man. Finally I said, "I had come to ask Sister Mary Joseph about a woman who died in the nursing home six months ago, a Martha Mahaffey, who was once secretary to my father. He had at one time placed a child for adoption. It has become important for me to find out with whom he placed it, and since he is dead and has been dead for a long time—I thought Martha might know."

"Did she?"

"Sister Mary Joseph didn't know. She told me she was going to talk to two of the nurses who had known Martha to see if she had confided in either of them."

"Do you know if she did talk to them?"

"No, she was going to call me back last night, but didn't. I called her this morning to ask her about it. And when somebody —one of the sisters, I suppose—answered, a man took the phone and told me Sister Mary Joseph had had an accident . . ." I paused.

"And you hung up." It was a statement, not a question.

"Yes."

"Why?"

"Because I didn't want to discuss what I had talked about to Sister Mary Joseph with anyone else."

"Was the child who you're looking for yours, perhaps?"

I hesitated, but how long could I hold out on that? "Yes."

"Would anyone want to stop you from finding out?"

"I've been asking myself that. The answer is, if so, I don't know why."

I saw Lieutenant Farrell's glance go past me and I turned. There, watching us, was Macrae.

"A friend of yours?" the lieutenant asked me.

"No," I said. "Someone I have . . . have worked with." As Macrae walked over I resigned myself and said, "This is William Macrae, author of an upcoming book and an ex-FBI man."

"What seems to be the problem?" Macrae asked. His question was courteous, his face cold and indifferent.

The lieutenant hesitated, then said, "Miss Covington had a long conversation yesterday with a woman who was knocked down by a car early this morning. The car drove away—left the scene of the accident—if it was an accident—and she died in the hospital."

Macrae's expression didn't change. "Sister Mary Joseph," he said. Again it was a statement, not a question.

"Yes. How did you know?"

"A . . . friend told me."

"What friend?"

Macrae sighed. "Sister Elizabeth, one of the other sisters at the nursing home. She is my second cousin. I was in Boston on business and called her." He paused. "I take it you don't think it was an accident."

"From eye witness accounts it sounded pretty deliberate. Apparently the car veered across the road to hit her."

"I see."

"You in town on Bureau business?" The lieutenant's voice was civil but his disbelief showed.

"No, something about a book I am currently writing. While I was here I called Elizabeth to find out how she was."

"And what's the book about?"

"Lieutenant, one of the things most writers learn early is not to discuss a work in progress—unless it's with one's editor."

"And who might he be?" The lieutenant was respectful—far

more so than when he was questioning me—but hanging onto his skepticism.

"You're questioning her right now." There was a glimmer of amusement in Macrae's cool blue eyes.

Farrell looked at me with momentary surprise. Then he turned back to Macrae. "So it was for family reasons that you called your cousin, Sister Elizabeth?" he asked.

"Mostly."

"And?"

"As I told you, Lieutenant, I prefer not to discuss works in progress."

"All right for now." Turning to me Farrell said, "According to one or two of the other nurses, during supper last night Sister Mary Joseph was called to the phone. Everyone, Miss Covington, assumed it was you, because they seemed to know she was trying to get information for you from two of the sisters, one of whom was visiting her family." His voice hardened suddenly. "What did you and Sister Mary Joseph talk about?"

"Hold it!" Macrae said. "You don't know that she did talk to her."

"As a former law officer, I'd think you would be interested in solving this crime," Farrell sounded aggrieved as well as annoyed.

"I don't think bullying witnesses or trying to catch them out is called for here, either. Come on, Janet. Let's get on the plane. If the lieutenant wants to reach you in New York, I'm sure he knows where he can."

"The plane just left," Farrell said with some pleasure in his voice. "And the next flight is an hour away."

"Just time to have a decent lunch." I felt his hand under my elbow and let myself be led towards the coffee shop near the corridor leading to the shuttle.

"You're very masterful," I said grumpily.

Macrae stopped abruptly, just short of the entrance to the cafe. "Do you want to go back to Farrell?"

"No, and you know I don't," I said.

"He's still watching, in case you haven't noticed. I thought we'd snatch a sandwich and sit down at a table. But if you prefer to go and sit by yourself at the gate, then by all means do so."

He had me there and I knew it.

I picked up a tray and started down the cafeteria line. My breakfast had been long hours ago and I was hungry, so I helped myself to a large hero sandwich and some coffee. When I got to the end I ostentatiously paid for my own lunch and walked to the window, sitting down at a table for two. Macrae was just behind me. When I sat down, he stood over me, tray in hand.

"Well?" he asked.

I submitted and pushed the other chair out. "Please sit down," I said graciously.

He sat down, put the dishes on his tray on the table and then put his tray onto a stand nearby. I waited for his opening statement or question, determined to be cool and uncooperative. But he said nothing, just opened his newspaper, propped it against the sugar bowl where he could read it and started in on his sandwich.

For a while we ate in silence, while I stared at the back of his newspaper and a headline that read, "Threatened Wildcat Taxi Strike in Big Apple." Then I said, "I don't think that will look very friendly to the watching Farrell."

"Is he still there?"

I glanced towards the door. "I don't see him."

"In that case we don't have to go on putting up a front."

"You're one of the rudest men I've ever met," I said, surprised at my own rage.

"That is certainly the pot calling the kettle black. What were those charming accusations you flung at my head when I came over to you at the hotel? Something about my having my snoops spy on you?"

"Well, didn't you?"

"No, I did not. For one thing I don't have any snoops, as you like to call them, for another, why should I? I was trying to help you find your daughter, not dig out the details of your life."

"Then who could have had somebody making inquiries about me at the office? Who could have had someone follow me in Boston?"

"I don't know. But since I didn't, you might turn your mind to who did."

12.

Against all my wishes and inclinations I believed him. But that certainly left me, at least in some respects, worse off than before. I chewed away at my hero sandwich and found I wasn't as hungry as I thought I was. I put half the sandwich down and sipped my coffee. "If it wasn't you, then who was it, and did he or she have anything to do with Sister Mary Joseph's death?"

"That's what your friend Lieutenant Farrell was trying to find out."

"What he was trying to do was pin the whole thing on me."

"Well, maybe with some logic. You show up and question the good sister and ask her to inform you about what she learned from the other sisters. Her secretary says she seemed upset by your visit. Then she gets run over—apparently deliberately—and dies. If you were Lieutenant Farrell wouldn't you be the least suspicious?"

"I've never found the workings of the police brain either interesting or inspiring."

"Ah yes. The former radical!"

"What are you talking about?"

"I'm talking about this: if you don't want people to leap to such an obvious conclusion, then you shouldn't make comments like that or the one the other day about federal agents not being heroes to your generation."

Plainly, I thought, safety and the respectable life had made me careless.

"They weren't heroes to any of my generation, not just the radicals. You should know that!"

"Since I got shot by one of your fellow radicals, I should."

I glanced at his large, lean physique. "You don't seem to have been scarred for life."

"Wait until you see me with my clothes off."

"An enticing prospect. I can hardly wait!"

He raised his eyes. "Am I to take that literally?"

"Of course not!"

Another silence ensued. I glanced up casually and saw Lieutenant Farrell stroll past the cafeteria door.

"Lieutenant Farrell is still here. I just saw him in the hallway outside the cafeteria."

"He probably wants to be quite sure you actually get on that plane."

"Why should he care?"

"He doesn't—at the moment—have enough to hold you, or he'd be holding you. But he probably wants to be certain that you're returning to New York and not doubling back when you think he's not looking to commit more mischief in Boston."

I blurted out, "Why were you really in Boston? I know you said it was because of your book—"

"But you didn't believe me."

"I thought—I thought it might have something to do with what I told you about . . . about me."

"Did anyone ever point out to you that that could be interpreted as paranoia?"

"You sound like my father. Although he would have called it self-centeredness. All right I withdraw the question."

"I realize you inherited my book, and you don't much like it. But you did read it, and surely you must remember that one of the defectors was born, brought up and educated in Boston and was probably here when he was recruited by his Soviet friends."

"But I thought all that was already written—finished. It seemed to me that it was when I read it."

"Something was called to my attention last week. I came up here to look into it."

"What was it?"

"If it has any relevancy to the book, you'll certainly be among the first to know."

"But you're not going to tell me unless it does."

"No. It involves other people. If it all amounts to nothing, why endanger a reputation?"

"And you don't trust me to keep my mouth shut?"

"Why should I? You don't trust me. And given your basic loyalties and assumptions I don't think you'd feel any need to protect at least one person who may—or may not—be involved."

"What do you mean by that—my basic loyalties and assumptions?"

"We both know your sympathies were with the campus radicals of the sixties—you've implied as much."

"And this person—whoever it is you're protecting—was on the other side? Pro the Vietnam War? Pro the establishment, whether the government, the military or the university?"

"You're taking a long leap. But it certainly shows, once a radical, you remain sympathetic to that side."

"And what side do you remain sympathetic to? The police

under Bull Connor who beat up Blacks trying to claim their civil rights?"

"As I said, a long leap." He put down his napkin. "I think I'll wait at the gate."

■ ■ ■ I sat there, staring out at the tarmac and airstrips and at planes landing and taking off. I hadn't allowed myself to be as easily goaded as this for a long, long time. What was it Jeff had once said? "You'll never make a good undercover person for the movement, Liz. Whatever's in your mind is on your tongue and out before you know what you're saying. There's a time to protest, to provoke, to incite. But you have to make the decision when to do it—so that you're the one in control, not some pig of a cop or government stooge on the faculty. But you have no control at all. You fight with the same passion whether it's with some kid who could be converted but who's still hooked into his family's middle-class values or somebody who's ready and could really help us."

"So what do you want me to do?" I had asked, disappointed and humiliated because he'd put me down.

"Right now, I want you to shut up. Don't go all around the place screaming your newfound ideas. Cool it. You may think you're a rebel, but you radiate the bourgeois mystique, and I'd rather use you that way. Smoke your pot and hang out with the kids who like to think they're radicals but'll be voting conservative by the time they're out of college ten years."

"Well, if that's what they're going to turn into, what do you want with them?"

"If all else fails, it'd be nice to have something on them. Useful." He smiled at me. "Also profitable."

In some way that conversation—and others like it—seemed so long ago it was almost as though it had all happened to somebody else. Yet in another way I remembered the scene and the words as though they'd been spoken last week.

And then, suddenly, there flashed into my mind the words Paul had flung at me: "I know more about you than you think."

Knowing he was drunk at the time, I didn't take it seriously. But what did he mean? I had never told Paul the gorier details of my radical past and I had studiously avoided all political talk when I could. It was true that Paul and at least some of his friends took certain attitudes for granted. And I had done nothing to disabuse them. But, surely, that was a far cry from positive information about certain episodes that could, indeed, spell serious trouble for me if they were known.

It could, I tried to reassure myself, be just drunk talk.

I turned as a flight attendant came rapidly across the cafeteria towards me. "Aren't you on this flight to New York?"

I glanced at the clock figured prominently on the wall. "Oh God! Yes. Thanks." I snatched up my bag and sped toward the door.

What were obviously the last passengers were slowly filing their way past another attendant standing at the desk, checking people's tickets and seat numbers. "Sorry," I said, running up, and thrusting my ticket at her.

"You almost missed it," she said cheerfully, "if that nice man hadn't told us you were supposed to be on this flight."

"Thanks," I said, and moved quickly down the jet sleeve to the plane. To my surprise the plane was full. I glanced around. Macrae was next to the window halfway down, reading a book. Two people were beside him. The only vacant seats were far behind. I went past his row and sank into the nearest empty aisle seat.

Was "the nice man" who had alerted the attendant Macrae, or someone else, like Lieutenant Farrell or the man who had been following me, who might have their own reasons for wanting me out of Boston? A sense of unease took me. I discovered I was sorry not to be sitting beside Macrae.

Angry at myself, I took out my own book and tried hard to read it for the forty-five-minute flight to La Guardia.

Just before we landed a cheerful voice announced that those who were planning to take cabs at La Guardia might have a long wait. The threatened one-day wildcat strike had struck. "But not to worry, they put on extra airport buses," she said soothingly.

■ ■ ■ I was one of the last to leave the plane and could see Macrae's tall figure well ahead of me, going towards the taxi lines and parking lot. The announcer had been right. There were few taxis and those who had shown up had been nabbed by people seated in the front and the middle of the plane who had got off before me. I looked around. The cabs were few and far between and the situation was not helped by the weather. It had been bright when I left Boston. Now the sky was gray and threatening. At that moment out of the corner of my eye, I saw what I thought to be Macrae in a private car driving towards the exit from the terminal.

The bastard, I thought. He didn't even offer me a lift. And I crushed down the inner voice that sneered, after the way you spoke to him, why should he? I stood there, staring both ways, hoping that, strike or no strike, someone in town would have been able to snare a cab to come to the airport but the only one that did drop someone off ignored my yells and took off. I was therefore desperate when a black car with a handprinted sign saying "Livery" stuck in the windshield came up.

In my years in New York I had once or twice taken a gypsy cab when I was in a desperate hurry in a rush hour or in a pouring rainstorm. And they had always carried me safely to wherever I was going. So when the driver stuck his head out and said, "Wanna ride to New York?" I said, "Yes. How much?"

He shrugged. "Whatever you think is fair."

I opened the door. Some sense of self-preservation made me hesitate. People had been known to be overcharged three and four hundred percent beyond the regular fare. But they were usually obvious foreigners, hampered by little English and no experience of New York. I neither looked nor sounded like an inexperienced foreigner. In some last gesture of defiance towards —towards whom? I wondered briefly—I got in and gave him my address. "It's in the West Village," I said.

I had made the trip numberless times, so I was aware, when the car made an abrupt left turn off the highway, that the driver was not taking the usual route.

"Why aren't we taking the Triborough Bridge?" I asked sharply.

"Lady, you said you lived in the West Village. Why go by the Triborough? That takes you uptown."

"What bridge are you taking?"

"The tunnel. What's the matter? I've done this hundreds of times."

I hesitated. Every taxi I'd ever driven in from La Guardia had taken the Triborough Bridge then gone down the East River Drive and cut across town at Fourteenth Street to the Village. But I knew that practically speaking there was no reason this man shouldn't take the Midtown Tunnel, go down Second Avenue to Fourteenth and then west. What I didn't like were the dark streets we were going through now. On the other hand to insist, at this point, that he turn around and go back, picking his way among streets that all seemed to be one way, seemed idiotic. "All right," I said. "We've come this far. I guess we'd better go for the tunnel."

"I know all the short cuts," he said.

It was only mid-afternoon but the rain was now streaming down and it had grown too dark for me to see his face in the rear view mirror. I had almost no memory of it from when he leaned out and spoke to me. I had the impression he was young, but that could have been his voice.

The streets seemed to get narrower and darker, the houses more run down. It was not that late, yet there were no people about. The rain was now coming down in buckets. There would have been no sign of life around us at all if it weren't for the headlights of the car behind us. It had been there since shortly after we turned off the main road. For some reason I took the presence of the other car as proof that my driver was taking me the right way.

But my faith in this was tested sorely as we twisted and turned in what seemed to me a crazy way. As the car swerved sharp left into a street barely wide enough for two cars and with half its street lights gone I became, suddenly, quite sure that the driver was not heading towards the tunnel or any bridge.

"Where are you taking me?" I asked, and could hear the fear in my voice.

"I told you. To the tunnel," he said.

I felt the car suddenly accelerate and was convinced he was lying. If we could only come to a stoplight, I thought desperately, I would then jump out and risk the streets because they had become less threatening than this man. But there hadn't been a stoplight for many minutes. The streets we were going through didn't sport traffic lights. I glanced behind. Even the car that had been following had gone, leaving me with no support at all.

And then, suddenly, as we approached a narrow intersection, just before we started to cross it, a car shot across our hood and stopped. My driver stamped on his brakes. We still crashed into the car but not as hard as we might have done.

Everything then happened so fast I was hardly aware of what was going on. The next thing I knew Macrae's face was at the window of the car.

"Open the door," he yelled.

I tried the door but it was locked. I looked for the gadget that was supposed to lock it, but there was none.

"Duck!" Macrae shouted again, and I saw some kind of instrument in his hand coming towards the window at great speed.

Just in time I realized what he was telling me, and ducked below the edge of the window as the glass shattered. Then Macrae reached in, wrenched in an odd way at the door handle and somehow got the door open.

At that moment the driver, whose head had been resting on the steering wheel straightened, looked back and lunged towards me. But with Macrae hauling on my shoulder, I slipped past the driver's hands and was out in the street. I saw the driver lean forward then and pick up something from under the wheel area. As he turned, I saw the gun, then I saw Macrae's hand slice through the air and strike back of his neck. The driver slumped forward over the wheel again.

"Come on!" Macrae yelled, grabbing me by the hand, and we started to run down one of the streets we were trying to cross. It was so dark and slick it was a miracle I didn't trip and fall.

We turned another corner and then a second, then we stopped.

"Be still," Macrae said. "Let me listen."

I could hear no sound, except the rain and, at a distance, cars and from behind some closed door, a loud TV or radio.

"All right," Macrae said. "Let's get back to the cars. With any luck he'll still be chasing us down some other street."

We must have run almost full circle. The cars were exactly where we had collided in the middle of the small intersection. The car I had been in was empty. Macrae's car was at right angles to its hood.

"Now is the moment to discover whether I outsmarted myself," Macrae muttered.

He went over to his car, opened the door away from the side

hit by the taxi and put his key in the ignition. "Come and get in," he said. "Quickly."

I got in. Macrae got in after me and turned the ignition key. Somewhat to my surprise, the engine coughed on. Macrae shifted the gear and then gently pressed the accelerator. Its windshield wipers going frantically, the car crept forward until it was finally free of the taxi. "That's a plus," he said, rolled the car easily until the next intersection, then turned and picked up speed.

We drove around another corner or two and came to a much wider, more brilliantly lit road.

"My God," I said, "that was a spooky area. I didn't see a light."

"It's mostly abandoned warehouses."

"And where in God's name was he taking me? And why? I don't understand any of this."

"No." Macrae was obviously concentrating on driving and didn't reply. After a minute, when some of the landmarks were beginning to look familiar I said, "He did kidnap me, didn't he? I mean, I thought I must be crazy to think so! But that's what he did!"

"Yes, I think he did."

His calm voice had the effect of calming me.

"But why?"

"I don't know. Do you have any idea?"

"What happened in Boston? Do you think it had something to do with my talking to Sister Mary Joseph?"

"It's possible."

We drove for a while. I sat going through the events, one by one, as though I could find something in them that would reveal who was behind it and why. Suddenly I sat up. "You were the car that followed us from the road away from the Triborough, weren't you?"

"I was indeed."

"But I saw you drive out of the terminal in your car minutes before I decided to take that wretched gypsy. I was furious at you for not offering me a lift."

"I was tired of having my various invitations thrown back in my face."

I absorbed that. Then I said, "But you were ahead of us. How did you see us and decide to follow? And why? Did you know there was something wrong with the car and/or driver?"

"Your driver pulled out of there at such a speed that he soon passed me, and I saw you drive past with him. The fact that it wasn't a regular cab made me uneasy. There's nothing wrong with most of the livery drivers, but—I don't know, something made me decide to follow and see what happened. Then he fooled me by turning off the parkway. I had to go to the next exit to turn off. For a while I lost you altogether. But then I caught up and decided that this was not what it should be. I tried the experiment of driving faster, on the theory that if he didn't want to drive that fast he could just motion me ahead. But he picked up speed, too. That's when I decided you were in trouble. I couldn't think of any way to stop the guy other than the way I did. At least not for sure. But this car is pretty sturdy, so I decided to take the risk."

After a pause I said, "I haven't thanked you."

He didn't say anything.

The shock of the whole thing was wearing off and I could feel myself starting to shake.

"Cold?" he said after a minute.

I shook my head and then realized he couldn't see it. "No. Fright, I think."

He lifted his right hand from the steering wheel and then put it back. "It'll wear off after a bit."

After we were back on the parkway he said, "Tell me what happened back there in Boston. I picked up bits and pieces from what my cousin told me and what Lieutenant Farrell extracted from you, but I'd like a coherent account."

So I told him about my visit to St. Jude, about the weird call I got in the hotel coffee shop and my impression that I was being followed. "In fact, at one moment in the car when I got kidnapped, I thought it might be the same man who seemed to be trailing me in Boston. But I really only saw his back so I couldn't be sure."

"Okay, now tell me what happened with the kidnapper and everything he said."

I did. "There's not much of it," I said when I'd finished.

"Somehow I don't think you were being kidnapped for money—you don't enjoy a reputation for vast wealth. You're an attractive woman and he could, of course, have uglier and more personal schemes in mind."

"But would he think he could get away with it?"

"Why not? Are you in the habit of noting license plates and their numbers?"

I thought for a moment. "No. Did he have plates?"

"Yes, nicely muddied over, so I couldn't begin to read them."

"So you think he could just have had rape on his mind?"

"He could, but somehow I don't think so."

"I thought at first he might think I was one of those unlucky foreigners who get off at the airport, take a cab and are then charged two hundred dollars. But I didn't sound like a foreigner and I told him that the address I gave him was in the West Village, so he could tell I knew New York."

"Not necessarily. Not until you objected when he turned off. The person whom you were visiting might have told you to ask for the West Village, so that alone wouldn't save you. But I agree, when you queried his route, then he must have known you were no outsider."

"So what do you think it was all about?"

"I have a feeling there have been other episodes in your early life you haven't told me. Not your having a child. Something more—something less personal. Do you want to tell me what it is?"

13.

So there it was.

Idly I noticed we were now on the bridge. Spread out in front of us were the lighted colored jewels of the New York skyline.

Once, when I noted casually to Jeff that I thought the famed skyline was beautiful and exciting, Jeff replied acidly that the noted skyline filled him with rage because to him it represented capitalistic greed at its most arrogant.

The memory of that moment, whole, filled my mind. Where were we at that time? Lying on our backs on a blanket in the foothills of the Sierras, having a picnic.

I still thought it beautiful and exciting. Without even thinking I said the words, "I still think it's beautiful and exciting."

"You sound as though you were defending something, are you?" Macrae said.

And I was back in the present with the man I'd thought to be the enemy sitting beside me, his question, unanswered, hanging between us. I couldn't—or wouldn't—answer his question, but he deserved an apology. I took a breath. "I'm sorry . . . I'm sorry I was so paranoid, thinking you were the one out to get me. I owe you an apology. Particularly since you rescued me."

We slid up to the toll booth. Macrae pushed his money into the man's hand and started down the FDR Drive. "It's all right." He paused.

"You don't sound as if you thought it was all right. You sound mad as hell. Not that anyone could blame you."

"I am mad as hell! I liked you. I liked you a lot. I've tried to show it, and all you've done is spit in my face!"

Torn in two different directions I stared at the buildings on my right as the car sped down the drive. Part of me was acknowledging—with considerable shock—how much I, too, had felt a powerful attraction. The other, of course, was my cautious shadow self. Don't trust him. He could send you to jail. When would you find Laura then?

Suddenly I forgot about being a fugitive. I only knew at this moment that I was having an overwhelming desire to touch the man beside me. I looked down at his long leg, foot on the accelerator, and without thinking put my hand on it.

"Whoa!" he said. His hand came down on top of mine. "Not here, not this minute!"

Humiliated I tried to snatch my hand away. He lifted it off his leg, but held onto the hand.

"If you—" I started.

But he interrupted. "Don't say anything."

As though watching a movie, I saw the car turn off at Ninety-sixth Street. "I live on the Lower West Side," I said, knowing perfectly well he knew that.

"I know. I live here."

I summoned more words, acid comments, angry questions as to what he thought he was doing. They didn't get as far as my tongue.

We stopped in front of a brownstone somewhere in the Nineties between Madison and Park avenues.

Pushing open his door, he walked around the front of the car and opened mine.

"I don't—" I started.

"It's up to you. Nobody's forcing you!"

I should have been furious. Instead, I got out of the car and realized with a shock that my legs were shaking. He locked the car, then walked up the steps of the house, and put a key in the front door. I followed.

There were four mailboxes between the inner and outer front doors. Then we were inside and walking up carpeted stairs. His apartment was on the second floor. Inside I saw a small multicolored cat come running forward, tail in the air, followed by a big black one.

But I didn't have time to take anything else in.

Macrae's arms seemed to crush the breath out of me. His mouth was warm and hard on mine. His body was urgent, and so was mine. And then we were in the bedroom and he was stripping off my blouse. And then, on the bed, his hands and mouth were on my body and mine on his.

■ ■ ■ In my early days of drugs and rock I had made love—although that was hardly the right word for it—many times with many boys and men. Often I didn't even remember what went on, or with whom. Deep in my Catholic-trained insides I still felt shame over that. I had considered myself in love with Jeff although I had come to realize that love wasn't exactly what it was. He had been a cool, skilled lover. Paul was more urgent. But neither had been as wonderfully exhilarating as Macrae. Outlandishly, in the middle, I heard my father's measured tones talking, as he often did at the dinner table, about thesis, antithesis and synthesis.

And I laughed.

"What's funny?" Macrae paused long enough to ask.

I told him, and he laughed.

■ ■ ■   Afterwards, when we were lying there, sated, content, I heard what seemed like a Siamese cat's voice on the other side of the bedroom door.

"I didn't notice that one of them was Siamese," I said.

"That's Waldo, he's a mutt, but I suspect he has Siamese ancestors."

"What is he saying?"

"He's telling me I haven't fed him or Samantha."

"Who feeds them when you're away?"

"I have a cat-sitter who comes in and feeds and plays with them. If I'm away long, she stays."

I wondered what she was like. I tried to keep my mind on that rather than on the astonishment I felt at what had happened between Macrae and me, at my being there beside him.

And then he said, "Did you decide you could trust me, or did that not have anything to do with what happened?"

In view of the way I had treated him, I knew I had no right to be angry at his derisive—almost sarcastic—tone, yet I was.

"You certainly don't let sentimentality stand in the way of your manners," I said.

"Do you?"

"I didn't know . . . I didn't realize how I felt . . . feel about you until it was happening."

I pushed up on one elbow and looked down at him. It was a mistake. There had always been a disciplined quality about his face, as though most of the feelings were kept well tamped down. Now there was a tender, angry, vulnerable look. The blue eyes seemed wider and bluer. My own strayed down. He was thin but muscular. I saw, under the ribs, the scar, still red, with lines going out. I touched it. "Does it hurt?" I said.

"Only when I'm tired or when it rains or sometimes both." He pulled me down, and everything started again.

■ ■ ■ The sky was still dark when I woke up. On his side, his face away from me, was Macrae. I lay there, thinking about what had happened between us. The miraculous part was that while it was going on the fear that had been with me day and night for so many years had lifted, which probably accounted for the giddy happiness that had filled me for a brief hour or two—something I hadn't even noticed until the fear returned.

But I should remember, my traitorous mind argued, Jeff had made love to me—and then deserted and threatened me. From my fellow radicals I had learned that sex and making love were often as much weapons to be used, vulnerabilities to be exploited, as anything else. Even though Paul and I had views more or less in accord—at least at the beginning—I hadn't been able to trust Paul, to the point where, in his own words, I could come out of hiding. And Macrae? If I stayed, I might—would—cross that line. And then I would never find Laura, not if he knew all there was to know about me. Or, if he found her, would he tell me, would he tell her her own birth mother was a felon?

Quietly I slipped out of bed and into my clothes and then, as quietly as I could, opened the bedroom door. The two cats backed off, watching me warily. Carrying my shoes and handbag, I went across the carpeted floor and out the front door, almost surprised at myself for successfully not waking Macrae.

I knew I couldn't get my bag from the trunk of his car. Well, that would have to wait. There was something to be said for the Upper East Side. Even at that hour it was possible to hail a taxi.

■ ■ ■ Paul was lying, fully clothed, on our bed in the bedroom. His face was red, his mouth open and he was snoring loudly. I found myself wishing violently he would move out, and remembered suddenly Claire Aldington's advice about seeing that he did. Then I recalled our truce of the past few nights, and the bed

I had just come from. It all seemed muddled and rather discreditable.

Evidently I made a noise. The snores stopped. Paul shifted around. Then he opened his eyes and lay there blinking at me.

"Welcome home," he said, slurring the words. Reaching out a hand to the alarm clock on the bedside table, he brought it up to his face, and then held it away.

After watching him do this for a minute or two I said, "It's about a quarter past one."

He put the clock down. "Out with your new author, I suppose, the supercop."

The temptation to say, Yes, I have been, was overwhelming, but caution prevailed. "I've been in Boston—on business," I added.

He grunted, stared at me for a moment, then flopped down again. In a few seconds, the snores started.

I stood there, staring at Paul, wondering what to do next. I could, of course, go into the study, but most of the time for weeks now it had been his room, his bed, and I found myself curiously reluctant to get into it.

There was the sofa in the living room, but it was not in the greatest condition. I'd been promising myself for a year either to have it resprung and reupholstered or to buy a new one. But I hadn't gotten around to it. So what did that leave?

It left my own bed. I could push Paul over and lie down under the covers. But I knew I wouldn't even consider it. So it had to be the sofa, bad springs and all.

I was in the shower before I recalled once more that the bag still in Macrae's car held my toothbrush and my robe. Fortunately, I had another robe hanging behind the bathroom door. I was rummaging in the hall closet to see if I had another toothbrush when something made me turn around. Paul was standing in the bedroom doorway.

"Where the hell were you?"

"I told you when I came in, in Boston."

"Yeah? I don't remember that."

"Considering everything, I'm not surprised."

His flush went a shade deeper. "What are you talking about?"

"Oh come on, Paul. You've been drinking and you passed out fully dressed on my bed. When I came in you woke up long enough to say 'Welcome home.' "

"It used to be my bed, too. And you weren't sorry to have me in it this past week. What's made you go back on that again?" He started forward.

"Paul, I'm tired, it's late. I'll snatch some sleep on the sofa."

He stared at me, at my wet hair. "You always shower in the morning. You said you liked it better. Why're you showering now? Who've you been in bed with?"

There were times when he was uncannily on target. "Nobody," I said. "You've been drinking. Now leave me alone!"

He stared at me for a moment, swaying a little. His skin flushed, then the color receded, leaving two bars of red across his cheeks. I knew it was a sign of anger. He began walking forward.

"If you come any further, Paul," I said slowly and clearly, "I'll scream so loud the entire neighborhood will hear."

He stopped. "You didn't say that two days ago."

"Two days ago it wasn't two o'clock in the morning after a long, difficult trip."

What he would do next was a toss-up. I felt my body stiffen.

Then he shrugged. "Suit yourself," he said, and went towards the study.

As I put fresh sheets on my bed, I knew I'd have to find a way to get him out and to do it soon. Before I got into bed I made sure the door was locked. When I woke up much later Sunday morning Paul was gone. To my vast relief he didn't return until after I had gone to bed Sunday night.

■ ■ ■ Monday morning I sat in a meeting which dragged on and on and tried to keep my mind on what was under discussion. But it kept veering between what had happened between Macrae and me and what to do about Paul. Finally, when it ended, I went back to my office and called Claire Aldington. Our lunch date was not until later in the week, but she seemed to know a lot about alcoholism, was a professional counselor and I suddenly felt I needed to talk to her a lot sooner than that.

Leafing through my messages before phoning, I was a little surprised to see that Macrae hadn't called me. But I pushed that from my mind as I looked up the number of St. Anselm's and dialed it.

"She's in session with a client," a pleasant female voice said when I was put through to the pastoral counseling office. "But I'll take a message and she can call you back."

The phone rang about ten minutes later. "It's Claire Aldington," she said, and I remembered her voice with something like relief.

"I was wondering if we couldn't have lunch earlier than our present date," I said.

"Has something come up?"

"Yes. But I'd rather talk to you about it in person."

"All right. How about today?"

I had a date with an author, but I knew I'd break that. "Fine. Wherever's convenient with you."

There was a short pause. "Why don't you come to the parish house and we can go across the street if you don't mind a rather ungrand place."

I took down the exact location, Lexington Avenue between Sixty-second and Sixty-third. "But I had a vague idea it was on Park Avenue," I said.

"The church itself is, and you can certainly come in through that way if it's more convenient, but the parish house is back of it and fronts on Lexington."

"I'll be there."

■ ■ ■ Since I'd left home I'd gone to church—to any church —only, in the classic phrase, when friends, or the children of friends, were being hatched, matched and/or dispatched, that is, for baptisms, weddings or burial services. And St. Anselm's Church hadn't figured among my particular set of friends in any of those ceremonies. I had, of course, read about it in news accounts and had a vague idea that there had been the dramatic suicide death of a previous rector and, more recently, some startling goings-on involving the death of an aging British dean. I was also aware that it was famous for its boys' choir, considered second only to the internationally acclaimed St. Thomas's choir.

From the outside the parish house was a dark stone building and seemed to comprise about three brownstones put together. The main entrance was on the corner of Sixty-second. I walked up the steps, through the gothic arched wooden doors and up more steps inside. A somewhat harried-looking young woman was behind a desk talking into the phone, trying to deal with what looked like a delivery of some kind and casting glances at a tall, good-looking young priest standing near.

"I'm sorry," she said into the receiver, "the rector's not in right now, and his secretary's at lunch. May I take a message?" The words were polite, the voice exasperated. Then, "I'm afraid I don't understand. Could you possibly speak in English?"

The young priest reached over a long arm. "Spanish?" he asked the receptionist.

"Yes. I suppose I should know it, but I don't."

"Yes, you should," the priest said severely. "It should be everybody's second language." Then he pulled the receiver to him and shot a volley of Spanish through it.

I waited for the receptionist to pay off the delivery boy, then approached. "I'm Janet Covington, and I have an appointment with Mrs. —" I hesitated, not knowing whether to use Claire's married or professional name.

"Aldington?" the receptionist asked.

"Yes."

The girl glanced at the switchboard. "She's on the phone right now. I'll tell her you're here as soon as she's off. And as soon as Father Martinez is through with the phone," she added, a bit grudgingly.

We waited. What seemed like an agitated conversation went on. My Spanish was not good, but I had heard enough, particularly when I was out in California, to be fairly sure that the priest's Spanish hailed from Spain rather than from the Americas or the Caribbean.

"You really should learn Spanish," Father Martinez said reprovingly, handing back the receiver.

"Why?" the receptionist said. "Why Spanish more than Japanese or Chinese or . . . or Italian or Polish? Why discriminate?"

The handsome face frowned. He opened his mouth. At that point a tall rotund man in a round collar ambled up. He glanced around, then smiled at me. "Can I help?"

"I'm waiting to see Claire Aldington."

The receptionist, who had been glaring at Father Martinez, put the receiver to her ear and pushed a button on her small switchboard. "Mrs. Covington to see you," she said.

She put the phone down. "She said she'll be down right away."

"What happened to the chairs here?" Father Martinez said belligerently.

"Some people are inclined to occupy them all day," the receptionist said.

"You mean the homeless."

"Yes."

"I think it is outrageous," Father Martinez started, angrily, "and totally lacking in compassion towards people who have no home, no facilities, no—"

"I tell you what, Joe," the rotund man said, "why don't you suggest to Sally here that they can all sit in your office while they're—er—resting."

Sally giggled. "I'll do that."

"I'll be happy to have them," Joe said angrily, "but my office is small and besides my desk chair there's only one other. Here, there's a big lobby doing absolutely nothing."

"It's holding people who come in and out of the parish house on various errands and missions," the other cleric said, "and—"

The elevator door opened and Claire Aldington came out. "Hello, Janet. Sorry to have kept you waiting. Have you met the others here?"

"No, not yet."

"Sally is at the phone, this is Larry Swade and Joe Martinez."

We shook hands all around.

"About the chairs," Father Martinez said angrily.

Claire put her hand on my arm. "Let's go across the street. As I said, it's rather ordinary, but the food is reasonable and it's moderately quiet."

■ ■ ■ "That's a rather fiery young man," I said when we were settled in a booth near the window.

She grinned. "Joe Martinez?"

"Yes."

"He burns on behalf of all the oppressed. Actually, he's a good guy, and when he isn't tilting at establishment windmills he's bright and can be fun. We didn't get along too well for a while. I think he thought I supported the power structure."

"Which power structure?" Claire didn't look to me like the average ardent right-winger.

"Any power structure. He's not particular. To be fair, he's done wonderful work with the Hispanic community which we inherited when we closed down our chapel, St. Matthew's, on the West Side."

I looked at Claire. "I take it you don't sympathize with his revolutionary zeal."

Claire, who was looking at the menu, glanced quickly at me. "I don't object to revolutionary zeal, far from it. But it's sometimes hard for me to take Joe's seriously because in his enthusiasm for some revolutionary principle he's inclined to apply it without regard to the particular. I'll give you an example. Once he got angry at me because he wanted to put signs around the church in Spanish. I said I thought the idea was to help them and their children to learn English as well and as quickly as possible. He was furious. And he was about to launch into a diatribe when I pointed out that I was quoting one of the Spanish-speaking members of the congregation who was extremely eager to have her son and daughter learn English. It's the 'this side is always right and that side is always wrong' attitude that goads me. Why, are you at heart a revolutionary?"

I'd brought the question on myself. I had discussed my daughter with Claire with no thought of concealment. Until this moment I hadn't considered talking about my radical past. But if I were to consult her, I'd have to open that up, too.

"Don't answer if you'd rather not," Claire said. I found the steady look in her gray-green eyes rather reassuring.

"No, I'll answer. But—" I hesitated, then seeing the waitress coming towards us, surprised myself by saying, "Do you mind if we order sandwiches and take them back to your office? I have something to tell you, but I'd like to be as private as possible."

Her pause was barely a second long, then she said, "No." She turned to the waitress. "Bonnie, there's been a slight change of plan. Do you think you could bring us a couple of sandwiches and coffee for us to take across the street to my office. Something has come up."

"No, but you'd better get up and stand by the door. There's a line of people staring at the tables and you know how the boss is."

She returned with our lunch in a surprisingly short time. We went back across the street. There was a different young woman at the desk, Father Martinez was talking to a man who looked as though he might be one of the homeless and the rotund priest had vanished. Father Martinez looked up as we passed and smiled. He might be an undiscriminating revolutionary, I thought, but he certainly packed a lot of charm into that smile.

"He's attractive," I said, as we were going up in the elevator.

"He certainly is, and no one is more aware of it than some of our upper-crust young women in the congregation."

We walked along a hall to a door marked "Pastoral Counseling." Inside was what looked like an ante room with a desk, now empty. What was plainly an answering machine with a green light blinking was on a small table beside the desk.

"You have a call," I said.

"It can wait until Susie comes back. Let's go straight into my office."

It was a pleasant room looking out onto the gardens inside the square formed by the brownstones. I glanced around the walls. Hanging there was a picture of a blonde young woman and another one of a serious looking teen-age boy, squatting beside a large dog of mixed ancestry. There was no resemblance between the boy and Claire, but something made me say, "Is that your son?"

"Yes, that's Jamie. Beside him is the creature that in my more depressed moments I think is the dearest of all beings to him—his dog, Motley."

"I'm sure you're a good mother," I said, believing it to be true.

She sighed. "I try. Sometimes I think I succeed and sometimes I don't. There's one sure thing I discovered: none of the ton of books I read both professionally and otherwise about bringing up a child remotely prepares you for the real thing."

"Is the girl yours, too?"

"No, that was my first husband's daughter by his first wife. She was very young when he died, so she and I had to go it alone for at least half her life. She's a darling and seems to have gotten through the shoals pretty well, but it was chancy there for a while."

"And your present husband? Do the two of you have any children?"

"Not yet." Claire had unpacked the sandwiches and put them on plates she'd taken out of a cupboard to the side. Sodas and coffee were on her desk. "Do you want to talk while we eat, or would you rather eat and then talk?"

As she said that I realized I had been chattering and shooting off my questions partly, now that the moment had come, to put off having to say what I had come to say. After years of secretiveness, confiding was not easy, not even when the confessor was as obviously reliable and sympathetic as Claire.

I sat down on the chair beside the desk, picked up half of my sandwich and then put it down again. "I'm having a hard time coming out with this, but I'm going to have to do it, or I'll be wasting your time and mine: I don't know how to get rid of Paul, whose drinking is horrendous and of whom, I suddenly realized, I'm afraid. And in addition to having to find my daughter—and I'm getting nowhere there—the police in Boston are out to get me, I was kidnapped by some creep when I got back to La Guardia and . . . and I seem to have fallen in love with a man who, if he discovers who I am, might well put me in jail."

To my horror I found I was crying.

14.

Claire said gently, "What did you do that could put you in jail?"

I took a breath and said shakily, "I hope this office isn't bugged."

Claire looked at me a moment. "Is that a serious question?"

"It must sound pretty paranoid."

"Yes, a bit. But just to reassure you, no, it isn't bugged."

We sat silent for a moment. The long years of silence were like a lock on my mouth. But if I wanted to find Laura, if I wanted to know how to deal with Macrae, or even more, my own feelings about Macrae, whatever they were, I had to break it. I stared down at the sandwich I was holding.

"Thirteen years ago I went to a rehab and stayed there for a year. Before that, I wasn't only into drugs and alcohol, but into radical politics. I—I drove a car for people who held up a bank. Somebody was killed. I was charged with conspiracy. Under my phony name, of course, and I was never caught. Macrae, the man Paul kept mentioning at that dinner, the one he called the supercop, the ex-FBI type, is an author. He wrote this book that I inherited. Somebody's been asking around the office about me —details of my life, and so on." I stopped. "This must sound not only crazy, but wildly disjointed."

"It's all right," Claire said. "Go on."

"A buddy of mine told me about the inquiries. I jumped to the conclusion that it was Macrae and did everything to insult him—hold him at arm's length. But the truth is—I guess I was also fighting finding him attractive. When I went up to Boston to see if I could get a line on my daughter, he showed up there. When somebody tried to kidnap me at La Guardia on the way home, he rescued me. So I'm beginning to think I was wrong. . . ." I paused, and then continued.

"Beginning is a deceptive description, I guess. I realized suddenly how attractive I did find him and I—well, I sort of made a pass at him. The next thing I knew we were in his apartment, on his bed, in fact, making mad, passionate love. That was last night. I crept out this morning when he was asleep and went home. Paul was passed out on my bed. To tell you the truth, I'm afraid of him. When he's been drinking he's fully capable of striking me. He hasn't yet, but I'm fairly sure he will. You told me to make him move out, but he doesn't have anywhere to go, he's going to lose his job, and I don't know how."

"Have you told him you want him to move out?"

"Not in so many words. I got as far as saying whatever we had was over, and he said that when the new job offer he's expecting comes through he'll move out. But that won't be till next fall."

"So you haven't told him to move now?"

"No."

As I was silent she went on, "Is your foot-dragging just in memory of the times between you or does he have some hold over you? Or is there another reason?"

"He said the other day he knew too much about me. It was a sort of a threat. That was when I suggested what we had was over with the implication he should move. He immediately put it on my goings on—which were then nonexistent—with the new author, and he suddenly came out with that."

"As though it were blackmail?"

"Yes." I hadn't given a name to it, but that's what it was.

"Did you challenge him?"

"Yes. I made a wild stab at . . . at an accusation about a former colleague of his—a priest who landed up in jail for his radical goings on."

"Did you accuse him of being responsible for the priest's going to jail?"

I nodded. Claire had a way of stating things clearly. "More or less."

"And that's when he threatened you?"

"Yes."

Claire took the last bite of her sandwich. "I can see that getting him to move is much easier said than done. Obviously I wish it were his apartment. Then you could do the moving. But I take it it's yours. Do you own it—rent it?"

"I rent it. It's rent subsidized, because it's an old apartment in an old brownstone. You can understand the complications. If I did move out, I'd have a horrible time finding another at the same rental, and new apartments, built in the past few years, are horrendously expensive. Even if I could just walk away from the lease, which I can't."

"In addition to which, even if Paul kept paying the rent, I'm not sure that the landlord wouldn't have cause for sueing you and forcing him to move."

At that point we heard the door in the outside room open.

"Hi!" a young voice said. "Are you in there, Claire?"

"Yes," Claire called out. "I had lunch in—with a friend."

The door opened and a tall, roundcheeked girl paused. "Sorry, I didn't hear that bit about your friend in time."

"Janet, this is Susan Morris, Susie—" she waved a hand in my direction, "Janet Covington. And yes, I know what you're about to say, my two o'clock appointment is due."

As though on cue the outer door opened again and an unhappy-looking woman started in, hesitated when she saw me, and looked a little helplessly at Claire.

I got up, scattering crumbs. Leaning down I tried to gather them up.

"Don't worry about that," Claire said. "Our nice cleaning lady will take care of it. I'm sorry the time passed so fast."

She sounded as though she meant it. I hesitated. "Could I have just one more moment?" I asked.

"Of course. Helen, I'll be with you in a minute, and we'll make up any lost time."

Susie went out the door of the office and I closed it. "I'm sorry—" I started.

"Don't be. I'm glad we've had this talk."

"I'd like to talk to you again." The words came out of my mouth of their own accord.

"I think we ought to be clear: is this personal, or professional?"

I hesitated. "I had therapy at the rehab, but not since, because . . . well, until now I hadn't seemed to need it, and I suppose I didn't want to reveal all about my past." Without thinking my voice had dropped. "Could I consult you on a sort of temporary basis? Ongoing problems. I don't think I want or need the kind of classical analysis that goes back to the beginning and starts digging, although the past does keep intruding."

Claire smiled. "It does indeed. When would you like to come again?"

The word on the front of my mouth was tomorrow. "Friday?" I said, which was the day after tomorrow.

She glanced down at her engagement book. "One o'clock?"

"Fine." I picked up my raincoat.

Claire started scribbling on a pad. "In the meantime, you might consider getting in touch with this man. I don't know him well, but he's one of the country's chief experts in adoption— both the children and the parents. Your father might have been referred to him. If he doesn't know anything about your daughter, he might know a couple of people in various parts of the country who are involved in adoptions who might have some thoughts and/or ideas." She tore the page off the pad and handed it to me. "See you Friday," she said and smiled.

■ ■ ■ I went back to the office feeling better—lighter, as though a burden I carried had been lifted a little, even though nothing had changed. Then, I glanced through my messages. As I ran through them a second time I realized I was looking for one from Macrae. But it wasn't there. The glow and elation from the hours I'd spent with him was still with me. But it suddenly seemed a little dimmed.

I stared at the phone and as I did so, it rang. I snatched it up. "Hello?"

"Hello." Macrae's voice had its aloof, almost ironic note back. "I have your bag—the one you went to Boston with."

I had completely forgotten about the bag. So he was not calling about our night together. I fought back a sense of disappointment that was out of all proportion.

"What would you like me to do with it?" he asked.

"You could drop it by the reception desk," I said, equally cool, equally remote.

"Fine. I'll do that." And he hung up.

Why, I wondered, was I behaving like a high school student after her first prom? I was a woman, a much-experienced woman of thirty-seven, almost forty. He was, I assumed, an equally experienced man of forty-two. Why couldn't we be civilized? Even amused?

I picked up the phone and dialed the extension of the receptionist. "Let me know when the author, William Macrae, arrives."

"Will do."

I sat at my desk and went back over my manuscript. When I had finished reading the final chapter, I found I had no memory of it whatsoever.

"Oh God!" I said aloud.

"What did you want to ask Him?" a voice from the door asked.

I looked up. Macrae was standing there, my bag dangling from his hand.

I was trying to summon a suitably detached expression when he said, "Just out of curiosity, why did you get out of my apartment like a bat out of you-know-what? Was it that awful?"

It hadn't occurred to me that he would put that interpretation on my furtive departure. "No, it wasn't. You know it wasn't." Getting up I closed the door behind him. "Mac, I didn't—it didn't occur to me you'd think that."

"What did you think I'd think when you sneaked out, carefully not waking me up?"

"I thought—I don't know what I thought. I'm sorry. I always assume people are more put together, have more confidence than I do."

We stared at one another. "Last night was wonderful," I said. "More wonderful than any other time in my life."

His face relaxed. "Yes, it was the same with me. So why did you leave?"

"I think—I think because of Paul." I saw his closed expression come back. "Mac, he drinks practically all the time, and when he's drunk, I never know how he's going to react."

"Why the hell do you put up with it? Why don't you leave?"

I sighed. "I've just been through this with . . . well, with a new friend cum therapist I've just met. The answer is that it's my apartment and I want him to move out, but he hasn't picked up my hints yet."

"Hints! Why don't you just tell him to go? I don't recognize this timid, self-effacing female. You've never had any trouble expressing yourself to me—no matter how suspicious, angry, not to say insulting, you've felt like being."

The urge to answer his question was there. But the old fear was back, staring at me. If I answered Macrae's question, then I'd have to tell him about my past, the past which Paul was using to blackmail me. The trouble was, to my old claustrophobic fear of being locked up in a cell behind bars was now added a new one—that I wouldn't find my daughter in time to warn her about the genetic flaw she was carrying. I glanced again at Macrae. It was a mistake. His face had closed down. The friend, the lover, had gone. What I saw now was the prosecutor and, behind his law-and-order exterior, the shadow, the ghost of my father.

"I can't do that, Mac. There're—there've been too many years and memories behind us. Also, he's losing his job, which means his income. That's one of the reasons he's been upset. I can't throw him out on the street."

He put down the bag. "It's your decision. No doubt we'll be in touch again over the book." He opened the door and walked down the hall to the reception area. Without looking back he went through the glass doors there to the elevators.

The impulse to run after him, to call him back was strong, but not strong enough. I closed the door after him and went back to work.

■ ■ ■ In the days that followed I thought about him almost all the time, certainly when I wasn't actively doing something else —like working with a manuscript—and often then, too. I knew it was I who had stopped the relationship, so it was I who could pick up the phone and begin it again—if he'd let me. Who could blame him if he didn't? More than once my hand was on the receiver, only to have me pull it back.

■ ■ ■ I started writing a letter to the man in Virginia whose name and address Claire had given me. Then, I stopped in the middle of a word and called information to get his telephone number. My daughter would be eighteen. She might marry at any time or, married or not, she might get pregnant. I didn't have all the time in the world.

As I was waiting for Information in that part of the country to come on, I stared at the piece of paper. In Claire's straight, up-and-down handwriting, I read "the Reverend Ian Wilson, St. Timothy's Church, Lawrence, Virginia." I'd heard of Lawrence, Kansas, I'd never heard of Lawrence, Virginia.

Information came on and supplied me with the number of the church, which I then called. What I got was a tape giving the time of services and inviting me to leave my name and number. Somehow I hadn't expected that. As a matter of fact, I hadn't really expected a church, although the address of the church was there on the paper. I supposed I had thought he might have a token tie with a church, but really be operating out of an adoption or child-location agency. So I did not leave my name and number when I heard the beep. I hung up. There was no reason for my sense of panic. If he had called Braddock and Terhune and asked for me, certainly somebody would have rung my office and, if I were not there, would have taken a message. But what message?

I thought of the person who had been making inquiries about me. Better to call again, or to write. But as I turned back to my typewriter to finish the letter I had started, my hands slowed down. If I asked the Reverend Ian Wilson to answer me at home, I had no real confidence that Paul would respect the old taboo against reading other people's mail. Until recently, he probably would have allowed his hand to be chopped off before sinking to that. But the last few weeks had produced behavior in him that I'd have sworn on all the Bibles in my original home he'd never have stooped to. So I wouldn't leave my home address. What about my office? And maybe have my secretary open the letter? I could, of course, tell the Reverend Ian to mark the envelope "Personal" on front and back. But my hands did not continue to write.

I decided I'd keep calling till I got him.

■ ■ ■ My second session with Claire went off without any seismic shocks to my system. At the end, though, she did ask, almost casually, "Have you told Paul to move yet?"

"No," I almost snapped.

"You're afraid of him, aren't you?"

"Yes."

"What is the worst that could happen?"

"The worst is very worst indeed, I'd be found by the FBI, taken off to jail, tried and put there on a long-time basis. One of the things I haven't told you is that I have a bad case of claustrophobia. Probably because I had a baby-sitter who would lock me in a closet when she wanted to punish me."

"And your parents let her do this?"

"I guess so."

"Don't you remember?"

I shook my head.

I stared at Claire, as a curious blank feeling came over me. It wasn't new, but I hadn't felt it for a long time. Along with the blank feeling came an urge to get off the subject. I glanced at the clock and saw with relief that the fifty minutes were up. I got up. "I'll see you next week," I said, and left quickly.

■ ■ ■ Paul had been quiet and rather remote for a while. He was usually out when I got home, and often still out when I went into my room and locked the door. On the evenings he came in, he would pour himself a drink, sit, look at television and then go to his study. But his silence was neither pleasant nor relaxing. I knew, and in an odd way, I was sure he knew that he was still there because of my fear of him, a fear that was both physical and psychological. I was afraid of the violence I could feel right below his silence. I was also afraid of what he knew about me and how he could use it.

And then one night he was visibly drunk when he got home. I knew that meant he must have drunk a lot, because he had the alcoholic's legendary hollow leg.

"So," he started straight off, coming out of the kitchen with a glass full of what looked like very dark bourbon, "you've been seeing your federal boyfriend."

I wondered whether that was a wild guess or somebody had told him. But who? And when? I started gathering together my papers. "I didn't say I had or hadn't."

"I was led to believe—deliberately led to believe—that you were not seeing him, not after you and I got together again."

"I didn't say or imply anything about him."

There were two bright red bars across the tops of his cheeks, and his eyes seemed to be unusually prominent and bloodshot.

"Oh yes, you did. Lying in bed there, making love with me like the slut you are! Don't think I didn't know where you'd been and who you'd been with! What are you trying to do— have another bastard?"

"But that was—" I almost spilled out that my return to Paul had been before I had spent the hours in Macrae's apartment.

"Don't be absurd!" I put all the scorn I could into it, to get his attention off the subject.

"Absurd is it! Don't think I didn't know where you'd been the night you got home from your Boston trip!" He started moving closer.

He was on target, of course, but, again, how did he know? I thought about the people in Boston who seemed to be watching me. I'd come to believe that that was mostly my own paranoia, but the gypsy cab driver wasn't. Had he been hired by Paul? But if so, why? Surely not just because of his jealousy.

I got up. "I have a lot more work to do. And I can't do it with you in this frame of mind." Suddenly the courage I hadn't had flooded through me. "And I want you to be out of this apartment by the end of the week."

"And where the hell do you expect me to go? The Plaza? The Regency?"

"I don't care where you go. I just want you gone."

"Why you—"

I saw his hand coming at me, but too late. No one had ever struck me before. Not even my father. I'd read about it, seen countless movies, listened to numerous accounts on television and in interviews. None of that was preparation for the real thing. The blows seemed to come from every direction from both open hands and bunched fists. The pain was excruciating. I couldn't get away, and then I managed to, long enough to let out a scream that must have been heard over the entire block. It stopped him for a moment.

"Shut up!" he yelled. "Shut up!" But all the time I kept dodging and ducking I went on screaming, I kept backing, then, as I found the apartment front door behind me. I yanked it open and ran. I had nothing with me, no coat, no handbag. I stumbled down the steps and, seeing a taxi cruising by, lurched into it.

"Where to, lady?"

Without thinking, I gave Macrae's address.

15.

The trouble was, when the taxi got there Macrae wasn't home. The possibility that he might not be hadn't even occurred to me. I rang again and again. But there was no answer. Aside from everything else, I had needed to borrow money to pay the taxi.

I started down the steps of the brownstone.

"Where do we go now?" The taxi driver, no fool, was beginning to see his fare disappear. "The fare so far is five seventy-five."

I started to shake. "I don't know. And I don't have any money."

"Now look—" He strode forward, and then, as my face came into the light of a nearby street lamp, stopped. "For God's sake, lady, what happened to you? Who did that?"

I began crying, hating myself for doing so. Where could I go? Yes, I had friends back in the Village, but an old sense of shame gripped me. I couldn't bear the thought of any of them seeing me this way.

"Look, maybe I ought to take you to an emergency room somewhere."

"No," I said, and then added, "I'm sorry about the fare."

"It's okay. I can't leave you like this."

Dimly I found myself thinking that New York cabbies had had a bum rap. Behind the righteous anger at being bilked of his fare, this driver seemed to be a decent guy. But I couldn't stop crying.

"Look, is there anybody you could call. Here, here's some quarters!"

I stared into his grubby palm. And out of the corner of my

eye saw a public phone. It would probably be broken. So often in New York they were.

"I'll try somebody," I said, and took a couple of quarters.

Information had nothing under Claire Aldington for residence, but at the last minute I remembered her married name. There was indeed a number for Brett Cunningham. As I pushed the quarter in, I wondered what time it was. My watch registered eleven thirty, but its glass was smashed and the hands squashed. It must be a lot later than that.

It was Brett who answered. I asked for Claire.

"It's a little late, isn't it?" He was courteous, but I could tell he was not pleased.

"I'm sorry. But—I've been beaten up."

"I'm sorry, too. Who is this?"

"Felic—" I paused, not believing what I was hearing myself say. Then, "Janet—Janet Covington."

"Just a minute."

Claire came on the phone. "Brett said you'd been beaten up."

"Yes," I said, and started to cry again.

"Where are you?"

I looked up and then remembered. "On Ninety-fifth Street, between Madison and Park. I'm sorry. Maybe the driver was right, I ought to go to an emergency room. But—" I hated admitting this—"I don't have any money. I can't pay his fare."

"Tell him to bring you to East Eighty-third Street," and she gave a number. "It's between Fifth and Madison. I'll be waiting and I'll pay off the taxi."

The rest seemed to happen in a blur. The driver accompanied me up to the door. Claire, in a coat and holding another one, was standing downstairs in the lobby of her building.

"Thank you for bringing her," she said to the driver. "I have money to pay you, but I think we'd better go to an emergency room."

"No," I said. "I don't want to go now. Please. It's not that bad. I'm sure nothing's broken. Please."

Claire looked at me for a moment. "I probably should overrule you, but I guess I won't. We can always get another cab. Here—" She turned to the driver and handed over some money, obviously adding a generous tip.

"And he lent me fifty cents to phone you," I suddenly remembered.

"It's okay, lady. Glad to help."

I saw Claire add another dollar.

"Thanks a lot," he said. "I still think you oughtta see a doctor, and whoever did that should go to jail."

"I agree," Claire said. And then to me, "Come on. We'll go upstairs."

■ ■ ■ A large dog was the first creature to greet me, his head thrust forward.

"Back, Motley," a young voice said. It seemed to come from a square, rather good-looking boy of fifteen or sixteen.

"Jamie, I really think you and Motley ought to go back to your room," Claire said.

"All right. But if she'd had a dog like Motley this wouldn't have happened."

"Probably true, but I think you and Motley should do what your mother says." The man who spoke was the one I'd met as Claire's husband. He seemed to be just as much at ease in robe and pajamas as he had in his banker's suit.

The boy's comment was so wildly off the mark, yet probably so right, I started to laugh, and then couldn't stop. When I finally got over that fit I was sitting in a kitchen, and Claire was boiling water and unpacking what looked like various first aid items.

"Paul?" she asked.

"Yes."

There was a silence. Then I said, "You were right, of course, I should have told him to move long ago."

"In fairness, he might have done this then. Anything in particular brought it on?"

"He was drunker even than usual, came home angry and ready for a fight and making accusations about Macrae. So I told him to get out."

"As I said, it might have happened any time."

The disinfectant stung as Claire touched various areas. "You're going to have a magnificent black eye tomorrow, if not two. I'm neither a doctor nor a nurse, but there don't seem to be any broken bones. That doesn't mean you haven't had a terrible beating. How do you feel?"

What I felt was numb and so tired I could hardly make myself talk. "Numb and exhausted."

"I'm going to put you in my stepdaughter's room with a couple of aspirin. Do you think you can sleep?"

"Practically on the floor."

"All right. Come with me."

The bed seemed like a haven and was neither too hard nor too soft. Just before I went to sleep, something jumped onto the bed. I put a hand out and encountered fur. I stroked it, and as I felt it burrow into my back, reflected how comforting it was.

■ ■ ■ I was in a small room with an immensely high ceiling, and I kept running frantically from wall to wall trying to find the door. But there was no door, even though I had come in by one. "I know there's a door," I cried out. "I came in through a door. There has to be one!" But the more frantically I looked the more it became obvious that the door I had come in by had disappeared and the opening had been sealed up. Who had done that? Who had that power? And then, of course, I knew. It had been my father. "Now you'll never find your baby," he said. "Yes, yes, I will," I screamed and looked up to the ceiling where his voice came from. There, staring down at me through bars, his eyes like black stones, was my father. "How often have I told you that the wages of sin are death," he said. Then he reached down an immensely strong arm and as he grasped my shoulder I knew he was going to beat me. I screamed as loud as I could.

"Janet, Janet, wake up. It's only me, Claire."

I opened my eyes and started up in bed. "Oh—" I said, and put my hand to my face. Then I winced. "Ouch!"

"Yes, I was right," Claire said. "You have a beautiful shiner."

I pulled my knees up and sat for a moment, absorbing the fact that what had been so frightening and real was a dream. Then I said, "I'm sorry. Did I make a terrible racket?"

"A moderately loud one, but, considering what you have been through, highly understandable. That was quite a dream you must have been having."

"That room! There wasn't any door, but I knew I had come in, so I kept looking for it. But it had disappeared. And then—" I stopped. "What gibberish! Sorry!"

"What happened after that?"

"When I looked up to the ceiling, there was my father. He was staring down at me."

"Did he say anything?"

Belatedly I remembered she was my therapist. "Ah yes, dreams!"

"They may come out like a crazy quilt, but they're a pretty good guide as to what's in your mind and feelings."

"He said, and it was as clear as a bell and I can still hear it, 'How often have I told you that the wages of sin are death?' " Without thinking I shivered.

"I see," Claire said. "Is that something he used to say?"

"Frequently. He alternated it with one of his favorite verses from, I think, Alexander Pope."

"A punitive verse, I feel sure."
I nodded, and recited:

> "Vice is a monster of so frightful mien,
>   As to be hated needs but to be seen;
>   Yet seen too oft, familiar with her face,
>   We first endure, then pity, then embrace."

"It's amazing," Claire said, "how many people who preach about your first quote, almost never think of one or two others I can think of."

"Such as?"

"Such as, to forgive until seventy times seven."

"I don't think my father ever heard of that."

"Have you?"

I stared at her. "Considering my condition—"

"All right, I was actually thinking more about your father."

"I'm no readier to forgive him."

"I understand."

"Do you?" For some reason, sore as I was, tired and beaten down as I felt, I also felt angry. "He was a total bastard. But maybe you disapprove of my saying that. I think of you as a therapist, not as a clergy—er—woman, but I should remember you're both."

"My rather virtuous sounding comments—and I agree, my timing could have been better—were as much from a therapist as from a priest. As long as you don't forgive, who and whatever it is will occupy rent-free space in your mind. By forgiving, you get rid of it."

"Right now I don't feel at all forgiving."

"I wouldn't either."

"By the way," I said. "Something warm and purring spent part of the night curled into my back."

"That would be Patsy, my stepdaughter's cat. She misses having someone to sleep with."

I glanced outside and saw daylight. "What time is it?"

"About nine."

"Good heavens. I should be at the office." I flung back the covers and put my feet on the floor. My head spun. "Ouch!"

"Are you sure you wouldn't like to take the day off? I think it'd be a good idea."

"I don't know—" And then, as I stood up, I caught sight of myself in the mirror. "Holy God!"

"Yes. You're very colorful!"

She was accurate about that. One eye had a purple and blue bruise that circled the socket and the eye itself. The other eye also had some red mixed in with the purple and blue bruise. Both were highly colorful. There were additional bruises on my cheekbone and at the jawline and part of my upper lip was puffy.

"I can't go in looking like this."

"I still want you to see a doctor. Yes, I know you don't want to," she said as I opened my mouth. "But since you've come here, I'd feel much better if we had assurance from a medical authority that you're not suffering more than visible damage. Sorry to put it on those self-serving terms, but I do feel somewhat responsible."

"All right," I said ungraciously. "Where is the nearest hospital, or do you have a doctor of your own who's near and reliable?"

"Don't you have one?"

Doctors, like insurance forms, were something I had left out of my life as much as possible. I hadn't been near one for ten years and the one I'd seen before that I didn't particularly want to go back to. "No, I don't have one," I said. "I've always felt they were for sick people and I've never been sick."

"Don't you have to have insurance forms and such like at your office?"

I made a face. "When I absolutely could not put it off any longer, I'd go to whoever they were using."

"All right. I'm going to suggest Dr. Brian Martin. He's attached to St. Vincent's, which is near your neck of the woods, and everybody tells me he's great."

"How do you know him?"

"Because his wife was my client for a while. Here's his address and number."

"What I really need," I said, looking back in the mirror, "is an expert makeup artist. . . . Oh God!"

At that moment the telephone rang. Claire went into the hall and answered it from an extension there. "Hello? Oh, Brett, what? What station?"

I saw her glance at me. Then, "Just a minute." She put down the phone, went into the living room and put on the radio. After a little adjustment the voice of the newsman came out clear and loud:

"Neighbors say that his companion, a woman who works in publishing, was screaming last night. This morning, when they came out their own door, the neighbors said they saw Professor Davenport's door open and his body lying half on the floor and half on the couch. The woman was nowhere to be seen. Professor Davenport had been stabbed several times and was dead."

16.

I lost the next few sentences the announcer said.

"Paul," I whispered. "Oh my God!" I sat down on the bed again. "I can't believe it. Dead. Did he say Paul was dead? He did, didn't he?"

"Yes," Claire said.

I jumped up. "I've got to get down there."

"Look, get dressed and come into the kitchen. At least have some coffee first."

"I ought to call somebody."

"Get dressed first and let's talk about it."

As I got out of the shower I saw a radio on the desk in the bedroom, and wrapped in a towel, went in and turned it on to an all-news program. While I dried off and got dressed I listened and finally, as the half hour struck, heard again the announcement about Paul's body being found. The announcer added that the police were looking for the woman who lived with him whom they now identified as Janet Covington, an editor at Braddock and Terhune.

A chill went over me. It was not the first time in my life that police had been looking for me. This time at least I was innocent of any wrongdoing. But how long would it be before they discovered that, under another name, I already had a record? And if they stumbled on that, would they believe anything I said?

At that point there was a knock on the door and Claire walked in carrying a tray holding juice and a cup of coffee.

"I've been listening to the news," I said.

"So have I." She put the tray down.

"They said the police are looking for me, and they identified me by name."

"I know."

I looked at Claire and she looked back at me. Finally I said, "You run and you run and you run, and in the end, it's no use." I paused. "That sounds callous when I think of Paul, but I can't help it."

"You'd have to be a saint not to think of it, given the circumstances of your life."

I drank the juice and sipped at the coffee.

"There's sugar or sweetener on the tray and some milk."

"No, this is fine."

"I have a suggestion, but I don't know how it would sit with you."

I looked at Claire and realized that, probably for the first time in my untrusting life, I trusted someone, or at least—always the proviso—I trusted her as much as I could anyone. "What is it?"

"It sounds like the commercial, 'I have a friend at Chase Manhattan,' but on various occasions I've gotten to know a Lieutenant William O'Neill and come to have confidence in him." She paused. "I'd be happy to call him on your behalf, but if I do, then I also have to be reasonably sure you'll be candid about your past—if it should come up. Under difficult circumstances he's been—well, he's been a friend, and—" She paused.

"You wouldn't want to recommend someone who lied about her past."

"It wouldn't be exactly fair to him."

I thought for a moment. "I mean if he's the one investigating the case, and asks me a lot of questions I've never answered, would you expect me to tell him the truth?"

"Only if I were the one to send you to him. If he's on the case without that, well—whatever I might think would be best, you're on your own."

"What if he gets to know you're my therapist and that I sought shelter here when Paul was beating me up?"

"Then the confidentiality between therapist and client would protect us both."

I drained the coffee and looked around for a coat.

"What are you looking for?"

"A coat—oh, I didn't bring one, did I. Nor a handbag. Speaking of all of which, thanks for the toothbrush."

She smiled. "We always keep one or two handy in case of guests who've forgotten to bring theirs."

"I'd better go," I said, and went through into the hall. At the front door I turned. "I haven't thanked you. You saved my life."

"I'm glad we were here. Here is some money to tide you over till you can get some. Do you want me to go with you?"

"No. I'll try it alone first." I opened the door and walked into the hall to the elevator.

"I'll call down and ask the doorman to get you a cab," Claire said.

■ ■ ■ Both the doorman and the taxi driver gave me odd looks. Having seen my face, I knew why, but I tried to ignore them.

The driver turned around. "Where to, lady?"

For a few seconds I sat there, frozen. The temptation to tell him to drive to the station or the bus terminal where I could get something going somewhere without having to hand over a credit card and thus identify myself—Except, of course, that I didn't have a credit card with me, nor did I have any money other than whatever Claire had just given me. I hadn't even looked to see how much it was.

The taxi driver was still staring at me. "Where to?"

I thrust my hand in my pocket and pulled out the bill Claire had given me. It was for ten dollars. You run and you run and you run, I thought. And I had spent most of my life running. In addition to which I now had to find my daughter. But it was no use. I knew that no matter what the complications were, I couldn't go on running.

Going to the office wouldn't solve the problem. They'd have police there, too, by now. I took a breath and gave my home address.

■ ■ ■ There were police cars in front of my apartment house. The taxi drew up. The driver turned around and stared at me. "Are you the one they're looking for?"

"I wouldn't know," I said, with all the chill I could muster. Then I paid him and gave him a moderate tip.

"There she is," somebody, I don't know who, said as I got out.

The two men who had been standing at the foot of the stoop turned. Seeing my bruised face, they stared.

"Janet Covington?" one of them asked.

"Yes."

"Would you come upstairs, please. The lieutenant would like to talk to you."

I knew at that moment that I should have accepted Claire's offer to talk to the lieutenant who seemed to be her friend. But it was too late now.

I went up the stairs. My apartment door was open. There were several men standing there, their backs to the door. But they turned as the policeman and I rounded the curve of the stairs. I saw the sofa and the huge red stain on it and on the floor and felt as though something had squeezed my heart. Paul's body wasn't there and the room itself it was a shambles, both a chair and a lamp overturned and books all over the floor.

"Where's Paul?" I said.

"Paul Davenport?"

"Of course."

"Who are you?"

"I'm Janet Covington."

"Where have you been these past hours?" one of the men asked. He was shorter than the other two, but there was something about him that spelled authority.

I looked at him. "Who are you?"

"I'm Lieutenant O'Neill," he said.

"Claire's friend," I said, without thinking.

He frowned. "Claire who?"

"Claire Aldington—priest-therapist at St. Anselm's."

"You her client?"

"Er—sort of. I mean, I am, on a sort of temporary basis." I paused. "I spent last night there. I ran out of here after, well, after I got these bruises, got into a taxi." Without my thinking about it, my hand touched my face. "I tried a . . . a friend's apartment, but he wasn't in. The best place I could think of after that was Claire's—Claire's and Brett's."

The lieutenant was staring at me very hard, his eyes in his square Irish face bright blue. "You just showed up there without calling first?"

"The cabbie lent me the money."

"You must have a more disarming effect on taxi drivers than most of us."

I was beginning to get annoyed. "Even a taxi driver responds to a woman who has . . . has obviously just been beaten up."

"Most of us do. Including me. In fact, your bruises and black eyes are so impressive I'd be inclined to think a jury would acquit you if you had stabbed Paul Davenport. Did you?" He shot the question out at me.

"No. I—he came home . . . well, drunk and started accusing me of . . . making accusations. I denied them, and told him he'd have to leave the apartment—move out, which seemed to enrage him more. He started hitting me then."

"Has he ever hit you before?"

"No." I started to shake my head and thought better of it. Aside from the pain of the bruises, a headache seemed to have started.

"This was the first time?"

"Yes."

"Why? Why now?"

I took a breath and felt my head start to spin. "Do you mind if I sit down?"

Somebody produced a chair. But there was still the overturned chair and the books on the floor.

"You okay?" the lieutenant asked.

"Yes."

"Do you have anything here—any brandy or anything I could give you?"

I shook my head, and again regretted it. "No."

"Sure?"

"I'm sure," I snapped. "But if you're longing to be helpful, then you could ask one of your men to put some water on to boil. I'd like a cup of tea. There are some tea bags in the middle cupboard in the kitchen."

An overwhelming sense of tiredness hit me. I closed my eyes and then, when everything seemed to swim around me, opened them again.

In a minute or two a man's voice from the kitchen said, "Do you want sugar or milk in it?"

"You can put some sugar in it, thanks," I said.

After I'd had a few sips I asked, "Where's Paul now?"

"At the morgue."

In my mind I saw his face. I no longer loved him, and I knew it would be a long time before I could think of him without seeing again the rage in his eyes, glaring at me, bloodshot and without a vestige of love or pity in them and the bars of red across his cheekbones. But he'd been part of my life for three years. We had loved and lived together and made jokes over the world of books and letters that we shared. Now he was a dead body with stab wounds lying in the city morgue, something I'd read about in newspapers and in mystery novels. "Do you have any idea who killed him?" I asked.

"No. We were hoping you would."

"When he started hitting me, I ran out. I never saw him after that."

He paused. "And where did you go then?"

"I went to—well, to the Upper East Side."

"What address?"

I didn't want to give out Mac's address. "An apartment between Madison and Park on East Ninety-fifth. Only the person I went to see obviously wasn't home. I rang the bell several times. Then . . ." My thinking wasn't as clear and orderly as I would have liked. "I went to the Cunningham's—"

"What time was this?"

My mind was a blank. I had no idea. "Some time after eleven-thirty."

"Do you know what time Paul Davenport was killed?"

I shook my head.

"According to the coroner, about twelve-fifteen."

"But I was in the Cunningham's apartment."

"Can you prove that?"

"Yes, I'm sure Claire would give witness to that."

"Yet a few minutes ago when one of the men here called her she said you didn't arrive until nearly one o'clock."

The trouble was, I had no idea what time I had gone to the Cunningham's, what time I had spoken with them, and what time I'd gone to sleep. I shook my head. "I don't know the times I ran out of here or went to the Cunningham's. But I didn't kill Paul."

O'Neill hesitated. "We're going to get some of the stuff here back to the lab, so I'll leave you for now." He hesitated. "If I were you I'd find myself a lawyer."

"But I didn't do it," I repeated stupidly. My headache was now a pounding nightmare.

He shook his head and walked out, followed by the other police.

17.

After they'd gone I got up, went to the medicine cabinet in the bathroom and looked for the aspirin bottle. To my surprise it was almost empty, but I was relieved to find a couple of tablets at the bottom. Then I took my tea into the kitchen, sat down at the kitchen table and swallowed the tablets as I sipped.

After a while the headache seemed to retreat a little. But as the throbbing pain left, a horde of thoughts, fears and impressions rushed in. The blood all over the sofa, the raining blows from Paul's hands, his angry eyes, my daughter, doubts and questions about Macrae, the feel of his mouth and body against mine, Claire's voice, my father's eyes above me and the agonizing memory of fears, old, old, old fears, formed crazy quilt patterns in my head I couldn't seem to stop.

Deciding that action—almost any action—was preferable to thinking, I started picking up the furniture and the books and tried to restore some order in the living room. The police had taken the sofa's slip cover, I noticed, but the splotches of blood were still discernible on the dark gray material beneath. It would have to be cleaned, or I'd finally have to get the new sofa bed I'd been promising myself. But in the meantime, I went to the hall closet, got out an old multicolored counterpane that had been used on my mother's bed at home and that I'd taken after my father's death, and threw it over the sofa, tucking it in at the back and sides. It didn't exactly go with the rest of the room, but it was better than the stains beneath.

I had forgotten that the front door was still open until I looked up and saw one of the neighbors standing there. She was staring at me, horror on her face. "Oh my God, Janet! We heard the noise, of course. I had no idea—I wouldn't blame you if you did kill him."

"But I didn't," I said.

She went right on as though I hadn't spoken. "Any jury would acquit you after that horrible abuse—"

"I didn't kill him!" I almost shouted.

She continued to stare at me. I had the strong feeling she still thought I killed Paul. Then abruptly she turned on her heel and went back down the hall.

I looked after her until she had gone into her own door.

Then I put on some more water to boil, checked the aspirin bottle just to make sure there weren't any more tablets and went on cleaning.

■ ■ ■ When I had cleaned and cleared up everything I could see or lay my hands on I decided to take another look at my face. I had not wanted to show up at my office one mass of bruises. But by now I knew that I wasn't going to be able to stay here alone with nothing to do except think obsessively about Paul's murder, the absence of any word from Macrae and the obvious fact that the police were simply waiting for lab reports before they arrested me.

And if they arrested and charged me, what then? I was innocent, but innocent people had been jailed, even executed.

The trend of that line of thinking was so unnerving I went into the bathroom and stared at my face in the mirror.

Oh God! I thought. It was worse than when I had examined it at the Cunninghams'. More bruises had come out and those that were already there were more colorful. "I can't help it," I said aloud. I could not stay in this now haunted apartment.

I glanced at my watch. It was about twelve-thirty. If I took a taxi to the office now I might hit the lunch hour and would not have to run the full gamut of fellow workers.

Putting on dark glasses and draping a silk scarf somewhat over my face, I put on a light raincoat and walked out of the apartment. The door locked automatically, but I carefully double-locked it anyway. As I did so I thought angrily it was no use wishing I'd had the forethought to double-lock it the night before when I ran out. If I were able to think about something like that, I wouldn't have run out in the first place.

Who on earth had come in and killed Paul? At this point, I was undoubtedly the only person in the world who knew beyond doubt that someone had. Everyone else thought I had done it, whether they sympathized with me and/or excused me or not.

Drawing the scarf around the front of my face as though it were an eastern yashmak, I hailed a taxi and gave the office address.

And why hadn't Macrae called me? Surely by now he would have heard at least one of the endless news accounts of Paul's death.

The huge stream of lunch-bound office workers had thinned by the time the cab dropped me on Fifth Avenue in front of the office. Keeping my face down, I was hurrying towards the elevators when the voice of my boss said, "Janet?"

I looked up. Jack Lederer, managing editor, had always been pleasant, if rather aloof and detached. "Hi, Jack," I said. He stared at me a moment. "Come here," he said, and, taking my arm, walked me to the side of the lobby where the phones were. Then he gently pulled the scarf aside. "Jesus!" he said.

I didn't say anything, because I couldn't think of anything to say.

"If you had killed him you'd have had my entire support," he said.

"Thanks, Jack. But that is what I'm afraid everyone is going to say, including the police and the courts."

"Do you have a lawyer?"

"Not yet. Do you know a good criminal lawyer?"

"No, just the firm that does our legal work. But I could ask them for you."

"Thanks. That'd be a help."

"Are you sure you want to come back here?"

"It's preferable to being by myself, free to think about this."

"Couldn't you go somewhere else?"

I stared at him. "Are you politely suggesting that my being here would be an embarrassment?"

"No, of course not. But you must be pretty shook up."

"I am. But if I can get my mind on something besides that I'd be better off."

"Whatever—let me know if there's anything else I can do. I'm late for lunch. See you." And he sped off.

I was relieved no one got in the elevator with me. When I reached the Braddock and Terhune floor, the receptionist was talking into the phone. For a moment I debated trying to slip past her, but decided that would not only be stupid, it would be unsuccessful.

"Hi!" I said as I passed. "Any messages?"

She was staring at my face, her own, pretty twenty-two-year-old face a picture of horror.

"Yes," I said, "it's pretty awful, I know."

"I wouldn't blame you if—"

"Thank you. But I didn't. Any messages?"

"Dozens." She reached over and picked up a pile of the pink telephone messages. "All these are for you."

My heart sank. "Thanks," I said again. And walked down the hall to my office. When I passed a couple of the younger clerical helpers and heard gasps I hurried. I was tired of hearing what was plainly going to be the standard response. Once in my office I closed the door and sat down. Being back at work was not going to be the island of calm I had envisaged.

After a moment or two I slipped out of my coat, removed the scarf and looked at my messages. Not one was from Macrae. My sense of disappointment was out of all proportion. I was about to indulge in some angry and recriminating thoughts about men who lost interest once their primary goal had been achieved, when I remembered that it was I who had left the bed and Macrae who had come to the office carrying my bag. He must have felt then what I was feeling now.

When I felt a little better I looked at the other messages. Every newspaper, news magazine and television news station had called, plus several talk shows. I had this sudden vision of myself saying into a camera, "And then he hit me for the tenth time and I knew I had to leave—"

"Was that when you picked up the knife?"

It was the same voice in my head, always questioning, reminding, taunting.

"No," I said aloud. "No!"

I remembered clearly, I told myself, very clearly. As the final blow reached my face, I ran towards the door and out. I did not pick up any knife . . .

The phone rang. I stared at it, realizing that after all those messages I did not want to answer. I pressed the button on the phone marked "Secretary," hoping that Jackie had come back, and if she hadn't that the receptionist would pick up.

But Jackie had. Her voice came over the phone. "Janet? I just walked in. Rebecca said you looked awful. I'm sorry!" I remembered that Rebecca was the name of the receptionist.

"It's okay, but would you pick up all my calls and let me know who it is. I really don't want to talk to anyone. And if it's a newshawk of some kind or other, you don't have to ask me, I definitely don't want to talk to them." And I hung up.

Working on the current manuscript was not easy. Paul's face kept intruding, as did Jack Lederer's voice. I was now reasonably sure that he would be grateful if I were not at work. So much for work therapy and the kind wishes of co-workers. What I was was an embarrassment! Why did that threaten to reduce me to tears more than anything that had so far occurred since I'd left Claire?

I wondered if I should call Claire and tell her that I had met her friend, Lieutenant O'Neill. My hand was out towards the phone when, without thinking, I withdrew it.

More than ever I knew now that I'd have to go it alone.

■ ■ ■ I don't know how much later it was that the name the Reverend Ian Wilson surfaced in my mind. Since Laura's disappearance was engineered by my father in Boston eighteen years ago I didn't have much hope that Mr. Wilson could throw much light on the matter. But as long as there was any chance at all I had to do something about it. I looked for the page in my diary where I had copied the number Claire had given me, then pulled the phone towards me.

The young woman who answered put me through immediately.

"Yes, can I help you?" a pleasant male voice asked.

I took a breath. "Claire Aldington at St. Anselm's here in New York gave me your name and number. I am trying to locate my daughter who was adopted eighteen years ago, but I don't know where or by whom."

"Why do you want to see her now?" There was a reserved note in his voice.

"Because I have discovered that I am a carrier of hemophilia, which means she therefore has a fifty-fifty chance of being a carrier also. She's now eighteen, and any time she could be getting married and planning a family. I have to tell her what she might face, but first I have to find her."

"I see. Well, let's start at the beginning."

■ ■ ■ I left out my radical past, seeing no reason to mention it. All I told the man was that my father and I had developed an implacable enmity, not improved by my years of drug-taking, and that he probably—undoubtedly—thought he was doing my daughter a favor when he took her from me at the hospital. "I was so ill I didn't even come out of it until the adoption had taken place. And he would never tell me who had adopted my daughter, where they were from, or how he had found them."

"I take it you got over the drug period?"

"Oh yes. Years ago. For the past thirteen years I've been drug free and sober. For the past twelve years I've been on the editorial staff of a well-known publisher."

"All right. I have two thoughts. One is that I would like you to come down here before I take any positive action towards locating the family that adopted your daughter. The other is that in the meantime you could give me a few technical details—your name, address, profession and the date and place of your daughter's birth and anything else you can remember to help me get started."

I told him everything I knew about Laura, which wasn't much, and then said, "But you're not going to start doing anything until I come to Virginia?"

"That's right. To do as you want requires the cooperation of your daughter's family—always providing I can locate them. And I would not do so before I could assure them that I had met you and become convinced you were being totally upfront and honest. There's too much at stake for them, for your daughter and for everyone concerned."

I hesitated a moment, but only a moment. "I'll take a plane down today."

But first, I thought, replacing the receiver, I'd have to do something about my bruises. I'd seen people's horrified reactions, and I didn't want the Reverend Ian Wilson deflected from his search for Laura by wondering, perhaps, what I'd done to evoke them and what threat that might hold for Laura, her adoptive family and their peace of mind. I knew I couldn't afford to wait for the bruises to heal. Staring out the window, trying to think what to do, I found myself looking down at the elegant door of one of the world's most famous salons. No matter what it cost, I'd get them to show me how to cover up the black and blue and purple.

An hour later, somewhat poorer and carrying in my bag a small kit of makeup tools, I caught a taxi to La Guardia. Evidently my foray into the salon was successful. To my great relief no one seemed to give my face a second look.

18.

Following the Reverend Ian Wilson's instructions I took a taxi at the small airport into the town. Here, in the mountainous western part of Virginia, the air was fresh and cool, a blessed relief from the sticky heat I'd left behind in Manhattan.

Mr. Wilson's church was a small, gray, not very interesting building a few blocks from the town's main street. A housekeeper let me into the parish house and left me in a small study. In a moment or two a stocky, quite attractive, youngish man of medium height came in.

"Mrs. Covington?"

"Yes."

"Thank you for coming. I know it sounds unreasonable to demand that everyone who wants information about an adoption come here, but as I told you on the telephone, I have to be able to personally assure all parties that I've met you and that insofar as I can tell you seem honest and well-motivated." He paused. I was about to make some innocuous comment back when he added, as an afterthought, "And of course Claire gave you a good recommendation."

It was natural, of course, that he would have called Claire. But I felt my throat tighten. "I'm glad to hear it."

"Now," he said, "tell me more about yourself."

I resisted an almost overwhelming temptation to ask, what did Claire say? and talked—about my upbringing in Boston, my period of drug-taking, my rehabilitation, my years in New York, and, finally, how I discovered that I was a carrier of hemophilia.

"So you had no idea of your sister's death, or of the hemophilia of the son she left behind?"

"No." Leaving out the years of radical politics left a large hole in my autobiography. I'd been aware of the hole before, but never so painfully. I was also finding the Reverend Mr. Wilson's hazel eyes uncomfortably penetrating. To be uneasy under close questioning was not a new experience, though I hadn't had it for a while. But in the past I'd always found that an excellent countermeasure was to ask penetrating questions of my own.

"How did you get so interested in helping adopted families and children?" I queried, with all the innocence I could put in my voice. "Were you an adopted child?"

"No, but when my wife and I found we couldn't have children, we decided to adopt three children who needed homes. That was when we ran into the various problems and hitches that can occur in the adoption process."

"How wonderful!" I said, with automatic admiration. Then, before he could ask another one, "According to Claire you're one of the best-known and most reliable agencies for locating natural mothers and their babies in the country. That must cost a lot of money."

He looked amused, as though he knew what I was up to. "It does, but fortunately we have an angel."

"An angel? You mean someone who donates money to the cause?"

"Yes. A local businessman—a very wealthy businessman who was adopted himself. My activities which—you're right—can be expensive, are funded by a trust he's put up. I—and children and families all over the country—can be grateful to him."

"How splendid." It was an automatic response. We both sat silent for a moment, then he got up. "I've taken the liberty of reserving a room for you at our local motel. If you can manage to stay a couple of days, it's just possible I can get some kind of an answer for you in that time. If you prefer to go back right away, then of course I'll telephone you."

If I went back, and was arrested for leaving the city—I was

fairly vague as to what the police could or could not do—then I might not be able to return. "No, I'll stay a couple of days. Time is important." As I encountered his probing eyes I added, "As I told you a few minutes ago, I don't know whether or how soon my daughter might be planning to marry."

And I still didn't know what Claire had told him, whether, for example, she had talked about the mess I was now in regarding Paul's murder. And I was afraid to ask.

■ ■ ■ I had arrived without baggage, simply because I was afraid that if I went back to my apartment to pack that might be the moment the police, lab results in hand, would decide to arrest me.

Luckily, the motel was across from the church and adjacent to a town mall which occupied three sides of a square. I was told by the man at the motel desk, when I inquired about shopping, that almost anything I wanted could be obtained in the mall. "I was so excited when Mr. Wilson called me," I said, in a feeble attempt at explaining my arrival without bags, "that I went straight from the office to the airport and took the earliest plane that would bring me here."

"I know."

Instant suspicion. "You know?"

"Yes." He smiled. "We've learned that a lot of people who are coming to see the Reverend Wilson don't even stop to pack. They're that excited!"

I decided to do some probing of my own and threw out a general fishing line. "It must be wonderful to have a benefactor in the town who gives so generously to such a good cause."

His smile broadened. "You mean Mr. Driscoll? Yes, it is. People who have despaired of ever finding their own natural babies have been helped by him. When you think of all the things rich people can spend their money on—yachts, parties, clothes, furs, luxury travel—and see what Mr. Driscoll does with his, well, it sort of makes you humble. Which is why we hope so much that the governor will appoint him to fill out Senator Chisholm—the later Senator Chisholm's—term." He gave a big grin. "After that, he won't have any trouble getting in on his own."

I suddenly remembered a billboard I'd seen on the way in from the airport—a big square board, bright blue, with white letters: "JAMES DRISCOLL FOR SENATOR."

"I think I saw a billboard saying something about somebody named Driscoll for senator."

"Oh yes. He has a lot of local support which, after all the good he's done, is natural." The clerk, overflowing with enthusiasm, rattled on.

"Mr. Wilson said Mr. Driscoll was himself adopted, so I guess he knows how somebody must feel not knowing who his natural parents are."

"Yes. Of course. He—"

But at that moment, somewhat to my annoyance, his phone rang. "Excuse me," he said, and picked up the receiver.

I wished the call could have come five minutes later, giving me more time to glean some information, but I was glad I had started the ball rolling. Now it would be easier to find out more about Mr. Wilson's angel.

Why, I asked myself as I went to my room in the motel, couldn't I just accept this kind and generous patron for what he was—a benefactor who wanted to do good?

The answer to that was easy: my experience with my own father who preached faith, love and charity—and practiced none of them—had given me an early cynicism. I had developed a knee jerk to look around for the underside of every philanthropic cause, and I usually found it, even if it was only the fact that whatever cause was ostensibly being benefited, received about thirty percent of the money raised. The rest went to the bureaucracy involved, including the direct mail experts and their accompanying promotion and publicity flacks.

"All this so-called do-goodism is the underside of capitalism," Paul used to say. "In a decently planned economy the state does that kind of thing."

Paul, I thought, and saw again the splotches of blood. The trouble was, my mind had become so confused that I thought—for a moment I was afraid—I had seen them, not the next morning when I had returned to find the police there, but before I ran out and into a taxi that terrible night. Which would mean—

"No," I said aloud, and then the phone rang.

For a frozen moment I stared at it, not wanting to answer. Then I shook myself, as the rings repeated themselves. I was here to find help in locating my daughter. This might mean Mr. Wilson had stumbled on something.

But it was Claire. "Are you all right?" she said. "Ian called me so I know where you are."

"Yes. I'm fine."

"Lieutenant O'Neill also called me," she said, "since he'd heard from you that you were my client."

"What did you tell him?"

"Nothing that you had told me in confidence. But I did gather you told him very little about your past, so one reason I am calling is to find out exactly what you did tell him so that I don't make a mistake."

I let out my breath. "Thanks, Claire. Nothing about—in fact, very little. Just where I'd come from and gone to school, and about the drugs and the fact that Paul was jealous of Macrae—although I don't think I mentioned his name."

"I think I should tell you that someone—a man—called me inquiring about you and where you were."

"Macrae?"

"He didn't give a name, although I asked him who he was."

"Your secretary put him through? Don't you usually have someone to screen your calls, especially if you're in a session?"

"Yes, but I'd sent her out to lunch, and he got through then."

"What happened when you asked him who he was?"

"He hung up." When I didn't say anything she went on, "Why do you think it might be Macrae?"

I was so confused about Macrae, among many other things, I didn't know whether I hoped it was he or feared it. "I don't know, Claire."

"Didn't you tell me that somebody had been making inquiries about you around your office?"

"I'm beginning to think again that this might also be Macrae."

"You also said he denied it and you accepted his denial."

"I'm not sure I do anymore."

"I see. Well, you know where to reach me if you need me."

■ ■ ■ I sat staring at the phone for a few minutes after she hung up. It was so easy to let my congenital suspiciousness reach out to her, to destroy what degree of faith I'd felt. It was, I decided, a little like feeling walls closing in around one.

Abruptly I got up. I'd go out to the mall now to look for some toilet articles and some underclothes and pantyhose. I knew it was highly fashionable to pour scorn on malls—Paul always had. But right now I was grateful that I could probably get everything I needed without having to go looking in a strange town or hiring a car.

■ ■ ■ In the end, though, I did hire a car from a local car rental agency. The mall had much that I needed, but not everything. Not, for instance, pantyhose of the kind I was used to wearing. But more than one storekeeper in the mall suggested I go to another mall about two miles distant.

"It's much bigger than here," one of them said. "The stores are larger and have more variety. After all, it was built two years before this."

So I hired my Chevrolet, which alleviated somewhat my frequent and ongoing sense of being trapped, and gave me an escape from my motel room.

It was a moderately prosperous little town, I decided as I drove, trying to follow the instructions about getting to the other mall given me at the rental place. As I went through one street after another, looking for signposts, hesitating at a main intersection where my instructions seemed anything but clear, I noticed the houses getting bigger and more lavish. Evidently the bigger and older mall serviced the richer section of town.

When I thought I'd left the last of the town and seemed to be passing through hilly fields and groves of trees, I saw suddenly some gates and walls branching out through the trees that bordered it.

Slowing the car I looked at them. Was this the home of the rich "angel" Mr. Wilson talked about? Leaning back and then forward I tried to see the house behind it, but the gates and more trees prevented it. After a few futile moments I drove on.

■ ■ ■ The second mall, at the top of a low hill, was indeed larger and glossier than the first, boasting the presence of some well-known New York and Boston stores. I found my pantyhose and then, discovering I was hungry, stopped and had some pizza and coffee.

By the time I had returned to where I had parked the car it was beginning to get dark. Considering how poorly marked the roads were, I thought, I'd do well to get back to the town I'd left before total blackness descended.

I'm not sure at what point I became gradually aware that there was something amiss with the car. Its engine gave an odd cough from time to time and then, abruptly, the steering wheel seemed to spin out of my control. The car shot to the side of the road which was at the head of a ravine. I slammed my foot down only to make another discovery: my brakes didn't work. I saw the huge declivity yawning before me and knew that within a few minutes—seconds—I could be dead.

But Providence, or something, reached out a hand. There was no question that my car would have slid off the rounded, pebbly slope into the deep ditch below, but something had deposited a thick concrete slab across that portion of the hill's edge. The car, thrusting forward, threatened to run over and past it, but didn't. My left front wheel teetered on top of it.

I sat there in the car, knowing I had been saved by a fluke from a nasty and almost certainly fatal accident.

I don't know how long I sat there, partly in shock, partly afraid to move. Finally, moving as gently and slowly as I could, I got the door open and stepped out. It was now almost completely dark. Off to one side, which I took to be the west, more low hills pushed up into a sort of golden glow. But where I was, there seemed to be no bottom to the ditch or ravine I had almost gone into.

It was in fact so dark I couldn't see clearly where the car's wheel was, and whether the other front wheel was also rammed up against the concrete block. Would there be a flashlight in the glove compartment, or in the back trunk? But I couldn't see well enough to fiddle around with opening the trunk. And I had to remember that there were no brakes in the car.

I looked around and discovered I was completely alone. No other cars were coming along the road, and though I stopped and listened, I couldn't hear any approaching from either direction.

I could, I decided, do one of three things: do nothing at all and hope that someone would come along and rescue me; start walking down the hill which led, I knew, to a crossroads where I might find more traffic; or get back in the car and try to maneuver it off the concrete block and back onto the road. But with the brakes gone, trying to take the car down the hill would be asking for disaster. Walking would be better than doing nothing. But I still wished I had a flashlight. I glanced at the large hulk of the car barely discernible against the faintly lighter sky. If the flashlight were in the glove compartment, it would be on the opposite side from the door now open. To reach it, I'd have either to open the other door, or crawl across the front seat, and what would either do to the balance of the car?

I stared down that dark road. Back in the days of my radical activities I'd heard some of my young companions, sickened by the machinations of a corrupt society, speak of the simplicity, truth and social superiority of country life over the decadent ways of the city. Not wanting to be considered a bourgeoise traitor, I never admitted that I found the country a big bore— when it wasn't frightening. And right now it was frightening. I started down the hill, barely able to see where I was walking, my city pumps slipping and sliding on the gravel and dirt.

How far did the man in the first mall say this one was? About two miles. To make myself feel better I decided to put it in the city terms. About forty north-south Manhattan blocks. I worked on Fifty-third Street and Fifth Avenue. Hadn't I walked the distance from my Charles Street apartment many times? How long did it take me? Even considering I was crossing town and with such city impediments as stoplights and traffic, only about an hour. Here there were no traffic lights, no traffic—unfortunately. And it wasn't quite as dark as I thought, was it? At that moment of positive thinking I put my foot down, felt my ankle turn and fell. It was then I heard my first car, coming towards me from the mall. Struggling to my feet I waved frantically. The car pulled up and stopped.

"Had an accident?" a hoarse voice said.

"I turned my ankle. Can you give me a lift into the town?"

"Sure. Climb in."

Whoever it was certainly wasn't Sir Walter Raleigh, guided at all times by the demands of courtesy. My rescuer sat in his car while I struggled to the opposite side, opened the door and hobbled in.

"Sorry I couldn't get out," he said, "but I'm afraid these impede me somewhat." He touched some crutches beside him.

Perhaps irrationally I felt better. It was a lot more pleasant to think the man was lame and unable to maneuver easily than to think he was a boor.

"That's absolutely okay. I don't think I've done anything very serious, but I wasn't looking forward to walking the rest of the two miles in the dark on a road that nobody seems to travel much."

"It's not the main road to the mall, that goes out from another angle."

"Maybe I got the man's instructions wrong. I will admit that I found some of them confusing."

"You want to be dropped at the motel?"

"Yes, if it's not too far out of your way."

It was at that moment that finally another car hove in sight, coming towards us. As it passed the headlights lit up the profile of the man beside me. I leaned a little forward to see him better.

I saw his eyes glide sideways. "Everything okay?" he asked.

"Yes," I said, and wondered why I felt vaguely uncomfortable.

Two miles on a highway in the country in a functioning car was nothing. We entered the town and I saw again the place where I could have mistaken the road leading to the bigger mall.

"The signs aren't too clear here," I said.

"No, one of these days we'll get around to fixing them."

In another two minutes we drew up before the motel. I opened the door and gingerly got out. Then I turned around. "I can't tell you how grateful I am that you picked me up. Thanks."

"A pleasure." Almost before I had the door closed he'd driven off.

I got the key from the desk clerk. As I did so, a man who had been sitting in a sort of reception area got up and came towards me. "Mrs. Covington?"

"Ms. or Miss if you prefer." My mouth was dry. The man was not in uniform, but there was something about him that said police.

"All right, Ms. Covington. A Lieutenant O'Neill of the NYPD asked us to keep an eye on you. So I just thought I'd come along and introduce myself."

I glanced at the desk clerk who was making a big show of filling out some forms. "That's nice of you. I hadn't realized I was under arrest."

"Oh, you're not. But we do like to keep an eye on people we're interested in who might decide to leave town."

"Is this a not so gentle hint I should go back to New York?"

"It's not for me to say," he said genially. He was tall, rangy and looked about fifty.

"Well, about half an hour ago I'd have been very glad to see you."

"Oh? How so?"

I told him what had happened to the car.

"And you say it's just outside the big mall?"

"Yes. And its brakes are gone."

"We'll send someone out to look at it." He picked up a wide hat from the chair next to where he'd been sitting. "Sergeant Lowry, Ma'am. Hope your stay will be pleasant. Maybe you should drop into the emergency room of our hospital and let them take a picture of that ankle. It's right down the road."

"Thanks, I might do that. Should I tell them to send a copy to you?"

"Oh, we'll get one if we need it." He waved and left.

I went into my room and slammed the door.

19.

I ordered dinner in my room, arguing to myself that if I ate with my ankle up on the bed it might get to feel better. My ancient dislike of hospitals and medical records held even here, though there wasn't much logic to it. Then I sat on the side of the bathtub for twenty minutes, soaking my foot in cold water.

When the waiter arrived, pushing a table, he obligingly went back for a tray and transferred my soup, sandwich and hot tea onto the tray so I could sit up in bed with the tray on my lap and distract myself with any television news program I could find.

This was not, I reminded myself, New York, so the fact that the national all-news program did not manage to mention Paul's murder within the first half hour was probably par for the course. I'd have to wait until the usual time for roundups. But just as I was about to find something else on the tube the announcer said, "This is just in: the police investigating the Davenport murder case in New York say the laboratory tests taken from the scene of the murder have been completed and they are now very near to making an arrest." The announcer glanced up from the paper he was reading and said, "As you may remember, Professor Paul Davenport from Columbia University, who lived with a woman, a senior editor at a well-known publishing house, was found stabbed to death in the apartment they shared in New York's Greenwich Village."

How near was near, I wondered? I thought about Sergeant Lowry. Would he be showing up at the motel with handcuffs on the ready?

Again, as though on a screen at the back of my head, I saw the stains on the sofa and floor. But they were the stains, not the body, I told myself.

It was years since I had taken my last drug. At the rehabilitation place I had lived in for months I had learned an interesting assortment of facts, among them, that drugs could and sometimes did have a lasting effect on the mind, or in the words of one of the doctors there, they could permanently destroy some of the brain functions. I had come to think that I was one of the lucky ones; that I had managed to escape without that. Occasional, almost dreamlike flashes of things that had happened in the past sometimes appeared in my dreams or in odd moments when I was tired or under pressure. I wanted to believe that it was not a remnant of drugs but my rage at Paul that had played such a trick on me, making me fear for a moment that it was I who had stabbed him and blocked it out. I knew that in the past years I had occasionally blocked out memories that were unpleasant or frightening. The psychiatrist at the rehab told me he thought I had blocked memories from much earlier. But I rejected that: by this time, and with all that therapy, I would have known.

I had not killed Paul, I told myself, although there was no question that I had wanted to. I must hang onto that.

■ ■ ■ The next morning my ankle bulged like an obscene cabbage. I stared at it dismally. Then I called Ian Wilson. A faint fear that he might have been watching the same news show and been alerted by the words, "a senior editor at a leading publishing house" made me grip the phone tightly, but his voice greeting me sounded normal. "No, Ms. Covington, I'm afraid I haven't had time since yesterday to get any more information for you."

Was there an understandable touch of reproach in his voice? Hastily I told him about my ankle and said I was just touching base before going off to the local emergency room to have them look at it.

Instantly his voice warmed. "Oh, I'm sorry. Why don't you let me call Dr. Foster? He's a member of St. Timothy's and I don't think you'd have to do all that waiting."

"That's kind of you, but I don't mind the emergency room." In fact, I much preferred the emergency room with its greater confusion and anonymity.

■ ■ ■ But two hours later I wondered if I had been stupid. This might be a country town, but the emergency room was full and the young doctors were going frantically from one patient to another. Finally one got to me. He stared at my swollen foot, asked a couple of questions, then yelled at a technician to get a wheelchair and take me for an X-ray.

When we got back he looked at the picture and said, "Well, I know it's a terrible sight, but it's not as serious as it looks. You have cracked the fifth metatarsal—that's the last bone on the top of the foot"—he pointed to it—"and we can do everything from putting the foot in a cast to simply suggesting strong shoes. It depends on your way of life."

Some insane impulse made me want to ask, "Which is the best for running from the police?" But I swallowed it. "How about a bandage and maybe running shoes?"

"Are you a runner?"

"No, but like a lot of other people in"—I decided not to say New York—"at home I wear them when I do a lot of walking."

"All right. Bathe the foot in warm salt water as much as you can. Stay off of it for a week"—he glanced at me—"as much as you can. I'll give you the X-ray to take to your doctor."

After being properly bandaged and dismissed, I stopped the cab in the mall, the little mall next to my motel, and bought a pair of dark, ugly, heavy-soled shoes with laces up to the ankle. They were a shade too big for my unbroken foot and didn't cause too much anguish to my wounded ankle. Then I limped back to the motel.

The next two days were a horror. The car rental service picked up the car that had almost killed me. Since the brakes were gone, they couldn't exactly charge me for the repair, but they also weren't eager to rent me another one. When I inquired if there were another car service in the area, I was given a number, but when I called them, they sounded evasive, too.

Knowing that I shouldn't go about—even in a car—I sat on the bed with my foot up and worked on the one manuscript I had shoved in my briefcase and brought down.

It was on the second night after my fall when the phone woke me up. My first thought, hastily abandoned, was that it was Macrae. My second, as I lifted the receiver, that it might be the Reverend Ian Wilson.

It was neither. A male voice said in an even tone, "I suggest strongly that you return home now. You're in enough trouble in New York. You'll be in far worse danger if you stay down here."

"Who are you?" I yelled, angry and—yes—scared.

But the phone had gone dead.

I jiggled the phone buttons and kept on jiggling them. Finally a sleepy voice said, "Yes?"

"Who was that who phoned me just now?"

"I don't know, Madam. After midnight we put the incoming calls on automatic. They don't go through the switchboard."

"What if somebody drives up and wants a room?"

"Well, if there is one, I'd assign it to him. Why?"

I was about to say that the phone call had been threatening when I decided I didn't want that piece of information put idly about. "Nothing," I said.

By then I was awake for good. My room was on ground level. I had drawn the curtains of my floor length windows and made sure no one could look in. But suddenly I felt exposed, at risk.

I drew up my feet—as well as I could considering my swollen ankle—and rested my head on my knees, letting my mind drift. After a while and going back to the beginning—if it was the beginning—certain facts stared at me:

Somebody had been making inquiries about me around the office.

Someone in Boston had attacked Sister Mary Joseph, killing her.

Someone had kidnapped me at La Guardia Airport.

Someone had killed Paul Davenport in the apartment we lived in and the police thought I had done it.

Someone had tampered with the car I had rented. I had carefully not allowed myself to think that until now, telling myself that this was a small town in hicksville and the car rental people probably didn't have too great a conscience about keeping their rental cars in good condition. I no longer really believed that.

And someone had made that phone call.

Who and why and with what purpose?

Cui bono? To whom the good? In other words, who benefitted?

Two faces swam into my mind at that point: Claire Aldington's and Mac Macrae's.

But I had deliberately sent him away. Why? Because until I had found my daughter I did not want to risk any possibility of not finding her by having my radical past with its legal charge being discovered by a onetime federal agent—however romantically or sexually he might be involved with me—and preventing me from locating her. I had done nothing else for her; I should do this.

It was true that my inability to help her was not my own fault. I had tried in every way I knew how to get my father to relent. Or had I?

It was I who had accepted that joint from my old boyfriend after months of abstemiousness, of trying to prove to my father that I was worthy to have my daughter. Afterwards, after the long drug-filled weeks that followed taking the joint, I had told myself that he wouldn't have relented anyway. But I didn't know that.

"It was your choice," I could hear the voice of the counselor at the rehab saying it over and over again. "You had a choice. Yes, yes, I know you were tempted, and yes I think your father irresponsible, manipulative and brutal, taking your daughter from you when you were too ill to know what was happening. But you still had a choice . . ."

I had come to hate those words more than any others I had ever heard. They shook the foundation of my life and faith, which rested on the belief, the certainty, that from the beginning I had been a victim.

After I had left the rehab, I had tried to make myself over as they had wanted me to. At least I had a job and had done well at it, at least I had not gone back into the drug world and I had stayed clear of politics. But I kept on rejecting, as I always rejected, the statement that when I had taken the drug that finally put my daughter beyond me I was acting from my own choice.

Why was that coming at me now?

What difference did it make?

Was it tied up with my relationship with Macrae?

Well, I thought, the man at the desk said calls were handled automatically. Let's see if this call would go through. But I didn't get as far as punching the number. By doing that I might be putting Mac in the field of fire. I'd have to do it from a public phone tomorrow.

I tried to go back to sleep, but the voice of the man on the phone woke me up each time I was drifting off, just as though I had heard it again.

Finally, around five, I gave up and sat up in bed, going over again the various points that I had listed in my mind. What, if anything, did they add up to or point to?

That I was a threat to someone or something?

That something or someone wanted me to stop doing something? But what? Since my Boston visit and my coming here to Virginia were both about finding my daughter, could it have something to do with that? It could, possibly. But not necessarily. Gil had told me about the inquiries around the office before I left for Boston and before I had told anyone I was going to go there for any reason whatever.

Was Paul's death part of this?

For some reason that possibility had not really taken hold in my mind. During his recent bouts with drinking, I had had no illusions about Paul's fidelity. And if he felt I was being unfaithful to him he would probably make a point of seeking out other diversions. But would one of them, possibly in a drunken quarrel, commit murder? Theoretically it was a possibility, but I had no feeling it was real.

For the next two hours I sat there breakfastless, coffeeless, my manuscript work done, closeted with myself, carless, with no means of getting out, running somewhere, finding some activity —almost any activity—to divert me.

"My dear, someday you're going to have to sit still and find your own center."

Where on earth did that come from?

I frowned. The words, spoken in a woman's voice, were as clear as though they'd been said an hour before. I scraped every corner of my mind, trying to make connections and contacts that would yield up the identity of the owner of that voice. Why did it fill me with anger? I didn't know. Nor did I know who had said it or where or when.

Let it go. It will come back. That was another piece of home-spun wisdom, not necessarily from the same source. But I knew it to be true. Whenever I had lost something in my memory I had learned long ago to stop trying to retrieve it. It would come back.

"Your unconscious mind is far brighter and knows far more than your conscious one."

That was said in the same woman's voice as before. Where, oh where—

"Forget it!" I said aloud.

I glanced at my watch. It was six-thirty. Hobbling from the bed to the window I pulled aside the curtains. Sunlight poured in. What chance was there that a breakfast place would be open in the mall? And could I get there? The hospital had sent me out with a cane and I could try my new hideous shoes. I stared left and right into the mall to see if I could locate a public phone. Yes, there was one—on the other side of the mall, of course. Maybe it would be good for me to try and walk!

The desk clerk looked at me with surprise as I walked past.

"When do you reconnect the phones?" I asked.

"Reconnect the phones?"

I sighed. "They're on automatic at night—or so I was told."

"Oh—oh yes. We reconnect them to the switchboard at six."

I hobbled out into the driveway and proceeded towards the phone booth across the parking lot that was now almost deserted. Except for the ever present sound of cars starting up and speeding along, what to any New Yorker would seem a deathly quiet reigned. It made me nervous, even as I explained to myself that this was, for the country, quite normal. Nevertheless and thinking myself stupid I turned around. And in doing so saved my life.

The car was low, amazingly quiet and coming at a deadly pace. For two stupid seconds I stood there and stared. Then I gave a shriek and jumped behind one of the few cars that was parked in the lot at that hour. The car sped away. Too late I thought about its license plates. I stared after the car which at that moment turned into the highway. Either the plates were obscured or the car didn't have any.

"That stupid jerk. What the hell did he think he was doing?"

The speaker was a man of about fifty in a plaid shirt and an old-fashioned hat, carrying groceries and what looked like a sack of dirt.

"He was trying to kill me," I said, and heard my voice shake.

The man turned his blue eyes on me. "I'll grant you, it sure looked that way, but why would he do that?"

"I don't know. I wish I did."

His round blue eyes stared at me a moment. "Not from around here, are you?"

I shook my head. "New York."

"New York, eh." The ensuing silence said louder than words that I should have left my New York ways and those of my fellow New Yorkers back there. "Even so . . ." he said, confirming my diagnosis. Then he looked at me. "You okay?"

While in danger of being killed, I hadn't thought about my foot, but now the streaks of pain shooting through my ankle and up my leg reminded me of it. In my leap to safety I had landed on my sore foot and it felt like a ball of fire.

"That shore didn't help your leg," the man said, staring down.

"No," I managed to say.

"Anything I can do?"

I was about to say no when I looked again at the wide distance between me and the public phone. "Do you have a car?"

"A pickup."

"I have to make a phone call and I want to do it from that phone over there." I nodded towards the public phone.

"Okay. I'll bring the pickup here and take you over."

Getting up into the pickup wasn't easy, but my knight got out, came around and gave me a helpful shove. "Ma wife sometimes has trouble getting in," he said agreeably. He also helped me get out when we got there.

"Want me to wait?"

It was a temptation, but I shook my head. I'd have to get back somehow by myself. I didn't want even the friendliest car to overhear my conversation. "Thanks, but this may take a while. I can get back all right if I take my time. Thanks anyway."

When he'd driven off, I got out my charge card and dialed Macrae's number along with his area code and the number on my card.

Amazingly, it hadn't occurred to me that he might not be there, not after my soul-wrenching decision to summon him back into my life. But after four rings his answering tape came on requesting me to leave my name and number and the time of my call after the beep. Hearing his voice, even recorded, had an unsettling effect on me. I was suddenly aware of tears flowing down my face.

"Mac," I said. "This is Janet. I need to talk to you. Could you call me at this number?" And I read the motel number I had carefully written down before. I still felt, given my unpleasant experiences in this town, that to talk to him on the motel phone might place him in some degree of danger, but I had to speak to him. My degree of urgency about that shook me.

Hanging up the phone, I set myself to hobble back to the motel.

20.

Stopping off and resting at various places—the Breakfast Nook where I had coffee and a muffin, despite almost tearful attempts to make me what was called "a real country breakfast" which turned out to include bacon, eggs, sausage, home fries and half a loaf of bread, a drug store where I bought some aspirin and sat in a chair put out for the infirm, benches here and there and another coffee shop—I managed to get back to the motel in about an hour.

"Your husband is here," the desk clerk said.

"My husband?"

"Yes." Alarm flooded the youthful face. "Aren't . . . aren't you married? He said he was your husband. He sounded like he really was."

"Of course," I said, but I didn't move. I could deny having a husband. (Why hadn't I?) I could ask the desk clerk to send for the police. The boy at the desk was staring, brown eyes widened with alarm.

"My foot is really giving me a bad time," I said. "Let me speak to him on the phone."

"Sure." He punched a couple of buttons and handed me the receiver from the phone behind the desk.

"Hello," the man said.

A nameless feeling flooded me. "Mac?" I said.

"Who else are you married to?"

"No one. I—er—have a bad ankle so it'll take me a moment to get there. Be patient."

"What else have I been? At this time I'd give Job a good run for his money."

I hobbled down to my room and unlocked the door. Mac Macrae was standing in the middle of the bedroom. For a moment we looked at each other.

"Who did what to your ankle?"

"I'll tell you about it in a minute. Did you know what I was doing out at this hour of the morning? I was risking life, limb and ankle to call you from a public phone on the other side of the mall. You'll hear me if you call in for your messages." I was hobbling forward as I spoke. Mac didn't move, making me come to him. When I reached him I dropped my cane on the bed and put my arms around him. "Mac, I'm sorry for—for not . . . for not—"

His arms went slowly around me. "For not what?"

I tried to think of a more palatable version of the truth.

"Come on," he said harshly. "Spit it out. It's worse if you don't."

"For not completely trusting you."

"Do I gather from your reticence you thought I didn't know you didn't trust me?"

I stared up at him. "It's a long story."

"It always is."

"Please kiss me."

"You know I'm not some kind of a bargaining chip to be put down and then picked up."

"No. I know." I felt the tears beginning to prick behind my eyes.

"I can't believe that it's just love, pure love that has overwhelmed you. There's got to be something you want me to do for you. What is it?"

I sat down on the bed. "No," I said angrily, as I saw his brows go up. "This isn't another come on. My goddamn foot hurts and I can't go on standing up so you can dress me down before the troops."

He stood for a moment looking down at me. "Why did you call me?"

I could not blame him for his skepticism. Yet, "Why are you here in my room, calling yourself my husband?"

"Given everything that has gone before, I had no idea how you'd react if you saw me, and it was important that I talk to you.

For some reason a small shiver went through me. "Why?"

"Because for causes I can't fully fathom, I carried on with trying to find your daughter. No, don't interrupt me or I won't get to it. I went through a friend of mine in Boston connected with the Church, who knew your father—"

"For God's sake!" I stood up and promptly got shoved back onto the bed.

"Remember your foot!" Macrae said. "The trail was not very clear and the . . . well, the man I asked wasn't too happy about cooperating. Evidently your father put the fear of God into a large part of the hierarchy. Anyway, he seemed to think that your daughter might have been adopted by a family up in Minnesota. They had relatives in Boston, and had been known to be looking to find a child to adopt. He suggested you might want to get in touch with them."

I found I could hardly breathe. "Did you go out there?"

"No. I thought I ought to tell you this instead. Questions would have to be asked that only you knew the answer to."

"I'll leave immediately. Where—where is this family? What town?"

"It's a small town about forty miles from Minneapolis. Here's the name and address and phone number." He handed me a piece of paper.

I took it and read, "Mr. and Mrs. Porter Anderson, 146 Elm Street, Northcliff, Minnesota, telephone 609 555 2980." The name rang no bell whatsoever. I never knew any Anderson in Boston.

"Sorry, my information didn't run to a zip code," Mac said. "You'll have to look it up if you want to write. But before you do anything I have to tell you that you're not alone in trying to find your daughter. Somebody else is."

I put down the paper. "Who?"

"I don't know. But a day or two after I talked to him my friend called back and said that two nights after our conversation somebody broke into his study and went through his files. As far as he could make out, nothing had been stolen, but the files that had been opened and the contents scattered were those to do with that adoption and one or two others. Evidently the thief or intruder had heard something or been frightened off because he left things lying around. My friend had called the people in Minnesota, feeling they ought to know that for some reason interest was being shown in the adoption of their daughter—i.e. that I had called and that someone had broken into his files."

"And they—?"

"I don't know what they did, but apparently they were extremely upset because your father, or whoever it was, had promised them total privacy. Apparently with all the birth mothers coming forward and demanding their rights, they were thoroughly alarmed."

"But my daughter would be almost eighteen by now. Why should they be so concerned about her knowing she was adopted, or about her seeing her natural mother?"

"I don't know. Maybe they never told her she was adopted. On another subject, I must also say that the New York police aren't at all happy about your skipping town." He paused. "For whatever reason, you didn't call me after Paul was found stabbed. I saw the headlines and heard the newscasts. I was in Boston when it happened, but when I checked my answering machine, you had not called me, so I had to assume you didn't want me to interfere." He paused. "I wasn't going to go rushing around offering help when it was obvious you didn't trust me and would only spurn it.

"Then my Boston friend called, so I tried to call you, couldn't find you and no one knew where you'd gone. So I called somebody I knew in the NYPD and learned from them you were down here. This is my final bit of running interference for you. Do I gather you were going to ask for my help again?"

"Yes," I said.

"Why?"

"Because weird things have happened and I don't know how to cope with them."

"They've got to be weirder than weird if they moved you to summon me back." He paused, glanced down at my foot. "Well, what did happen?"

I told him about the car and my ankle and about the phone call from the man telling me to leave. "I'm beginning to feel that something is closing in on me—"

"Only now? Not after the man at La Guardia, to mention only the most obvious?"

"Mac, I know you're angry, and you're right, I didn't trust you with the whole truth."

"You don't say!"

"Please don't be sarcastic."

He stared down at me for a moment. Then, "I've done the job I came here to do. I think, for your own sake and safety, perhaps telling all to the police might not be a bad idea. You might give it some thought."

I watched him go towards the door. Asking for help had never been easy for me. Being completely straightforward about the messy details of my life was something I'd never done—not even completely with Claire. I had hoarded the most damaging truths, having had long practice with that—far longer than the years in California. Even thinking of giving words to one particular secret made me break out into a sweat at the same time I also felt icy cold. I watched Mac pick up the raincoat thrown over a chair and open the door. If he went now, then I knew he would never come back.

"Mac!"

With the door partly open he stopped.

"Come back. Please. I'll . . . I'll tell you."

He half turned. "You'll tell me what?"

"All there is to know."

He came back in and closed the door. "Why?"

"Because I desperately need your help, not only with the whole muddle you've been talking about, but also to find my daughter. I have to keep that in the front. It's her life. I haven't been able to do anything else for her."

He threw his raincoat back on the chair. "All right. Speak!"

So, slowly, dragging my sentences, I told him about the years in California, the bombings, the holdups, the deaths of innocent people. Finally my voice ran down.

"Were you charged?"

"Yes."

"What name were you using?"

"Liz Porter."

"And what group or groups did you operate with?"

I stared at him. The one thing that no self-respecting revolutionary did was betray any of the others. If the pressure became too much, you were supposed to lie and keep on lying until you found a way to escape. And what about Jeff—Jeff the one love of my life until then—or even afterwards, at least until now? Even in our best days I never thought what Paul and I had was anything like the wild romance with Jeff, interspersed, of course, by political forays. But Jeff was neither romantic nor sentimental when he walked out on me or threatened me if I told anyone about the things we'd done.

"Jeff Dysart."

"Hmm!"

"You know the name?"

"I think anyone in the Bureau knew that name even though it was obviously a phony one. After all, Jeff Dysart, or whoever he really was, was responsible for killing at least one government agent."

What was it Jeff used to say, those long ago days in the sixties and seventies? "Killing the pigs is not killing. It's legal extermination." And we'd all laughed.

I closed my eyes. Anyone who worked for a law enforcement branch of the government—whether federal, state or city—was automatically an enemy—an enemy, one of the pigs, one of Them. Killing them was a necessary sanitizing act. They weren't people with families, wives, children, friends. Needless to say I'd never known a cop or federal agent so depersonalizing them was easy. Now I knew an agent, or at least a former one. It made a difference. I wondered if it would have made one then.

"Had you heard of me?" I asked.

"No. Not that I can recall. What things—holdups, bomb-ings—were you actually involved in?"

"I drove the car once—for a bank holdup. Because somebody —a bank guard—got killed, the federal prosecutor charged me in absentia, so to speak."

Mac got up and started to walk around. "What made you break with them? What happened afterwards?"

So I went back and put together the events following the day I came back from shopping to find Jeff and his friends gone and his note on the packing box we'd used as a table.

"I went back to drugs and to the druggies I'd run around with before I got into the political groups. Only I went into it more . . . it was much worse than before . . ." I paused, the memory of those horrible final weeks—the degradation—rushing back. "I was twenty-four years old, but I had been using drugs for most of the nine years since I was fifteen. I was destroyed mentally and physically."

"So you decided to go to the rehab?"

"It was decided for me. It was that or jail."

"You were sent to a state place?"

"At first. Then I got a . . . well, it was like a scholarship to a place in Minnesota and spent a year there."

"And that did it?"

"Yes. Finally."

He got up. "I've known several people who have been to one or the other of those places in Minnesota. Apparently they were able to turn their lives around. I take it you were able to do that."

I nodded.

"I suppose you didn't tell me before because you thought I'd turn you in and you'd finally have to face that charge."

"You make it sound so easy. After twelve years of a straight life in a good job doing moderately well, I wasn't much attracted by the thought of going to jail." I shuddered. "I couldn't take that."

"Nobody likes jail. But you'd probably only get a year or so."

I turned on him. "You're very casual. Have you ever been in a cell behind bars?"

"Yes. I was a prisoner of war. I didn't like it. But I survived. That doesn't mean I don't sympathize with your desire to avoid it."

I said slowly, "I think I'd have killed myself first."

He frowned. "You must have at least considered jail a possibility when you went into your political activities."

I was silent.

"Didn't you?"

Suddenly, as though I had never seen it before, I saw now

that my political ardor sprang, not from carefully thought out views or convictions about the body politic, books I had read, lectures I had attended, arguments I had heard that had won me over. It sprang from two purely emotional and symbiotic sources: my rage against my father and my falling in love with Jeff. My father treated me with cruelty. He was also a rigid, dogmatic conservative who demanded brutal control of those around him. That made me a radical in the making. All I had to do was encounter the trigger, and Jeff was the trigger.

"It's a little humbling," I said.

"What is?"

I looked up at him. "To realize that my revolutionary zeal was nine parts filial defiance plus falling in love with a radical activist and one part—if that much—political conviction. In answer to your question, no, I was too far gone in both my emotional orbits even to think about jail. It wasn't until I walked into a mall post office one day and saw my name on a wanted poster that it became real. And it was shortly after that that Jeff walked out on me."

"Maybe he realized the basis underlying your revolutionary conversion."

"Probably," I said.

"Have you seen him since?"

For some reason I was astonished. "Of course not."

"Have you wanted to?"

"No!" I almost shouted the word. "I just told you, he walked out on me."

"And you weren't—er—mollified by the thought that with your unreliability—as a driver and so on—he was acting unselfishly to preserve his own safety and that of his political group?"

"What are you doing? Playing devil's advocate?" I looked back at him. "What's your stake in all this? Love, pure love?"

"Which you don't believe in."

"What reason have I to believe in it?"

"Did you ever love anybody? Or maybe that's the wrong question. Did you ever feel complete and unconditionally loved by anyone?"

"My mother."

"And how old were you when she died?"

"Nine."

"And she was the only one?"

"Except for Jock."

"Who's Jock?"

"A dog I once had. I had to find a home for him when I went to the rehab. I deserted him just as I did Laura." I paused, then asked, "What's the purpose of all these questions?"

He sighed. "I guess to see what I'm up against."

"What do you mean?"

"I mean, Janet, Felicity, whoever you are, it's been my misfortune to fall in love with a former revolutionary who is still being sought by the police and who, incidentally, has lied to me almost from the beginning, who has been nice when she wanted something, and removed herself when she didn't, all with a complete disregard for my feelings."

"Your feelings?"

"Yes, my feelings. Men have feelings just as women do. But you've never really believed that, have you? There was your father, and then there were the various tools to get back at him, of which your ex-love, Jeff, was one."

"What did you do, major in Psych I? Don't tell me you're feeling sympathetic towards Jeff, who would have blown you and your Bureau sky high if he could!"

"No, I don't have any use for Jeff. But as for your relationship, I think you were two of a kind. You used each other."

Disregarding my foot I stood up. "Thanks a lot. Is this what you call love? What do you do? Collect character references on the women you love? Decide whether or not they're worthy of you?"

He turned and walked to the door. "I've done what I came to do," he said. "I've told you what I've found out. The rest is up to you. Like I said, the best thing you can do is tell the police. But it's up to you. Good luck."

And he walked out.

21.

The telephone awoke me the next morning around seven. "Sorry for the early call," Mr. Wilson said. "And I certainly don't want to raise your hopes in any way. Unfortunately, on the contrary. My first line of inquiries—sources that can often produce adoption information—have come up with nothing about any eighteen-year-old girl who could be your daughter. And I thought I ought to tell you this now so you won't feel you're wasting time down here. How's your ankle, by the way?"

"Much better," I said, without bothering to check. I paused for a moment, my eyes on the piece of paper with the Andersons' address that Mac had left. Should I mention it? If Mr. Wilson's inquiries would verify Mac's story, the answer would be yes. Yet something held me back. Instead I asked, "Could you give me any idea as to what your first line of inquiries is—that is, if you can. If it's confidential, then I understand." Liar, I thought to myself. If it were confidential I'd do my best to find out who and what his sources were.

"There's no secret about that. There are the major adoption agencies and services in each state, plus others that work on a smaller scale, but are still known to the government. But you have to realize that a certain percentage of adoption is done privately by doctors, lawyers, friends and so on. It takes much longer to find those out, who the children were, who their mothers were, and involves detective agencies and so on. It takes not only time, but money, and of course we're always in need of more of that." There was a wry note to his voice.

"I thought you said you had an angel."

"We do. He funds our basic functions and we call on him for extra from time to time, but I prefer not to call on him unless it becomes obvious that only with his help can we find out whose child somebody is, or which child is the son or daughter a woman is looking for."

I swallowed. I certainly couldn't blame him for not wanting to rush in and pour extra money into one particular search simply because I was feeling anxious and frustrated.

He went on, "I can't say I'm certain we'll find out where your daughter is, I can never guarantee success. All we can do is try. But it will take a while, and I think it would be better for you to return to New York and your job. Sitting here, waiting for a result that may take who knows how long, can do nothing but produce frustration."

There was something about what he was saying, or perhaps the way he was saying it, that bothered me, but I couldn't figure out what it was.

"So," he said, "we'll be in touch as soon as I have the faintest sign that we're getting anywhere. Have a good journey back. And get your doctor to give another look at that ankle." He hung up.

Did he seem anxious for me to leave? I got out of bed and

wobbled to the bathroom where I had a long hot shower followed by a short cooler one. Then I dressed and packed the few things I had acquired in a zip bag and took a taxi to the airport.

■ ■ ■ It was a small airport, but it would have been perfectly capable of changing my return ticket to New York for one to Minneapolis. But as I stared at the one ticket counter, two things stopped me from making the change: the near certainty that I would have to take a flight either to New York or some other major center and then another to Minneapolis, and, again, Mac's statement about someone else being interested in the Andersons' adopted daughter. This was a small town. I might be paranoid but buying a ticket to Minneapolis would be a lot less anonymous here than in, say, La Guardia.

The flight to La Guardia was uneventful, and I was unbelievably glad to look down and see the familiar streets of Queens and the small island with the towering peaks that made up Manhattan.

But when I tried to get a flight to Minneapolis, I discovered that, unless I wanted to change twice, the next flight was four hours off, which left me with a tiresome dilemma. Either I killed the four hours sitting at La Guardia, or I was willing to spend two of them going to and from La Guardia and midtown Manhattan.

It would be nice, I thought, to get out of this wrinkled and, after my tumble, somewhat grimy suit and to get some of my own underclothes from the apartment. Unless, of course, police were there waiting to nab me when I walked in. Or, they could be watching the airports, hoping to pick me up there. A chill went over me. In my eagerness to check on the Andersons and their adopted (my?) daughter in Minnesota I had let my fear of the NYPD's interest in me recede a little. Trying not to be obvious I glanced around me, reflecting wryly as I did so that any undercover cop watching me would, if he were worth his/her salt, not be detectable.

Then, of course, there was whoever had been trying to locate/impede/kidnap and otherwise damage me. As Mac said, my sense that I was being watched and followed and inquired about was hardly imaginary. So, I thought, hovering over the newsstand, what did I do? Stay here for four hours or risk going back to my apartment or the office.

The thought of Mac depressed me. I had certainly done nothing to win any confidence he might have had in my feeling for him. But I wished—how much I wished—that he were here! Hanging around the airport and brooding over lost causes was not doing me any good. Action, however hurried and perhaps pointless, was better. Next decision: Did I want to return to my apartment and get clothes, or to my office? I had to turn in the manuscript I had been working on in Virginia and might pick up another to work on in Minnesota. There was also the slight question of whether or not my office, i.e., Mr. Jack Lederer, wanted me back. At this point, I could well be a major embarrassment. Who could I trust?

No one, I decided. I could have trusted Mac, but was too paranoid to do so when I should have. Then the thought of Claire Aldington came into my mind. There was a bank of phones to the left. Picking up my bag I went over to one and dialed Claire's number. I realized the chances of her being free were dim, but I thought if she knew I was on the other end she might pick up the receiver.

I was right.

"Where are you?" Claire said.

"La Guardia. I . . ." How could I put this with reasonable brevity? "Mac—Mac Macrae said he might have located a family in Minnesota who might have adopted Laura. I'm going to take a flight out there in four hours. But I'm afraid to go home in case the police are there. I don't know whether I'd be welcome back in my job, or even if I still have a job. And I don't know what to do."

"Why don't you come here. The police are looking for you, I know, it's been in all the papers. But there's something I want to talk to you about and I'm not sure anyone would think about the St. Anselm's parish house."

"All right. I'll take a cab there."

■ ■ ■ The receptionist at St. Anselm's stared at me when I said Claire was expecting me, but did she stare more than previous times? I didn't know.

When I went into Claire's office she was standing by the window. Hearing me, she turned. Her eyes traveled from my face to my ankle. "Don't tell me you've been further in the wars!"

"I'm afraid so. Can I sit down?"

"Of course." She looked at me with a slight smile. "Were you imagining that I'd have Lieutenant O'Neill here to make an arrest?"

I thought about that a moment and could honestly say, "No, I wasn't. I guess that's some kind of a marker."

"What happened?"

I told her in every detail I could remember about everything that took place in Virginia.

"So you and your ex-FBI guy are still on the outs?"

"Yes. He got fed up with my distrust of him."

"How much did you tell him?"

"Everything except—"

Silence.

"Except what?" Claire asked gently.

"Except the details of some of the holdups I was involved in."

It sounded reasonable. Only I knew it was a lie, a rush for

cover at the last moment. Since it was Claire asking, I felt terrible.

"All right. I had a couple of reasons for suggesting you come here. One was that I know Lieutenant O'Neill was not a bit happy when you left town. He kept tabs on you, of course."

"I know he did." And I told her about the sergeant down in Virginia.

"I know that if he spots you he'll order you not to leave again."

"I'm just surprised he didn't have people at La Guardia. It was the obvious place I'd return to."

"Maybe he did. Maybe he had his own reasons for not having you stopped. But I'm not at all sure that if you go down to your apartment there won't be a policeman there."

"And they've found nobody else who might have done this?"

"Not to my knowledge, but then beyond a certain point I'm not in their confidence."

"Did you ask me here because of that?"

"Yes. I at least wanted you to know what you might walk into." She paused. "It's up to you now, of course. Anyway, I'm glad you saw Ian. Did you like him?"

I hesitated.

Her brows went up. "No?"

"I didn't dislike him. I just had an odd feeling that he wanted to get rid of me."

"That's very strange. I've sent several people to see him, and I never heard anyone say that or anything approaching it."

I shrugged. Suddenly I felt overwhelmingly tired. "Maybe I have chronic paranoia applicable whether there's the slightest reason or not. By the way. Did you ever meet his angel?"

"Angel? Oh, you mean the man who funds his work."

"Yes."

"No. Why?"

"I don't know. I don't know why I even asked."

"Who is he?"

"A wealthy businessman named, I think, Driscoll—James or John. He lives there. According to the motel manager he's in line to be appointed by the governor to a vacated senator's seat."

"Well, if he's helping Ian, he deserves to have everyone vote for him when the time comes. What time is your flight?"

"In about two and three-quarter hours. I'd better just go. You know Mac said also that somebody else was making inquiries there, in the Minnesota town."

"What town?"

I rummaged in my pocketbook for the paper with the address on it which I had put in the side pocket, I thought. But it wasn't there. I searched the pockets of my suit jacket, then got up and unzipped my bag. I searched every corner of it and then emptied the contents out onto the floor. I even opened the portable tube which I bought to carry my toothpaste and brush.

The paper wasn't there.

"I can't believe this," I said slowly. "Mac wrote the name and address down on a piece of paper and left it on the bureau in the bedroom."

"Do you remember packing it?"

"I thought I did. I thought I put it into a side pocket of my handbag. I do remember clearly putting it on the night table beside the bed."

"Do you remember the name and address?"

"I remember the name, Anderson, but not the address. You'd think it would be burned into my mind, but—obviously it wasn't. Maybe it was because—well because of Mac's walking out on me. What on earth am I going to do?"

"You can try and call the motel from here, if you want to. The trouble is, they'll almost certainly have cleaned out to the room by this time. But do you want to try?"

I looked at her and she looked back at me.

"All right," I said. "I'll charge the call to my charge card."

She got up. I went over to her desk and went through the necessary steps of finding the area code, then calling Information down there and getting the number of the motel. Finally I got through. I felt foolish as I broached the subject. By the time I got finished with a bored and faintly amused desk clerk I had learned that the rooms were, of course, cleaned out shortly after the guests left.

"What would the maid do with a piece of paper carrying a name and address on it. Would she give it in to the desk?"

"She might. On the other hand she might have just figured you had finished using it. But I'll see if there's any paper here that she might have given to the desk." Silence for a minute then, "No, I've found a hairbrush, some toothpaste, a portable radio and two earrings. But no paper with an address on it. Sorry."

I put down the phone. "Nobody handed it in."

I stood looking down at the phone. I knew perfectly well what my next step had to be: call Mac Macrae. A spurt of rage went through me. Until this moment what I had most felt was disappointment and hurt and depression. Now I knew I was also angry. It would sound like the lamest excuse going—an excuse to call Mac and see if this time I couldn't get him back. But my daughter was at stake.

I didn't have to look up his number. Evidently I had burned it permanently into my mind. I thought his phone might be busy. I thought I might get away with leaving a message on his tape. But he picked up the receiver. "Hello?" His voice sounded abrupt.

"Mac, this is Janet. I feel a thousand fools, but I failed to bring that piece of paper with the Anderson's address in Minnesota back to New York with me. Could you give it to me again?"

"If I can find it." He sounded more than abrupt. He sounded grim and angry.

"What do you mean?"

"I mean I don't think there are two books, two pieces of paper, let alone two items of furniture or plates or cutlery or glasses left together. I don't know and can't find out for the moment if anything's missing or not. Somebody has gone through this apartment with a winnowing and chopping machine."

22.

"My God, Mac. What an awful thing! Why, why would anyone do that?"

"I haven't the faintest idea. What I've been writing in my current book—mostly notes at this point—is in the public domain, though requiring some tedious work to get it out. And the same's true of any notes or research on *Exposé*."

"Do you think—is it possible that someone was looking for that address—the one you gave me? After all you said the study of your friend in Boston had been broken into, too."

"I've wondered that. The only place I had that address was in a notebook which I can't find, and on the paper I gave you."

"So it could be that—the notebook—that whoever trashed your apartment was after."

"It could be. I don't know. I only just got back myself and I haven't been able to get things cleared enough even to know what's missing. I do remember the name of the people in Minnesota was Anderson and the town was Northcliff. You can go out there on that, I should think."

"Yes." I had a curious and fleeting feeling that I couldn't identify.

"Then you'd better get out there, hadn't you?"

"Yes. I'll call you from the airport."

"All right."

I tried to make myself detect a note of welcoming in his tone, and failed. But then his apartment had been rifled. I replaced the receiver and looked at Claire. "They live in a town called Northcliff, about thirty miles from Minneapolis. I can go out now and look them up."

But I just stood there.

After a moment Claire said, "Tell me something. Is there any reason you can think of—any at all—why you might prefer not to go out?"

I felt irritated. "I'm busting a gut to get out there, and you ask me why I don't want to go. Why?" I paused and looked at her. "Because I lost the paper?"

"I just wondered."

"That's just a bunch of psychononsense!"

"You seem very violent on the subject," Claire said mildly.

I picked up my bag. "I'm going out to the airport now." I glanced at my watch. "In fact, I'm going to have to hurry." And I walked out of the room and down the hall to the elevator.

■ ■ ■ All the way out I felt my anger growing. Of all the stupidities, that took the cake! And for Claire of all people— Claire whom I had liked and trusted . . . I chewed on that half the way to the airport, then switched to my other grievance— Mac's dumping me. It was only as we approached the ramp to the departure flights entrance that the memory of Paul's murder suddenly flooded my mind and I felt a stab of fear and pain. The mark of his blows were now only faintly on my face, easily covered with makeup. But my panic and rage were there, and I saw suddenly again, the spurt of blood that stained the sofa and the floor.

But I didn't see it, I said to myself. I saw the stain the next morning. And then I became aware that the taxi had stopped and the driver was staring back at me. I glanced at the meter. The fare was now fourteen fifty plus the bridge toll.

After I went into the airport I glanced at the clock and saw I still had half an hour. I stared at the arrow indicating the departure gates and then let my gaze drift to a nearby newsstand. I'd get a paper for the flight to Minneapolis.

As I approached the first thing that caught my eye on an afternoon tabloid was my own picture, under it a headline: "New Developments in Village Murder Case. Police Now Seek Editor."

For a moment I froze, then I turned quickly on my heel and walked towards an area I knew contained a coffee shop. But when I got there I saw through the window someone sitting at the counter reading the same tabloid, with my picture staring at him. Turning away I was about to go back towards the departure gates when I saw two men approaching. Actually I saw them reflected in the coffee shop window. They had not seen me, so I plunged into a phone booth, closed the door, put a quarter in the phone and sat with the receiver covering my face. The first number that occurred to me was, of course, Mac's. I dialed it.

When Mac answered I plunged straight in. "Have you seen the afternoon papers?"

"No, but I've been listening to some radio news. They're out after you."

"I saw my picture in a tabloid somebody was reading when I got to the airport. I don't even dare go to the departure gates. I don't know what to do."

"The chances of your getting to Minneapolis are pretty small. You'd better lie low for the time."

"Mac, I know you're angry with me and you think, maybe

rightly, that every time I've called you it's been because I needed your help—"

"Are you about to tell me that's not true?"

"Maybe it is true, technically, but it doesn't mean that I don't, well, I don't care for you."

"It doesn't?"

"Damn you!" I said, and burst into tears. He was saying something when I hung up.

I sat there for a long time, long past the time for my flight to leave. I didn't dare go to the counter to cancel it. I'd just have to lose the money. Since there was the threat of a far greater loss—my freedom—the money didn't seem to count that much.

Where could I go, without being arrested? What were the new developments? Did anyone believe me? Claire?

Yes, I thought, Claire believed me, but she had placed that doubt in my own mind about whether I truly wanted to find my child and I found that unbearable. Why? Something picked at the frontier of my consciousness and I was aware of my own rapid breathing and a fear so great I couldn't think or sit still. Yet I couldn't leave the phone booth.

Finally a possible way out occurred to me. I looked in my bag. I'd drawn some money in Virginia and had plenty of cash. If I could get to the shuttle building without being stopped I could take a shuttle to Boston and try and think of some way to get to Minneapolis from there.

I glanced over my shoulder to the hall beyond the phone booth. The only people visible were an elderly couple pushing a small luggage carrier. Across from them was a ladies room. I waited until I could see no one, then I darted from the phone booth and across to the ladies room. There was only one woman in there, a young woman with a baby. I went over to the line of basins and while I was washing my hands looked at myself in the mirror above them. Maybe a hat and some larger and more concealing dark glasses would provide a reasonable disguise. It seemed to me that near the ladies room was a gift shop in which every conceivable thing a traveler might need was offered in some form or other.

Usually I used little makeup. However, a touch of lipstick, a dash of rouge and a faint line around the eyes did wonders for my neutral coloring and, no matter how hurried, I generally managed to get that much on. Since Paul's attack, though, I had also smeared an all purpose mask over my face to hide the bruises. Taking out a tissue, I smeared some off and looked for the bruises underneath. They were still there, so I groped in my bag for more to put on. However, I did remove the lipstick, the rouge and the eyeliner. To my own eye I looked plain beyond plain, the use of the mask without those touches giving me an all-one-color look that I considered totally boring. However, it was better than getting stopped.

Picking up my bag I went across to the shop and managed to find a beret, some hairpins and huge dark glasses. There, in the gift shop, hidden behind a few display cabinets, I pinned my hair on top, pulling it as hard as I could to straighten out its natural waves, then put on the beret, pulling it forward and down over my forehead, and put on the dark glasses. Since I had never worn a hat when I could possibly avoid it, I didn't think any pictures of me wearing a hat existed anywhere. Then I pulled a traveling canvas bag and a handbag of a different color and shape from my own off the rack. I repacked my possessions in the new acquisitions, paid for my purchases and left as quickly as I could. When I passed a large litter basket, I stuffed the former bag and pocketbook inside. I had done the best I could to throw off any possible followers or arresting cops. I didn't think my so-called disguise would stop anyone for long, but even a few minutes could get me on a shuttle flight.

I caught a jitney bus to the shuttle building. When I arrived there I went over to the desk where I filled out a form, writing in the space for my name and after a moment's hesitation, Claire

Driscoll. Then I went through the security gate, remembering again to keep my head down and devoutly hoping that no sharp-eyed attendant would connect my face with that on the front of the tabloid.

It was fifteen minutes before we were waved towards the plane, during each of which I expected to hear my name over the public address system, and kept reminding myself that if there was a call for Janet Covington, I was not to respond. Finally we got on the plane and it took off. When the ticket wagon came around I paid cash. Less than an hour later I was in Boston's Logan Airport.

Lining up at the right ticket counter, I waited my chance to buy a ticket to Minneapolis, praying that there would be enough money left over from the shuttle to buy it. There was, but only just. And I knew there wasn't enough to hire a car or take some means of transportation from Minneapolis to Northcliff. This time, with no betraying pauses, as the attendant made out my ticket, I made up a different name and a bogus address.

My flight didn't take off for an hour, so I went into a cafeteria and brooded over a cup of coffee. I had, of course, known that if I handed in a credit card at the ticket counter the chances were certain that they had been told to watch out for anyone of my name. But what about the bank cash machines? Would the banks be told by the police to watch for my card even after the banks closed? Probably. But the risk was far less. And while it would certainly tell them the location of the cash machine I had used, it would not tell them where I was flying to. The only people who knew that were Claire and Mac Macrae. Lieutenant O'Neill of course knew of my connection with Claire. Would she consider my destination within the boundaries of legitimate confidentiality? I thought so, but I didn't know the ethics of the situation, and this was a murder case. My old, old mistrust of people prodded at me, but I tried not to pay too much attention. I had come to realize I had to trust someone. However, it wasn't easy for me. As for Mac, since he was friendly enough with someone or some people in the NYPD they might very well come after him. Would he tell them I was on my way to Minnesota?

Again, I didn't know. But cashing money now in a large international airport was better than cashing it in Minneapolis, even supposing my card would be honored there.

Finishing my coffee, I kept looking till I found some cash machines, then went in and withdrew as much cash as the machine would allow.

No one stopped me before I got on the plane.

■ ■ ■ For safety's sake I did not take off my hat or dark glasses. When the drinks wagon was passed, I took a soda, but was glad of the dinner. I had often complained of airplane food. Since I hadn't eaten since breakfast, it tasted Lucullan. And I took everything offered. Who knew when I would get another one?

For three and a half hours I had plenty of time to think and a variety of subjects that offered themselves: would I still have a job when I got back? Would there be cops in Minneapolis waiting for me? How could I get to Northcliff without hiring a car, and did I have to show a driving license? The answer to that was easy. Yes, I'd have to show my license. Cancel that, I thought. What other means could I take?

There might be a local train or busline. If not either of those, then it would have to be a taxi or limousine—expensive but certainly safer than driving a car.

And Mac—don't think about Mac I told myself, and tried to get my mind on something else. Considering what I was facing, it shouldn't have been difficult. Nevertheless, it was. Not since Jeff—cancel that, I told myself again. I didn't want to think about him now.

Why? He was long gone out of my life. I now knew nine-tenths of my feeling for him had been fueled by fury towards and defiance of my father. But there was something else—a sort of sick feeling. My mind slid away. I found myself thinking about the piece of paper with the Andersons' address that I had lost. And I got angry all over again at Claire.

I put my head back, forced my mind away from the piece of paper, closed my eyes and drifted off to sleep. I was in a car driving along a dark country road and Jeff was sitting beside me in the driver's seat, laughing. I started to laugh, too, and then realized why he was laughing: he had a loaded gun pointed at me and I knew that just as surely as we were driving too fast he was going to kill me. I screamed, and woke to find someone shaking my shoulder.

"That must have been a bad one," the flight attendant said, smiling and in a kind voice. "I do hope it wasn't the dinner we served!"

I felt foolish. "Sorry," I muttered. Had I screamed aloud? I didn't dare ask. Any hope that people traveling with me would forget me as a nonentity was gone. Somebody who managed to have a nightmare on a relatively short flight would not be forgettable.

"Like some coffee?" the attendant asked.

"Yes, thanks."

I stayed awake for the rest of the flight, mindlessly thumbing through one of the magazines in the pocket of the chair in front of me.

"Do you often have nightmares?" my seatmate, a middle-aged man inquired.

"No. Practically never," I lied.

"I'm only asking because that's part of my job. I'm a sleep therapist."

The last thing I needed was a therapist of any kind (excluding, of course, Claire) probing my sleeping habits. "Really," I said, putting a chill into my voice. "The attendant was probably right. It was the dinner."

■ ■ ■ I got off the plane with my carry-on luggage and walked as purposefully as I could to the exit. I didn't know if anyone—or who—might be waiting. To think that meant either Mac or Claire had talked, or possibly the New York bank controlling the cash machine in Boston had been watched. I would prefer to think the latter, but I was taking no chances.

When I got out to the ramp I looked around and saw an airport limousine. According to the driver it stopped at one of a chain of well-known hotels located in the town. Since it was now almost midnight by local time I decided to register there. I had cash, of course. But would they demand identification?

My heart sank when we stopped in front of a large and imposing hotel. It looked too expensive and too overwhelmingly respectable not to demand every kind of identification and creditation—beginning with a handful of credit cards. What would they think of a woman in dark glasses who slapped the money for one night down but claimed she had no identification?

They'd probably think she was some kind of prostitute. At that thought I gave a slightly hysterical laugh. Prostitute seemed a benign category beside murderer.

"Is this okay?" the limousine driver said, obviously a bit taken aback by my laugh.

"Fine," I said, and picked up my bags and walked in.

23.

The hotel desk accepted, albeit not too graciously, my tale of having my wallet lifted in Boston. "Luckily," I said, "I had put my cash in the side pocket of my handbag."

"You were lucky," the clerk said, deftly counting the money I had put down. "Your name?"

It was a legacy of my radical days, this blankout when somebody asked me my name suddenly. I should, of course, have had one ready when I was sitting in the bus. As before, the clerk looked up when I hesitated. "Claire Driscoll," I finally blurted out. Unfortunately, he'd remember my hesitation. I wondered if any Minneapolis papers carried my picture.

"Address?"

I made up a street and a number for Boston. And hoped that nobody on the hotel staff knew Boston. From his accent the desk clerk was a westerner.

I was shown to my room by a sleepy bellboy to whom I gave what I hoped was the exactly average tip.

Once inside with the door locked I breathed a long sigh of relief. It was, of course, true that the desk clerk or the limousine driver or the bellboy might come across my picture and be able to see through my not very convincing disguise and call the police. If they did, I was finished. There was no way out of this twelfth-floor room. Or was there?

I went to the window and looked down. It was a straight drop to the lights below. And the only part of the window that opened was a small side panel—not that I had any intention of jumping.

On the right was the bathroom, on the left a closet and—

another door. I went over to it and turned the knob. Surprisingly, it opened. I found myself in a dark room. Which might, of course, be occupied by someone now asleep in the dim shape of the bed just in front of me. Or by someone who would shortly return to his/her hotel room. I waited a moment or two, hoping my eyes would get used to the darkness in there, a darkness somewhat alleviated by the light from my own room. After a few moments I saw that the bed was definitely not occupied. Walking in, I opened the closet door, there were no clothes. I then turned on a light. There were no personal articles around, nor were there any in the bathroom. I stood there, debating and tempted to double-lock the inside of the door so that no one could get in. But if the unoccupied room was found to be locked, it would cause more of a hullabaloo, with bellboys and hotel staff with keys running around, than I wanted. So I sent up a prayer that the room would not be given to a new guest who arrived even later than I. Then I turned off the light and went back to my own room, closing the connecting door and locking it from my own side.

Quickly I showered and washed out the underclothes I had worn. If for any reason I had to make a fast getaway, then I would simply put the wet clothes in the shower cap supplied by the hotel and pack them.

I thought I was so tired I'd fall asleep before I was fully in bed, but I lay there, my mind racing and my heart beating.

I tried to think about what I'd do tomorrow. The first part was easy: I'd look up bus terminals to see which, if any, went to Northcliff. And if none did, then I'd inquire about taxi and limousine services. I'd see if the hotel had a suburban telephone directory so I could get the exact address. Would I call first?

I felt then the first trickle of another kind of fear, a fear I couldn't really identify. And if I found someone in, what would I say? "Do you have a daughter who was adopted approximately eighteen years ago in Boston?" And if they didn't want to acknowledge they had, or didn't want their (adopted/my) daughter to know? What would I do in such a situation? Pile her into the car and take off?

Furthermore, Mac said there was someone else looking for her. Who? The same person or persons who dogged my footsteps in Boston? Who arranged for me to be kidnapped in New York? My mind went around and around. Finally, a little to my surprise, I went to sleep.

The country road was black and the car was going very fast. I stared at the driver and didn't recognize him, but something about his face terrified me.

"Let me out!" I screamed. But he laughed and then I saw what he was going to do. He was going to run over a woman who was standing there in the road with her back to the car. Then the car crashed into her. As it did so, I suddenly knew who the woman was. I screamed and woke myself up.

I sat up, my heart pounding with fright probably from the dream but also from fear that there'd soon be pounding on my door and a voice demanding to know what was going on.

But all was quiet. I sat there, hugging my knees, and became again aware of my ankle. It had had quite a workout during the day and I could see that it was swollen. I picked up my watch from the night table. One-thirty. It was already a long night.

Getting up I turned on the television and sat doggedly watching some mystery made in the 1950s. Things were neater then, I decided, including men's haircuts and happy endings. The women looked overdecorated in makeup and hairdo, but they were much sweeter and more compliant. I found myself wondering if that was the kind of woman Mac wanted. Then my mind wandered from the increasingly boring picture onto wondering what his divorced wife was like. A pianist and piano teacher. I wished she'd been an ordinary, homemaking housewife, like the heroine in the epic I was watching. Why? Because she'd have been easier to defeat. Or would she? Was I just being condescending towards a lifestyle of another time? And anyway, was she one to defeat? Why did I assume that she left him?

Because I couldn't imagine any woman unencumbered with an embarrassing, not to say alienating, past leaving him of her own accord. Suddenly I saw his angular profile and long blue eyes. He was not handsome, but he was mightily attractive. This wasn't helping. I turned off the movie and lay down. Eventually I drifted off to sleep again. My last thought was to wonder if I still had a job. I couldn't see Jack Lederer holding warm the seat of a murderer and an embarrassment to the company. Not when there were so many talented editors out there, wanting jobs, having lost theirs in the mergers and buyouts that seemed to have hit book publishers like a plague.

I was up at six and dressed, complete with pulled up hair, pulled down beret and makeup mask, by seven. My underclothes were almost dry, but I put them in the shower cap anyway. It was now seven. Did I dare order breakfast? Might not the waitress have also seen a picture of me? It would be better, wouldn't it, to postpone coffee until I could go to some anonymous coffee shop or cafe?

I decided to fill the time by looking in the directory under the phone on the night table. At least I could call the bus terminal. Yes, I was told when it was answered, I could get a bus to Northcliff. It would be leaving at twelve-eleven.

"None before that?"

"No, not unless you want to go to Stanton and change buses there. That would get you in at—er—ten thirty-four."

"All right. I'll take that. What time does the bus leave from your terminal?"

"Eight forty-eight, because there's a small stop over in Stanton. You have to buy the ticket at least a half hour before."

"All right." I hung up and decided not to ask how to get to the bus terminal. I'd take a taxi there. No need to advertise to everyone that I was an obvious stranger.

Then I looked up Anderson. There were pages of them. I should have realized this was Scandinavian country. Nor was I helped by the fact that no matter how hard I tried, I couldn't remember the Andersons' first name—at least his first name, or even the initial.

Finally, knowing it was a slight risk, I called the operator and asked if Northcliff had a separate book. Oh yes, she said, I could find that in the lobby. I debated going down right away, but it was still early. Not too many people would be about. I preferred to be there when there were more.

Finally I gave in and ordered coffee, orange juice and a muffin. It arrived shortly. The waitress did not give me any strange looks, and I got rid of her with a tip as fast as I could. Then I took my bags and went downstairs to the lobby, trying hard not to limp.

When I checked the Northcliff phone book I immediately found the Andersons I was looking for. The moment I saw "Porter Anderson, 146 Elm Street," I recognized it, and wondered why it had disappeared from my head. I turned in my key and walked out. The desk clerk checked my card, said I owed for the phone call and the breakfast. When I paid that I left. He never even looked up. I wondered if that were good or bad.

There was one thing to be said for Minneapolis as the taxi drove me to the bus terminal: the cool air. By comparison with the sticky heat of New York it was crisp and refreshing. I saw the newsstand as soon as I walked in the terminal. The papers were stacked so that I could see. None showed my picture, at least on the top half of the first page, or on the front of the tabloids. Keeping my head down, I bought all those from New York I could find, plus a local one, *USA Today* and the Chicago *Tribune*. Then, because it looked so strange walking with all those newspapers, I also bought a tote bag and put them in.

In what seemed like the long ride first to the town of Stanton, then during the waitover there and the next ride to Northcliff, I read them from front to back, always glancing furtively between the pages to make sure I didn't open it up so that any of my fellow riders across the way or behind could get a full view of my likeness.

A long time later, when someone asked me what the Minnesota countryside was like, I realized it could have been anything from the Antarctic to the Sahara and I wouldn't have known. Not only was I reading every single item in each paper with obsessive thoroughness, I was also keeping my head down. I had a vague idea of the sun shining and occasionally a group of tall trees and that was the extent of my intake of scenery.

When we arrived in Northcliff I pushed my bags and papers in a locker and left the little terminal. To my relief it seemed to be in the center of the town. Which meant I could walk, if Elm Street weren't too far. But how could I find out? I could walk back into the terminal and ask if there were such a thing as a map, which, of course, should there be any inquiries later, would mark me as a stranger. Still, I had either to get a map or ask someone, or take a taxi. There seemed to be one of the latter parked outside the terminal. But there was no driver.

On impulse, I stopped a woman passing. "Could you tell me where Elm Street is?" I asked politely.

"Of course." She glanced at me. "It's quite a distance. Were you planning to walk?"

I had forgotten how pleasant and helpful people outside New York can be. "I can take a taxi," I said.

She glanced back. "Steve seems to be taking a break. He often is," she said drily. "I'm just going to get my car and go home. I'll be glad to drop you. It's not far from where I live."

Again that panicky hesitation. Would this make her remember me? Would it be better to take a taxi? Wouldn't it be more memorable if I offended her by refusing?

"If you'd rather take a taxi, I'm sure you can find Steve over in that diner over there."

"No, that's very kind of you. Are you sure it's not out of your way?"

"No, as I said, it's near where I live. My car's parked here. What number are you looking for?"

"One thirty-two," I said, devoutly hoping there was such a number.

"Hmm. I know most of the people in that area, but I can't remember the name of the people who live at that number."

"Ballinger," I said, prepared, for once, with the phony name.

It was about a ten-minute drive. I decided to take up her attention by asking a lot of questions about the town, Minnesota, and anything else I could think of. It might just prevent her from asking a lot of questions I didn't want to answer.

For the next twelve or so minutes I learned that the town's chief industry was lumber, that there was a threatening fight between the local lumber company and the Environmental Protection Agency, and that not too many townspeople, whose living depended on the industry had good words for the EPA though she, herself, was all for it. Then she sighed. "I suppose opponents could easily claim that thanks to my family, which made its money in cutting down trees, I could now afford to sit back and be virtuous, and there's truth to that, I'm afraid."

I liked her honesty, and the slight question in my mind that she might have been hired by my previous kidnappers vanished. As a matter of fact I hadn't even been aware of it until the moment I let it go.

"It must be around here," she said, slowing the car. I looked out and now noticed that the houses were somewhat larger than those nearer the center of town.

"Yes, there it is!"

I sent up a sigh of thanks that there was, indeed, a one thirty-two. "Thank you so much," I said, getting out as fast as I could. "I really appreciate your help." And I shut the door and waved.

"Will you be all right now?"

"Oh yes, absolutely."

For a moment the car stayed where it was and I stood there. Then realizing that I'd have to look as though I were going inside, I waved again, and started up the short path to the front door. I walked slowly and listened for the car to move on. Finally it did. I slowed even more, then quickly turned and went back down the path and even more quickly walked down the road past a curve.

One forty-six was going to be several houses on. I kept up my pace and marveled there were so few people about. I have been told that walkers in such palladian suburbs as Beverly Hills are arrested on suspicion because nobody walks. Elm Street was not that different. And then I remembered that living for so long in New York distorts the perception. Even in crime-infested New York where women now try not to carry handbags that can be ripped off their shoulders people walk. In that we're unlike the rest of the country. Everywhere else people are born with wheels, not legs.

I had let my mind run on that topic because I could feel myself beginning to get panicky. Why, why on earth? I was about to see the daughter I had longed to see and sought so earnestly, at least recently, but had thought about and yearned over in absentia all the years before.

Why did I feel like I was going to be sick, like what I wanted to do was to turn around and run, like finding her was the last thing on God's green earth I really wanted to do. Where on earth did I get the idea I wanted to find her?

"Oh my God," I said quietly to myself, standing in front of a house that I now realized sported the brass letters one forty-six on the white front door. "What am I going to do?"

I could hardly breathe and my heart was pounding. The door with its numbers seemed to recede and then get nearer as though I were adjusting a zoom lens. I was aware of my ankle hurting. How would I get back? Questions, to none of which I knew the answers, poured through my head.

"You always were a coward." The words were my father's. That was one piece of loving support I had forgotten until this moment. Then, another time, in another mode, he said, his voice strained and almost loving, "The only way to go through it is to go through it."

I started to walk up the path.

24.

I don't know how many times I rang the bell. I could hear it ringing in the house. But there was no answer. Finally I walked across the grass to one of the front windows and tried to peer in, only to realize that the curtains had been drawn. I walked over to the other side and peered in windows there, to be met by the same curtained wall.

I stepped back. There were no lights on anywhere, but then it was the middle of the day. I could, of course, go behind the house. On one side the garage extended the area of the house, so I decided to try the other, and realized as I got there that an extra extension had been built on that side, too. However, by walking over some of the next door neighbor's ground I could get around it, which I proceeded to do.

Behind the house was a fairly extensive lawn with flower beds and trees. The back windows were similarly curtained. The house, somehow, did not seem alive. I became quite convinced, without any real evidence that not only was it empty, but that no one was returning to it. That it was not just empty at the moment; it was closed.

"There's no one there." The man's voice was quite near. He was standing at the end of the extension, one hand against the wall, watching me. In his zip jacket and jeans he could have been anyone: a gardener, a neighbor, a delivery man, a security guard, a cop, the other person who had been trying to get in touch with my daughter.

"I was trying to find the Andersons," I said, and added, "They told me they'd be here."

"Oh? When did they tell you that?"

"Last week," I lied quickly. "Do you know when they'll be back?"

He removed his hand from the wall and started coming towards me.

I stood there, frozen. I didn't even dare glance behind me to see if I could make a run around the end of the garage or if there were something there to stop me. I felt if I took my eyes off the man coming slowly towards me then I'd be lost.

And then a door opened in the house on the other side behind the man.

"I'm afraid they're away," a woman's voice floated out.

Relief washed over me. "Oh, thanks," I said, and started walking towards her giving the man a wide berth. Whoever he was, I didn't think he'd attack me in front of her.

Then he turned, facing the woman. "Thanks a lot," he said. "We'll come back another time."

I knew then that my suspicions were right. "Just a minute," I called out. "I'd like to talk to you." I walked quickly past the man and towards the woman who was standing in the door of a small porch.

"Could we go inside?" I asked in a low voice.

"Of course," the woman said, but she looked surprised. Then, "Isn't that man with you?"

"No. I don't know who he is but I do have a feeling he's up to no good." I sounded as virtuous as I could. "And I would like to ask you one or two questions."

"Oh. Are you related to the Andersons?"

She seemed your average middle-American middle-aged lady, mature, matronly. But she was far from stupid. "Yes," I lied again. "I'm related, and since I hadn't heard I thought, since I was in the area, I'd come and check on them. Have they been away long?"

"A few days. It was rather sudden. Karen announced one day when we came out of our houses at the same time that she and Porter and Hilda were going abroad. I was surprised, because I thought Hilda had been so involved with going to college this fall, but Karen said her husband had won some kind of company contest and they were giving him a vacation abroad—maybe Hawaii, I can't remember."

Hilda, I thought, not Laura. "I've always been particularly fond of Hilda," I said. "Do you have daughters of your own?"

"Oh yes, Hilda and Carol have been friends since they were in school, and, of course, Hilda was in my Bridget's wedding."

"It was sudden wasn't it, their going away," I said, hating my guile but building on my sense of a slight grievance in her voice.

"It was. Oh well, one mustn't be jealous of others' good fortune."

"It's been so long," I said, "and I was so fond of Hilda when she was a baby. Is she as pretty now as she was years ago?"

"She certainly is. I sometimes think it's hard for my Carol to be around her, but neither one seems to be conscious of it. Which is nice, of course."

"You wouldn't have a picture of her, would you? Karen said she was going to be in a wedding and promised me copies of the pictures. I'm her godmother, you know."

"Oh." The faint surprise that showed in her face for a moment cleared. "As a matter of fact, I do. Come into the living room and I'll show you."

She led the way, so I was able to glance back quickly. The man wasn't in sight, but I didn't think for one moment he had just obediently walked away.

As I watched her take an album out of her desk the fear that had receded now came over me again. I could feel my heart pounding and I had trouble breathing. The temptation to get up and run out of the room and of the house was overwhelming. No, I told myself, no. I had no idea why I felt this terrible fear. There was no rational reason for it, but it was there, making me grip the edge of the chair I was in, holding myself down by force.

"Here," she said. "I'm not sure this does her justice, but it'd be impossible to take a bad picture of her." And she laid the album in my lap.

The girl was, indeed, pretty, small and petite, with dark brown curly hair, a roundish face and very dark brown eyes. My pounding heart slowed and the stifling feeling left my throat. The relief was unbelievable. At least I could breathe now.

"Yes," I said. "She's lovely." I took a breath. What I was going to say could not only ruin my little act but cause my nice hostess to call the police. But I had to find out as much as I could. "You know, of course, she's adopted."

"Yes. Of course I know."

I was trying to phrase my next question as carefully as possible when she answered it for me. "Well, what I mean is, Karen told me. That was years before they moved here. They believe that the child should know right from the beginning if it's adopted and I agree with them. I can't tell you the trouble there's been—I was a school counselor for a long while—with children who didn't know and then wanted to get in touch with their birth mothers."

I couldn't get away with much else. Although the woman

was pleasant and helpful I wasn't sure how long I could maintain this charade, nor was I entirely convinced that her doubts and suspicions had been allayed.

I closed the album. "I can't tell you how grateful I am to you for showing me this. Now I wonder if I could impose on you once more by calling a taxi. I'm afraid my car gave out and I had to leave it in a garage."

"Would you like me to take you to the garage? I'll be perfectly happy to."

Inwardly cursing her kindness, I said, "Oh no. A taxi will be fine. I have other errands to do. Shall I find the number in the phone book?"

"Yes. Here." And she put the open directory in front of me.

"We'll be there in about ten minutes," a laconic voice informed me. Good as his word, he drove up in nine minutes.

"Thank you so much," I said getting up when the taxi appeared. I had spent the intervening minutes listening to tales of the woman's daughter, Bridget, now married and pregnant, and the general adventures of Carol and Hilda. She was hardly a gripping tale spinner, but whenever she threatened to run down I had encouraged her with helpful expressions such as "Do go on," but nothing particularly helpful had come to light.

"I'll tell Karen you dropped by," she said, waving from the door. And then shouted, "What name shall I tell her?"

"Penelope Dyer," I made up and shouted back, glad that I'd had the forethought to invent a name ahead of time. The poor Andersons, I thought. This would be the third mystery within a short time and might send them away altogether.

I glanced quickly around as I walked to the taxi. I couldn't see the man but I didn't for one moment think he couldn't see me.

"Where to, lady?" the driver asked as he pulled away from the house.

What I wanted to do was go directly to Minneapolis. I didn't feel hanging around the local terminal for an indefinite length of time was good for me. Cities were safer. But there was the problem of my bags. "The bus terminal," I said finally.

"Going far?"

"Minneapolis."

"I'll take you there for fifty dollars."

That was thirty more than the bus trip cost. "I'll think about it," I said. "I left some bags in the locker at the terminal."

I got out the bus schedule that had been given me when I picked up my ticket. In one sense, a bus was safer. Who'd want to quarrel with it on the road? On the other hand, if that man were watching me, he could drive in his own car and be waiting for me at the terminal in Minneapolis. Unless I bought a ticket somewhere else.

The matter was resolved when I got to the terminal. I saw the man before he saw me. He was watching one entrance to the terminal and we had come by another. I ducked down.

"Avoiding someone?" the driver asked.

"Yes. That man has been harassing me." My voice came from below the seat level.

"If you want to give me your locker key I can go in and get your bags and bring them out."

Wordlessly I handed the keys over.

"Better keep your head down," the man said. "I'm going to park behind those cars where he can't see."

While the driver strode in I raised my head a little and saw the man still staring at the other entrance to the terminal. In a few minutes my own driver was back. He put the bags in the trunk and got in.

"Minneapolis?" he said.

"Yes," I said. "The airport."

After we had left he said, "You can sit up now. He's not following."

"Thanks," I said. "You'll be appropriately rewarded."

The man grinned. "That's nice."

I was aware that I had no more reason to trust this man than any other. But at this point I didn't have much choice.

With a slightly aching back I sat up and watched the countryside pass. I had a lot to think about. But of one thing I was fairly certain. Hilda was not my daughter.

■ ■ ■ I am not a scientist, least of all a geneticist, yet I was reasonably sure that blue eyes are recessive and brown eyes are dominant, which means that two brown-eyed parents can have a blue-eyed child, but two blue-eyed parents cannot have a brown-eyed child. My daughter had two blue-eyed parents. Hilda Anderson's eyes were brown. Hilda could not have been my child.

This meant that Mac's informant was wrong in naming the Andersons as my daughter's adoptive parents. It also meant that whoever else was trying to track my child down was getting information from the same source.

And it left me no nearer finding my daughter than I had been when I had set out to Boston what seemed now so long ago, but was only—what?—a month?

■ ■ ■ The certainty that it had all turned out to be a wild goose chase had the effect of making me so tired I could hardly drag myself from the taxi into the airport. I knew that theoretically there could be police waiting there to nab me, but I could no longer work up much steam for dodging them. But I bought a ticket to New York without any trouble. I even got a newspaper. No one seemed to look up and there were no pictures of me hidden in the inner pages of the paper. If the police didn't know I was in Minneapolis, that meant Claire had not told Lieutenant O'Neill and I felt a spasm of remorse for having doubted her.

When I had finished looking around I put down the paper and my eye caught sight of a bank of pay phones. I walked slowly over and started depositing change.

"St. Anselm's," a cheerful voice said.

"Claire Aldington," I said.

In a moment another young and cheerful voice announced "Pastoral Counseling."

"I'm calling from Minneapolis airport," I said. "Is Claire still there?"

"No, she's gone home."

"Thanks." I dialed Claire's home phone number.

"Motley's residence," a young male voice said.

I was about to curse myself for having spent money on a wrong number when I remembered something Claire had said. "That's your dog, isn't it?"

"Yes. Numero uno in this house."

"I'm sure. Can I speak to your mother, please. I'm calling long distance from Minneapolis."

In a moment Claire said, "Sorry about that. It's Jamie's way of reminding the rest of us how important Motley is. Did you find your daughter?"

"I'll tell you more about it when I get back, but the answer is I'm almost sure not. Not if my knowledge of genetics is right. I saw a picture of her and she has brown eyes. Both . . . both of my daughter's parents have blue eyes."

"Yes, I think you're right about that."

"Are the police still after me?"

"Yes, officially, although I can't help feeling that Lieutenant O'Neill himself doesn't think you did it. Don't ask me how I can tell, but I still think that."

At that point the operator interrupted requesting more money. I started shoving in quarters.

"Look," Claire said, "I don't know whether this makes me some kind of accessory after the fact, but I have an idea where you can stay until—well, at least another day or so, that is, if you want to."

"Where?"

"With an eccentric lady named Letty who lives in the Village and is devoted to cats. She's also psychic. She called me to tell me you were in some kind of danger but not from the police."

"Do you believe her?"

There was a silence. Then Claire said, "Under the general aegis of there being more things in heaven and earth than are accounted for in your philosophy, Horatio, I guess the answer is I don't not believe her. And in the past she has sometimes been uncannily accurate. Are you allergic to cats?"

"No, I don't think so."

"Well, do you want to go there?"

"Yes," I said. "I do. A while ago I was so tired I didn't think I cared. But I feel better now."

"All right. Here's her address. What time do you expect to get in?"

"Around nine."

"I'll tell her to expect you at ten. Call me when you get in. For some reason I'm glad it wasn't your daughter."

"Why?"

"I don't know."

25.

"Here it is," the taxi driver said, drawing up in front of a brown-stone on a narrow, tree-lined street in the Village.

I got out and paid him, noting as I did so that not a lot of the money I had extracted from the machine in the Boston airport was left. Well, it would have to do.

Then I walked up the steps and looked for the name Dalrym-ple. Before I could find it the door was buzzed open.

"Up here," a clear, rather English voice said from some-where above.

I started climbing the stairs and saw a white head bent over the bannisters about two floors up.

"It's a long climb so take it slowly," the same voice cau-tioned. "I have some nice tea waiting."

It was a long climb, and my fatigue of a few hours before had come back. Pushing myself, I finally got there and found myself confronting a thin lady with rather wild short white curly hair standing up around her head and very blue eyes. She had on sneakers, jeans, and over that an apron. Sitting regally at her feet was a large, long-haired tabby cat with a white front and white paws. "This is Andy," she said. "He always likes to greet visi-tors."

I had never had a cat and did not know them as I had known various dogs. But I bent and held out one finger. Andy sniffed at it for a few seconds, then turned his head and rubbed against my arm. I could both hear and feel his purr. It was oddly reassuring. "I like you, too," I said.

"This is your first acquaintanceship with a cat?" Ms. Dal-rymple said.

"Except for Patsy at Claire's house." Andy's purr grew louder as I scratched behind his ear. I smiled. "Andy's wonderful!"

"He thinks that about you, too. It's hard to think you didn't know cats before. Perhaps another life?"

I glanced up.

"Yes, I know you were brought up to think all that rubbish. So was I. But it isn't."

I got up. "How did you know? I mean, you're right. My father was a ferociously strict Catholic. My mother was less ferocious but still orthodox, of course."

"But then she died when you were small, didn't she?"

I was surprised that Claire would talk about the details of my life to that degree. "Yes," I said.

"And it's not what you're thinking. Claire didn't tell me anything. I just had this very strong feeling that someone connected to her was in danger, and when I called her to tell her, she thought you might come here. You mustn't think she isn't totally descreet about her clients. She never reveals anything she shouldn't!"

The blue eyes trained on me were full of reproach. I'd spent a life mistrusting everyone, even those, as I'd come bitterly to see, that I loved. Such as Mac Macrae. Yet standing there in that upstairs hall I knew, beyond any question, that what this woman was saying about Claire's trustworthiness was true.

"Then how did you know—about my father and mother, I mean?"

"I don't really know. But suddenly, there it was in my head and coming out of my mouth."

I could think of absolutely nothing to say in reply to that.

"Come along in," she said. "You're tired and bewildered and all this is new to you. And you must meet the others."

I almost stopped. The thought of meeting other people was

new and unwelcome and nothing Claire had said had indicated other people would be there.

Ms. Dalrymple was walking into her apartment. I picked up my bags and followed her.

The room I walked into, once probably an attic, was large—surprisingly so in so narrow a brownstone. Doors led off, one showing a kitchen. There seemed to be a myriad of colors, on cushions, on a sofa, on chairs, on the floors. Books were on shelves to the low ceiling. There was a small fireplace. But the main decoration of the room was cats. At quick glance I saw five: a black, a white, a ginger, a multicolored one and a long-haired gray one. Slowly most of them got up from where they were adorning the various cushions and chairs and came over. "The gray one's Peter. He and Andy are brothers. The ginger is Emily, the white is Cordelia, the tortoiseshell is Widget and the black is Francesca."

All except Francesca seemed very friendly and willing to think the best. Francesca, having got up from her cushion on the floor, jumped on the arm of the sofa and sat there looking regal and disapproving.

"I don't think Francesca likes me," I said.

"She had a difficult kittenhood. But she'd probably be that way anyway. I call her the Reigning Empress. Now, I've put you in the bedroom so that you can be free of cats if you prefer, and it has a connecting door to the bathroom. Just there, the third door on your left. Put your bags down and come back and I'll give you some herb tea to make you relax."

Feeling as though I were in the hands of a very kind nanny, I did as she suggested, and came back into the big room.

"Now tell me as much about yourself as you want to," she said cheerfully, going into the kitchen.

I couldn't help grinning a little. "I'm surprised you need me to tell you. You seem to have other sources. How does it come to you?"

"I don't know. It isn't always clear, and usually time—the past and the future—are rather muddled. But sometimes things are clear."

I wondered what my father would make of her. Even thinking casually about him filled me with anger and fear.

"Yes, well, you must realize that he himself was a product of some terribly strict teaching," Ms. Dalrymple said. It was exactly as though I had put my thoughts into words and said them out loud.

"Ms. Dalrymple," I started.

"Letty," she said. "And please don't call me by that awful Miz. I find it quite, well, insulting."

"I'm sorry, Letty. It was invented because some women felt that—er—women should not be immediately designated as married or unmarried. That Mr. refers to all men, married or unmarried, and the same should be for women."

"Oh, I know the argument, but I could argue equally truly that that implies some kind of inferior status to spinsters."

"I haven't heard the word 'spinster' used for years," I said.

"No, quite, for the same reason. It's considered insulting, whereas 'bachelor' is all right. Such rubbish! When I was growing up and going to our village church, I used to hear the banns read all the time as 'I announce the banns of marriage between Mary Smith, spinster of this parish, and John Jones, bachelor of the parish of Huyton cum Roby.' And the two of them would be eighteen and twenty."

"Where was Huyton cum Roby?" I asked. "It's such a delicious name."

"Outside Liverpool. Here is your tea."

I took it without much enthusiasm, but it tasted delectable and as I sipped I seemed to feel calmer. A pleasant silence ensued. Emily jumped on my lap, turned round and round and settled herself. Cordelia came and sat at my feet. "I wonder if it's cats in general or your cats here, but they seem to have a peaceful and calming influence."

"They do. They're wonderful and mysterious beings."

The phone rang.

"That'll be Claire to see if you've arrived safely. Do you want to answer it?"

I was getting a little used to Letty's extraordinary ability to know what was happening before she was, so to speak, officially told. I crossed the room and picked up the receiver. "Hello, Claire."

"How did you know it was me?" Claire said.

"I didn't. Letty did."

"Of course. I should have remembered. Everything okay?"

"Well, if you discount being looked for by the police on the suspicion—if not conviction—of murder, plus being followed, plus . . ." Suddenly the thing that had haunted my dreams since I was seventeen, that I had buried deep, so deep that I had spent most of my life not even being aware of it, was there, in the front of my mind. Before I could stop myself I gave a sort of gasp.

"What is it?" Claire asked sharply.

"Nothing," I managed to say, and had this mental picture of myself burying something deep, deep in the earth. "Nothing."

There was a short silence at the other end of the phone.

"I'm tired," I said almost crossly. "You know how people are when they're tired."

"Or busy suppressing something that threatens to come out."

"I'm not suppressing anything," I almost shouted. Then a kind of numbness seem to take possession. "I'm sorry, Claire, it really is fatigue. I feel like I've traveled a thousand miles."

"It's all right," Claire said.

"How's the murder investigation?"

"I'm not sure. Lieutenant O'Neill is perfectly aware that I'm withholding things about you—"

"He is?"

"Of course. Such as where you are right now. I've never denied knowing where you are—"

"But you didn't tell him, did you?" The words were out before I knew I was going to say them and I could hear the panic in my voice. What had happened to my trust? "I'm sorry," I said again. "I trust you, I really do."

Another pause. "I'm glad of that," Claire said finally. "And there's something else I have to report. I mentioned to Brett the name you gave me of Ian Wilson's angel, Driscoll—you know, the philanthropist who supports Ian's efforts at finding lost or adopted children." Claire paused, and then went on. "Brett, who has a lot of contacts in the business world and has been a banker most of his life, couldn't find too much about your Mr. Driscoll."

A little trickle went down my back. "What was he looking for?"

"How he got his money. Did he inherit it, make it, get it from investments? He apparently turned up in Virginia about seven years ago, built himself a large mansion and became the local benefactor. Brett's here and wondered if you'd talk to him for a moment."

"Sure. Put him on."

It was amazing, I thought, as he came on and said hello, how much or how little you could tell from a voice. I had been so distraught when I met him in their apartment none of this had registered, but I found now I remembered how he sounded. I had never thought bankers were among the more interesting or creative of our citizens. My own portrait of them was that they were greed machines who sat and took in money eagerly and gave it out grudgingly. Yet Brett Cunningham's voice was clear,

crisp, even vibrant. Somehow one knew there were more levels
to this man than someone who only took in and gave out money.

"Did you get to meet him?" Brett was asking.

"No. I just heard about him, and when I went to a neighbor-
ing mall to do some shopping, saw his large—very large—
house." I paused. "Is it unusual that you can't find any record of
how and through what or whom he got his money?"

"It's not that there's anything wrong, necessarily, but usually
money in that magnitude leaves trails, and in Driscoll's case,
there aren't any. I don't suppose you met anyone who knew him
or talked about him."

There flashed into my mind the man who had picked me up
on the road and driven me back to the motel. But did I ask him
anything about Driscoll? I didn't think so.

"No. It's true that one of the local citizens picked me up
when my car went haywire and drove me back to the motel. But
I'm sure I didn't mention Driscoll to him."

"I wonder then what made you think about him in particular. Did he have some connection to Driscoll? Wait, here's
Claire."

There was a brief conversation between Brett and Claire
before she picked up the phone. "You told me about your car
breaking down and the man who picked you up. But what connection did he have with Driscoll?"

"None, as far as I know. I don't know why I thought of
him."

I heard another phone being picked up. "I'm here on the
other phone in the study," Brett said. "Did you have any idea
whether the car that broke down was just poorly serviced or had
someone tampered with it?"

"I have no proof, but I think someone tampered with it."

Claire asked, "Did you leave because Ian said the search for
your daughter was going to take a lot longer or what?"

"He called me the last morning I was there and said that his first line of inquiries hadn't worked out and the rest would take longer. Has . . . has he always found the adopted children of other people you've sent to him right away?"

"In all cases except one, yes. In that one, he urged her to stay longer, saying he might hit on the right sources any time."

I said slowly, "As I told you, I felt he wanted to get rid of me."

"Are you sure?" Claire asked.

"Yes. I realize now I'm sure, although I didn't think it at first. Maybe I didn't want to. But he seemed very definite that there wasn't any point in my staying longer, and when I asked him about Mr. Driscoll—his angel—he was careful to state that the angel only got called on in rare cases."

I hung up the phone and was aware of a feeling of discomfort. Something was nagging at the back of my mind, but the more I tried to look at it, the more whatever it was hid from me. Aware of something rubbing against my leg, I looked down and saw Andy, his tail upright and plumey, gently massaging my leg with his ear and jaw.

"Good boy," I said and reached down to scratch him between his ears. A deep, rattling purr filled the immediate vicinity. "What a nice cat," I said.

"He's wonderful," Letty said simply.

Something made me say, "Something's bothering me, but it's just out of reach. Do you have any advice on how to get it out?"

"Just ask whatever God you pray to to let you know what it is, always supposing, of course, that it is His Will. After all, it might be the last thing on earth you should know at the moment. And then forget it and stop trying to worry it out. It will come."

I thought, how wonderful to be so sure! All my years in Catholic schools had not given me that faith. What they had given me was a sort of heavenly legal schema: this sin to be paid for by that prayer or series of prayers. I sighed and said, "Your faith seems so direct and uncomplicated—and believable. I was brought up to go by a specific theological legal balancing act. You tell a lie and you get five Hail Marys and a good act of contrition. I don't know what I'd have gotten for adultery. Probably five complete rosaries and several eons in purgatory. But by the time I would have been confessing that, I'd stopped going to church."

"I don't suppose the Catholic faith is any different from mine, but I think people have sometimes had an unfortunate way of teaching it, which is true of all Churches. And people and ages have different temperaments. One age will harp on the punishments and another on the love and compassion. In this age of insecurity and science we need the latter. From the secure ramparts of the Victorian age they could talk about punishments. And some people only feel safe if they have such a detailed edifice that every last human failing and tendency is accounted for. Like a detailed shopping list."

"But you believe in all kinds of other things, like psychic intuition."

"If it's there you have to make room for it."

"May I make a phone call?"

"Of course. You can take the phone in the bedroom if you want to be private. It's got a very long cord."

"No, that's all right." I dialed Mac's number and found my heart beating as I waited. But eventually his answering tape came on. He wasn't there. He wasn't there I told myself at—I pushed my sleeve up to look at my watch—at eleven at night. But after all, he was a bachelor. Why shouldn't he be out? But I put the receiver down hard. The last time I'd talked to him had been when his apartment had been ransacked. I wondered now if he had been able to find whatever was missing. Including, I remembered, his notebook. I owed him an accounting of my finding Hilda Anderson and the rest of her family gone, and my conviction that she was not, anyway, my daughter. Plus, of course, an accounting of the man who was there, waiting for me.

But he could wait.

"Bed, I think," Letty said. "You look tired."

And, all of a sudden, I was. So tired I could hardly move.

I took a shower and crawled into her deliciously comfortable bed. My last impression was of something warm and solid settling itself against my back, just like Patsy at the Cunninghams', I thought, and then I was asleep.

26.

I was walking between rows of trees. An extraordinary peace and happiness filled me and I wanted both to laugh and cry. This seemed to go on for a long time and in my dream I thought, I am now in Eternity. And even though that meant I was dead I didn't mind.

Then, with dreadful suddenness, the happiness had vanished and I was almost suffocating with fear and rage. There between the trees a few feet from me was my father and I was rooted where I was. I wanted to run, but I couldn't.

"You've been trying to tantalize me for years now," he said. "Like a whore. So I'm going to treat you like one." And then he was on me . . .

I wanted to scream but I didn't. In my dream I knew I ought to scream, because any truly innocent girl would. But my dream self, like a twin, a doppelgänger, knew I wasn't innocent. I'd been drinking and drugging since I was fifteen. And I knew that what he was saying was true. When I came home drunk and he'd be waiting up in his pajamas and dressing gown, then it was sweet revenge to . . . well . . . his word was best: tantalize him. And how did I feel about it? Somewhere far in the mists I knew that I had loved him and wanted desperately for him to love me. But he had never loved me. Maybe this was the only love he could achieve . . .

The old arguments went through my head as he held and groped and ripped his way into me . . .

And then nine months later I had Laura.

I was sobbing when Letty woke me. "There now, there now," she said, almost crooningly. "It will be all right. Truly."

"You don't even know what I was dreaming about," I sobbed.

"Not in detail, but from your mumblings and shouted words, it wasn't hard to guess. Was it really your father?"

"Yes," I said. And it was like opening a gate that had been straining against its locks for years. I had never told anyone. It had been the most horrifying secret of my life. Or rather, I had never told anyone but Jeff. Because this had happened right after he had left Boston for California the child I was carrying could also have been his child. I told him because he got me high as a kite and when I told him he laughed and laughed . . .

"I only told one other person," I said.

"And where is he now?"

"I don't know."

After a while she got up. "See if you can go back to sleep. You need it."

After she left Andy jumped back on the bed and I lay there drained. I knew I needed sleep yet, frightened by my dreams, I was afraid to let myself go to sleep again.

After a while, despite my fear, I drifted off. What I hoped to find myself in again was that allée of trees where I was innocent and loved and guiltless. But there was no allée this time. It was Jeff I dreamed about and it was not a dream to make me much happier than the first one I'd had. He was laughing and laughing. Like the previous dream, I was dreaming of something that had happened. But this time I knew I was dreaming, and I kept trying to wake myself up to stop it, but I couldn't anymore than a swimmer can push against a tide that is stronger and is going out.

"Don't laugh Jeff," I kept saying in my dream. "It was horrible. And it was probably your child."

"But you don't know, do you, love? And you'll never know. And it's the kind of thing your daughter can't ever know. How would she like one day to find out that she was the child of a girl and of her own grandfather? Talk about incest!"

He started to laugh again, and in my dream I shivered uncontrollably. Then again the dream shifted and just before I awoke I dreamed about the good Samaritan who had picked me up on the road in Virginia. Curiously, although I could hardly see his face, his voice reminded me strongly of someone, but before I could figure out who, I woke up. I lay there in Letty's bed, my arms wrapped around myself, still shivering.

I was as tired as though I hadn't been to sleep at all. Perhaps more so. Slowly, dragging myself, my sore ankle swollen again, I went in and took another shower, first hot, then cool and then cold to see if I could shed the numbing fatigue.

When I got out of the room all the other cats were lined up waiting to see me come out of the bedroom. Letty was busy putting crumbs into a plate.

"I don't think it's fair to the bird or the cats to feed them on the window sill, but I do like to put crumbs in the feeder in the big tree. Then they can eat and be safe." She glanced at me. "Coffee's on the stove and there's some orange juice on the kitchen table and a muffin in the oven."

I drank the coffee and the juice and munched on the muffin

while Letty was out feeding the birds. Obviously she did this every morning, because, hearing the cries and squawks and squeaks of every kind of bird I glanced out the kitchen window and saw battalions of them on the branches of the big tree in the common garden behind Letty's house and those around and back of her.

Then without thinking I went to the phone and dialed Mac's number. I got the tape again. A great sense of unease filled me, although I didn't know why. There was no reason Mac shouldn't be away—doing research, interviewing people, visiting friends, seeing a new girlfriend—I didn't want to think about that, I decided, and tried to obliterate that last thought. But there were plenty of justifiable reasons why Mac could be away.

That obvious fact did not make me feel better.

I sat at the table sipping coffee. Wondering what developments there had been in Paul's murder I looked around for a radio. I could see absolutely none. Nor did there seem to be a television set. Then I looked for and failed to find a newspaper.

At about that moment Letty came back up the stairs.

"You don't have a radio or television, do you?" I said. "Nor a newspaper."

"No, they just muddle things and get people excited, most of the time for no reason at all."

"I wonder how the society of newspaper editors and journalists would feel about that. You should go and make a speech at one of their gatherings."

"They'd just laugh at me, since public stoning has lost popularity. 'There's that silly old English biddy,' they'd say, 'with her ESP and psychic vibrations and New Age rubbish.' "

I looked at her curiously, almost admiringly. "It doesn't seem to bother you."

"No, why should it? Every age has its wise men. Two thousand years ago, according to the Scriptures, they were astrologists. Today, they're called the media. I imagine the accuracy level would be about equal, but I'm quite certain that the media cause far more trouble."

I grinned at her. "They might bring stoning back."

She smiled at me.

After another minute I said, "I've been using your phone freely. Please let me know how much I owe you when your bill comes in."

"All right, but I don't think it's much."

I dialed Claire's number at home and didn't even get "Motley's residence" from her son. A tape clicked on, so I hung up. I wasn't entirely sure what I wanted to say or whether I wanted to say anything.

I could call my office. I could call my own phone and pick up the messages. Both of these would alert the powers that be that I was in the city, and I wondered how long it would take Lieutenant O'Neill to get to me. I didn't have much doubt he'd put pressure on Claire.

But the thought that Mac might have forgotten his anger enough to call me made me forget everything else. I called my own number and heard my own voice telling me to wait for the beep. After which I punched in the code that would give me my messages.

There were plenty of them: newspapers, television stations, the police, Jack Lederer from the office and a voice that I knew I had heard before telling me that if I weren't careful my daughter would be killed. That voice, I was fairly sure, was the one that had called me in the motel in Virginia and told me to leave.

Finally, at the end, was Mac's voice. I stiffened and heard him say, "I don't know where you are at this point or whether you want me to know or what kind of luck you had in Minnesota, but I'd be interested to hear from you. By the way, not knowing where you were and knowing from what you said that the one person who might know was your shrink, I called her, without much hope that she'd shed any light on your whereabouts. She must be concerned about you, because she came on the phone immediately and told me, among other things, what her husband had told you about not being able to find any trace of her friend's benefactor's wealth. I'm not sure why that struck me, but I decided to do a little digging. So I'm going to Washington and then on to Virginia if it seems warranted. I hope you can manage to stay out of trouble." There was a pause, and I was sure the announcement would come to an end. But the tape was voice activated, and he started speaking before he could be cut off. "I'm doing this partly because I agreed to help you with your search and partly because my own curiosity is aroused. It's not any kind of bid to restart a relationship that seems to have caused you nothing but grief and is obviously not something that either of us finds pleasant or rewarding. If I've been a pain in the ass, I apologize. Loving, or its various simulations has never been easy for me. *Arrivederci,* or perhaps more accurately, good-bye . . ."

I sat there, the tape finished. The trouble was, Mac didn't give a date. If it was the same day as the previous messages, it would have been yesterday evening. Theoretically, it could have been this morning.

So, he had gone to Washington and Virginia to see what he could find out about Ian Wilson's angel, Mr. James Driscoll, benefactor to all natural mothers and adopted children interested in finding their own genealogy. And rounded his message off by telling me to get out of his life.

In the meantime the police were still looking for me and were no doubt monitoring all Claire's calls. Could they trace any call to her from me? According to all movies and television cop shows it would take a while, which was why the central villains (or heroes) always rang off before the telephone trail could be completed. Which meant that they could then come and harass Letty. Had I given them enough time to do that while I was picking up my messages? I didn't know. But I was fairly sure it would not be a good idea to call Claire again except from a pay phone.

And then I wondered if they would be monitoring Brett Cunningham's phone with the same doggedness? And anyway, did I have an office phone for him? A telephone directory was on a shelf near the phone. I flipped over the pages to Cunningham and with no trouble found "Brett Cunningham, offc." followed by a number.

I dialed the number and tried to think what name I'd give if —as was certain—a secretary or assistant answered. At that moment the phone was picked up and a cheerful young man announced, "Brett Cunningham's office."

"Is Mr. Cunningham there?"

"Who is calling?"

My mind did its sticking thing and, panicked, I hung up.

My anxiety was now unpleasantly high. The tendency to space out when confronted was a fairly accurate sign of that. Then the phone rang. I looked at Letty, who was in the living room wielding what looked like a fishing rod with a cloth mouse at the end to the vast pleasure and exercise of her menagerie. She came over and answered the phone.

"Yes, dear, she's here." And she held out the phone.

"Brett said someone tried to reach him and hung up. Was that you?"

"Yes. I wanted to talk to him because Mac Macrae has left a message on my phone saying when he tried to find me by calling you he'd learned from you about Brett's being unable to trace Driscoll's money and has gone down to Washington and Virginia to see if he can trace it himself. He also firmly said this was good-bye."

To my horror I found tears flowing down my cheeks. "I don't know why I'm crying," I said.

"Don't you?" Claire said drily. Then, "And Lieutenant O'Neill would like you to get in touch with him."

"Has he been putting pressure on you?"

"You could describe it that way."

"All right. I'll call him. My next call will probably be from a cell."

"Brett knows a lot of good lawyers."

"I can't afford anything but Legal Aid," I said. "I'm going to get off this phone before they trace it. I'll call you."

I didn't want to get Letty, kind Letty, into trouble either. I had collected my things into my bag. So I turned to her. "I'm going to go down and call the police from a phone booth," I said. "I don't want them knowing you've helped me. In the mood they're in, they might come and arrest you as an accessory."

"Oh I don't think they'll do that," she said, her calm unruffled. "And anyway, what about Claire?"

"She has at least the out that she is a priest and a therapist and is abiding by the laws of confidentiality."

"I know they'd take it from a male Roman Catholic priest. I wonder if they'd be as obliging towards an Episcopalian priest who is also a woman."

"I didn't know you were a feminist, Letty."

"All women are feminists, whether they know it or not," she said. "And anyway, there are my cats to think of."

"Would that make you a catalyst?" I said, and winced. "Sorry."

"Oh dear," she said. "I wonder if Widget is feeling quite well. She just threw up."

It didn't take penetrating psychological insight to know that her attention had switched from me to her main interest.

I leaned over and kissed her cheek. "All my thanks to you and the kids."

When I got out I had every intention of walking to the end of the block where there was a phone booth, and if that had been recently vandalized, a grocery with a public phone in it, much more liable to be in good condition.

But the first thing I saw were two police cars turning the corner. I stopped. It was true, I realized, that my own apartment was a lot nearer than I had realized in my exhaustion last night. And they would undoubtedly be keeping a watch both in and out of my apartment. Which meant they knew I had picked up my messages. But would they know from where? And, considering I was planning to call Lieutenant O'Neill anyway, what did it matter?

But I did not go to the end of the block. I flagged down a taxi that was cruising past.

"Where to, lady?" the driver asked as he continued down the one-way street.

And out of my mouth came words that, two seconds before, I hadn't even known were in my mind.

"La Guardia Airport," I said.

27.

I waited till I got out there to go to the money machine again. If my account was being watched, would they get to the airport in time to stop me? I didn't know. They could, of course, call security people at the airport. I had to risk it. I was almost moving on automatic. I didn't even know what I was going to do when I got to Virginia, if I managed to get there. But I was certainly going to give it a good try.

Miraculously, I was not stopped, either at the money machine nor at the gate to the Washington shuttle, and I was in the nation's capital within a short time. No one arrested me as I got off the plane. I then paused to consider which would run the greater risk—buying an air ticket to Virginia, or hiring a car and showing my driver's license?

An urgency was pushing me although I didn't know why or what caused it. But I felt driven by the need to get to that Virginia town as fast as possible. I went over to the appropriate desk and asked for a ticket on the next flight. Then I held my breath. The young woman at the counter did not seem to push any buttons or throw any questioning glances at me. The only thing that seemed to surprise her at all was that I was prepared to pay cash. In a few moments the ticket was in my hand, and my flight was due to take off in an hour.

I decided not to risk going to a newsstand, so I spent the hour at the cafeteria, sipping coffee and looking at an out-of-date magazine someone had left on the seat. Something was pounding at my brain, but after futile efforts to figure out what it was I decided to take Letty's advice and put it on a back burner somewhere and think about something else. I studied an article on the differences in hair care, according to age, sex, race, ethnic origin and a few other subdivisions. Not since I was a child having to study algebra had I applied myself to something I found less interesting.

Finally the flight was called and a half hour later I was getting out at the same airport I had flown from two days ago. This time I hired a car, waiting with held breath while she looked at my name and license. She, also, appeared to find nothing unusual in it.

A short time later I was handed the keys to another Chevrolet. Now all I needed to decide was where I was going next.

Perhaps I did make a decision. But in some ways it seemed as though the car took me to the Reverend Ian Wilson's rectory office.

I gave my name to the parish secretary. She pushed a button and gave my name. Then, with an odd glance at me, she murmured an excuse and disappeared through a door which led from her office.

Curious, I thought. I had expected trouble at both airports and the car hire agency. The one place I had not expected trouble was at Mr. Wilson's rectory. Yet my feeling that there was trouble here was getting stronger and stronger.

Suddenly the young lady was back. "I'm really sorry. Mr. Wilson isn't in and doesn't know how long before he'll be back. It might be several days."

I said slowly, "If he's out, I wonder why you didn't tell me that right away."

Her cheeks reddened, but she didn't say anything for a moment. Then, "I'm sorry."

I got up. "So am I."

In this small town the rectory door was kept unlocked, so it was easy for me simply to leave. I had no idea whether or not she was watching from the window, but I had a firm conviction that she had probably returned to Wilson's office as soon as I was through the front door. So I waited for about the length of one minute and went back in. The reception room was empty. I went straight through the door that led to his office. Her back as she stood in front of his desk talking to him, shielded me from his eyes for a few seconds. Then she turned around. "Oh!" she said.

Mr. Wilson saw me. "This is really unwarranted," he said sternly.

"That's a very interesting statement from a Christian minister who has just been caught in an outright lie, Mr. Wilson. Your secretary, acting no doubt from your instructions, told me you were out of town and would be away for several days. Why?"

To do the man credit, he was obviously not a skilled liar and looked as uncomfortable as any moralist could wish. His face flushed and then went pale. "I really don't feel I owe you an explanation. You came here without an appointment, demanding to see me whether it was convenient or not. You put my secretary—and me—on the spot—"

"I'm looking desperately for my child, remember? A girl who might be a carrier for a terrible disease, which she ought to know about before she marries and has children."

"I told you—"

"You told me that it would take some time for you to find anything and suggested—no, ordered me to go home."

"I did not—"

"You were polite about it, but it amounted to an order. What I want to know is why. Did your angel, Mr. James Driscoll, instruct you to?"

The red flowed back into his cheeks. "How dare you suggest such a thing!" But his voice lacked the authority of conviction. And I saw him move his arm over a piece of paper.

My eyes riveted on the paper, now mostly covered, but not the two initials at the bottom of the page: "J.D."

James Driscoll, I thought. All my fears and intuitions were right. "Tell me something, Mr. Wilson, where did he get his money? How did he make it—" The memory exploded in my brain, the words as clear as they had been all those years before: "If you ever let on that you know any of us, you'll have the same fate as that security guard. And so will Jock."

And the signature? J.D. Jeff Dysart. James Driscoll. He once said that some numerologist had told him to hang on to his initials, even if he changed his name.

"My God!" I said weakly.

As though from a distance I heard Mr. Wilson's angry words. "You have no right to ask such a question, no right whatsoever, especially in view of the help he's given so many women, which he would willingly have given you—"

"Are you sure of that, Mr. Wilson?" I heard my own voice ask. "Or did he say in polite terms the equivalent of 'Get her out of town if you want more money for your charitable works'?"

Wilson and I glared at each other. Vaguely I realized the secretary had disappeared.

"No wonder Brett Cunningham couldn't find any trace or trail of Driscoll's money. Whatever it is, I'd be willing to bet anything its origins are illegal, if not actually criminal. That's not his real name. I knew him years—almost twenty years—ago as Jeff Dysart. And that wasn't his real name."

"You're insane—you must be! This man comes into this area and gives his money and time and work to any number of good causes, the adoptive agency is only one. He's a leading member of my vestry, he supports the church. The governor is seriously thinking of naming him to Senator Chisholm's old seat, and you accuse him of being a criminal and a felon."

"Was an ex-federal agent called Macrae here, asking questions?"

His silence was my answer. Then he said, "I consider myself under no obligation to tell you anything. And now please leave at once, or I'll call the police to come and get you. I have learned that you yourself are wanted for murder in New York, so you're hardly in any position to come here, making outlandish accusations against a man I've known and respected. If the police lay hands on you here, you'll be shipped back to New York and find yourself in jail—where, I am convinced, you should be."

So Mac had been here. "Where was Mac—Macrae going from here? Did you send him to Driscoll's house?"

"I don't see why I should—"

"Just answer that question and I'll go immediately."

"I certainly gave him Driscoll's address and told him how to get there."

There was a slight commotion outside. I heard a voice and knew where and when I'd heard it before—when he was driving me back from my stalled car, in years gone by, in my dreams.

There was a door behind Wilson's desk as well as the one I had come in by. Without asking him, I ran around the desk and ran through it, praying that it didn't lead to a closet. It led to another study and through that to the kitchen. I was out the back before I stopped to figure what I'd do when I got there. From the back I could see Jeff's car drawn up before mine. Luckily for me it was empty. I ran then, as fast as I could, knowing I'd be visible through the windows, but I had to get to the car. I was in it and starting the engine before the rectory door opened again. I drove away from the rectory, and made right and left turns, driving as fast as I dared. Finally I turned down an alley, parked the car in the shadow of the adjacent building and turned off the engine. A few seconds later I saw Jeff in his car race past the end of the alley.

My chance of getting back to the airport and on a plane was nil. But that wasn't what I planned to do, anyway. Where was Mac? Where would he head after his visit with Wilson? To Driscoll's house, of course. Would he by then know who Driscoll really was? Maybe. Maybe not. For me to try and get in Driscoll's house was like signing my own death certificate. I hadn't seen much of his face in the car that night, but I had seen enough to know that he must have had considerable plastic surgery, which was what threw me off. I knew now I recognized his voice, which he probably tried to disguise, but you can't perform plastic surgery on a voice.

I remembered the Driscoll house well. Set back from the road, with open lawns around. I'd have about as much chance of walking in there unseen and/or unrecognized as a snowball in a skillet. At night? If I knew anything about Jeff, he'd have that place so wired and tapped that a cockroach couldn't wiggle in on the blackest night.

So what was left?

Drive up there, walk up to the door, ring the bell and when the door was opened, walk in. And get killed.

What about my life?

What about my daughter's life?

What about Mac's life? If Jeff knew he had been a federal agent at any time his chances of survival were about like mine.

I sat there for a long while. Once or twice police cars sped past, their sirens going. I had no illusion that I could push this car one foot out of the alley and not get caught. Sighing, I got out of the car. What I hadn't noticed was that there were one or two other cars parked in the alley. Without thinking I glanced in each one, checking to see if it had a key. One of them did, and the key was in the ignition. This was small-town middle America. People, to some degree, still trusted one another.

I returned to the hired car, got my traveling bag, went back to the other car, opened the door and got in. I still had my dark glasses and the beret that I had worn before and put them on, twisting my hair up so that it followed the curve of the back of my head instead of resting on my collar as it had before. Then I turned the key in the ignition and, not waiting to see if someone tore out of one of the buildings, drove into the road. After that I kept going until I found myself outside the town heading towards the Driscoll manor house.

When I got there I turned in the drive, parked and left the key in the ignition as I found it. Then I walked up to the front door. I didn't expect it to be open, as the rectory's was, and it wasn't. I rang the bell. In a few seconds a man servant opened the door.

"Is Mr. Driscoll in?" I asked, banking on the fact that I didn't think he had returned.

"Not at the moment, Miss. Who shall I say is calling?"

The words were there on my tongue. "Mrs. Macrae. I'm looking for my husband."

I knew I had won a round when the man hesitated.

"He's here, isn't he?" I said. "He said he might drop in on James." And I pushed the door further open and walked in.

"Mac!" I called loudly. "Mac!"

"I must insist," the man said, getting in front of me.

And then a figure came through a door on the left and turned towards us. "It's all right, Matthews. I'm delighted to see"—He smiled and the smile was very much the same—"Mrs. Macrae, isn't it? Come in!"

The old butler stepped back.

Jeff had obviously had plastic surgery. His nose, which had been long and a little curved, was now shorter and blunter and not the better for it, I thought. His forehead was higher, but that could have been the inevitable working of time on his hairline. But his height, very close to mine, and slight body could not be concealed, nor could his voice be changed. My first thought was, not how different he was, but how much the same. His voice had always had an almost musical element, a quality that somehow lent greater threat to some of his more violent rhetoric.

He stood, holding the door. I went into a room that plainly served as a study. The desk, the two eighteenth-century portraits, the prints, the French doors that led to a walled rose garden immediately outside, were set pieces in a civilized stage setting for a country manor.

"I'm surprised you're not smoking a pipe and don't have a retriever or a lab or a hound stretched out before the fireplace," I said.

"As a matter of fact, I do. Or rather, my wife does. She's very fond of animals. That's one of her charitable works."

"Good for her!"

Somehow I had gone, or been maneuvered to the desk, while Jeff stood, squire-wise, in front of the fireplace. I picked up a framed picture that was resting on the desk. There they were, the happy family: blonde wife dressed in riding clothes, three children, the girl also in riding clothes and the two boys in jeans. I put the picture down.

"I feel like I walked into a play by John Galsworthy or Somerset Maugham or Philip Barry."

He stared at me. He was still smiling, and I stared back at him. "Or is it from the works of some modern chronicler of the drug trade?"

Why I said that I wasn't sure. Except that something Jeff had said in the past, one day when we were lying on one of the brown hills of California, came as vividly to my mind as though he had spoken it yesterday. "The drug dealers," he'd said, "aren't any different from the old robber barons or your local respectable banker or manufacturer, they're just better at it— capitalism in action."

"But the man who banks money or . . . or makes cars doesn't deal in things that kill people!" The moment I'd said that I knew I'd made a mistake.

"Oh no?" Jeff asked. "How many car-related deaths are there a year, as compared to how many drug deaths?"

"But even the socialist states make cars!"

"But they're less concerned with profit and more with turning out a decent object! And do you think the bankers care where the money comes from, that they use to so-call launder other money?"

I could never win an argument with Jeff.

"You have no reason whatever to say that," Jeff now said mildly.

"Yes, but when the husband of a friend of mine, a man in finance himself, tried to find the . . . the origin of your wealth, it all seemed curiously mysterious."

"That would be Brett Cunningham, wouldn't it?"

I stood, stunned. But why was I surprised? Obviously someone was watching everything I did and everywhere I went and now apparently everything my friends did.

"You're the one who's been watching me, following me."

"Well, not me personally, friends and well-wishers."

"What are you going to do with me?"

His brows went up. "You're free to go."

"Am I? And where is Macrae?"

"Ah, yes. The former federal agent. I haven't—yet—decided what I'm going to do with him."

A chill went through me.

"If I'm free to go, why isn't he? I assume you're holding him."

"Sentimental reasons, of course, er—Janet. Except that I remember you as Liz! If you want to go, go. You don't have to go through the front. Just use the French doors there!"

"I don't believe you! After all the following, all the interference, the kidnapping, you're just going to let me go?"

He shrugged. "Why don't you try it?"

I had walked around the desk to see the photographs, and I was now two feet from the French doors. The roses outside, of every color and type I had ever seen in an expensive florist, were beautiful and out of another world. Behind the arbors and rows red brick walls protected them.

"Your roses are lovely," I said.

"They're the other enthusiasm of my wife."

"The first being riding."

"Yes. We have a stable at the back."

"Why are we having this conversation, Jeff. It isn't real. I remember you when we were running from the police, pigs you called them."

"That was another time, another place. I thought you wanted to leave."

I knew I couldn't desert Mac, wherever he was, but my old claustrophobic fear of being trapped was pushing my hand towards the French door handle. After all, I thought, I could get the police to help me find him.

But when my hand was three inches from the door, I knew I couldn't run myself now, not without Mac. For a moment, as I stared at the door, fear shot through me. I snatched my hand away. I turned suddenly, and I saw the old Jeff, clever, manipulative, ruthless, staring at my hand. And I also knew that if I had touched that door handle I wouldn't be alive five minutes later.

28.

"If I'd touched that door," I said slowly, "I really would have escaped, wouldn't I—to another world?"

He sighed, reached into his jacket and pulled out a small revolver. "In the long run it would have been easier for you."

I stared at the revolver. How often in the past had I seen him with far larger weapons—big guns and pistols—in his hand!

"Why?" I said. "What happened to you? I know you, but I don't know you. What happened to the revolutionary, the terrorist on behalf of the people? The man who used to quote to me from—who was it? Franz Fanon—'Property is theft.'" I indicated the room and the garden. "You seem to be surrounded by a lot of theft. Who did you steal it from?"

"You know that old saying, Liz, 'There are more ways of killing a cat,' etc. Sometimes to destroy it, you have to join it."

"It being the establishment."

He smiled again, and for all the changes in his face and everything I now knew about him, the old charm was still there. At the same time as I felt it, I wondered how I could have missed seeing the evil also in him. "The capitalistic establish-ment," he said gently.

"You know, I don't believe you. I think you got tired of being a revolutionary. After all, it stopped being fashionable after the middle seventies. According to Ian Wilson, whom you seem to have in your pocket, you're going to be appointed to a vacated senatorial seat by the governor. What then, Jeff? The presi-dency?"

He didn't answer at first. Then, "You see now why I had to find you and stop you. You have an—unfortunate—memory."

"So did a lot of others. What did you do, get rid of all of them?"

"There weren't so many. Three died in the course of a few holdups and one thing and another. Two more went to jail and suffered unhappy accidents there. Our group was always small. So that left you."

"So you set out to find me."

"I didn't even have to do that. You did it for me." He grinned suddenly, and I knew he was the real Jeff, the one I remembered.

And suddenly I knew. "The *Newsweek* picture."

"One of the rising stars of publishing!"

"Did you kill Paul?"

"Again, not me personally. And it wasn't hard. Anybody who drank like that was an easy mark—to talk, to vent his grievances —mainly at you, but also the man he considered his rival—"

"Macrae."

"As you say."

"But why did you kill him?"

"Because he drank too much, and when he did, he talked too much. The night you ran out he followed his usual habit and went to his favorite bar. He drank some more and talked loudly to the guy, the man who'd become his buddy, his confidant, that we'd planted there. Then Paul started yelling about how he was fed up with faithless women and, almost without pausing, wanted to know why the hell our guy was so interested in you and had been asking all those questions about you. We decided the time had come to do something about his running off at the mouth that way. So our guy coaxed him back to your apartment. Then, when Paul provided him with all the excuse he needed by attacking him, the guy picked up a nearby knife and polished him off. Thus, if you'll excuse the expression, killing two birds with one stone. You should have been arrested. Unluckily, because of slow police work and your jumping around the country, you got away long enough for them to back off a little. Now I'm going to have to do the job."

Fascinated, I watched Jeff, his eyes never moving from me, his gun never wavering as he moved towards me and the desk. When he reached the front of it across from me, he slid his hand in the upper drawer and pulled out something I didn't recognize. But as he screwed it on the end of the gun's muzzle, I knew it was a silencer.

"I'll scream," I said.

"Nobody will hear you."

"What about your loving family?"

"All away, attending a horse show in another county. And the servants have the afternoon off, except for Matthews. And he had special training." He grinned again.

"And what do they think when you stay behind and the servants are let off?"

"Just that I'm hard at work on my career and am a generous employer."

I was putting my foot back an inch or so, backing just a little. "And how does your lady wife, the gardener and equestrian, deal with your double life?"

"Easily. She doesn't know it's double."

"What are you trying to do, burrow from within?"

"It worked for the barbarians, didn't it? The splendid Romans were so corrupt and effete and dedicated to pleasure—and drug ridden, for all I know—they couldn't be bothered to mind the store. So when the barbarians made their umpteenth raid on mighty Rome, their cousins—now most of the Roman army—let them in." Jeff laughed. "I was naive and young and in a hurry. I always thought the means of changing society was at the end of a gun or a bomb. Now I know better. It can be done by the right laws, or the right lobbying with the right people to effect or hold up the right laws so the drugs can come in. They'll do the job for us. Then, when people's morale, their ability to fight back, is destroyed, we can make the changes we want."

"And the nun was another impediment that had to be cleared away."

"She was going to find out for you where your daughter—possibly our daughter—was. I couldn't allow that."

"Why the hell not—what would it matter to you?"

"Before I knew I was going to have to kill you, I thought she might be a way to keep your mouth shut. If I found her first I could hold her safety over your head. After all, would you want her to know that she's the daughter of your father?"

"You don't know that."

He started to laugh. I remembered him laughing before. At that moment I'd have given anything—anything in the world—to be holding that gun. "You don't know that it isn't true, do you?" he said. "Then your federal snoop found her. That nice girl in Minnesota. But it was easy to get in touch with them and put the fear of God into them that she was going to be injured by a deranged natural mother."

"And one of your delegates was there, waiting for me."

"Yes, not the sharpest operator going. You got away."

My mind was working overtime. Obviously Jeff still thought she was my daughter. "So what are you going to do to her now?"

"Nothing. I don't have to. With you out of the way, there's no need, is there."

I became aware of a curious bumping.

"What's that?"

"What's what?"

"That bumping."

"You're imagining things." He sounded as completely in control as before but I knew he wasn't watching me as carefully as he had been and I slid back a few inches around the desk. He was now behind the desk and I was on the side.

"Slithering around's not going to do you any good," he said.

There was another muffled bump.

"I suppose Mr. Wilson was part of your plan."

"Of course. Before I knew where you were, it was the best way I could think of to find you and/or your daughter or both so I—er—insinuated the idea of such a search agency in his mind. It wasn't hard. Children frantically searching for their mothers, mothers searching for their children has great charitable appeal."

"Is he part of your master plan?"

"Don't be an idiot. That pious and not very bright priest? He was a sitting duck, waiting for me."

I prayed. I forgot my rage at God and the Church. Whether my prayer was answered or I was just lucky I don't know. But the phone rang. Jeff answered, his eyes still on me. "What?" he said. "What d'you mean?"

The paperweight was sitting there on top of a pile of letters marked with distinguished letter heads, "United States House of Representatives, United States Senate," and so on.

"But you couldn't really get started and appear on television till you had me settled, could you?" I said, moving forward, my eyes on the letters, edging back behind the desk. "You really are going to follow your master plan, aren't you?"

Then came my second stroke of luck. Suddenly Matthews came in. "Mr. Driscoll—" he said, alarm in his voice.

Jeff's attention went off me for a crucial second. I swung the paperweight with all my strength, blessing the fact that Jeff had never been more than an inch taller than I. I felt it crash onto his skull.

"Mr. Driscoll," the old butler screamed. But Jeff was lying across the desk and I had his gun in my hand.

"Move back, Matthews," I said.

He hesitated.

"Move back!"

He moved. I ran past. As I heard him behind me I turned and fired the gun, aiming at his leg, and not waiting to see if I had hit him. I went on going, up the imposing staircase and could hear him pounding behind me. Obviously, I hadn't hit him.

"Mac," I yelled as loud as I could. "Mac!"

When I got to the second floor the noise was unmistakable, a series of bumps and knocks. It came from one of the rooms off the upstairs hallway. As Matthews reached the top of the stairs, I turned and pushed and he fell backwards. Then I opened a door, saw nothing, and opened the next.

Mac was tied and lying on the floor, a piece of tape across his mouth.

I went over and ripped it off.

"Knife, in my pocket," he gasped. "Right pocket." I wasted valuable seconds trying to get it open, but eventually the blade emerged and I hacked at the rope around his hands. Then he took it from me and cut through the rope around his ankles.

"Driscoll?"

"I knocked him out, but I don't know how long he'll stay out."

He saw the gun I'd put down. "Okay. Let's go."

We started down the stairs. Sitting on the bottom, his head in his hands was Matthews. He started to rise.

"No. Stay where you are," Mac said. He made for the study door, with me behind him.

Driscoll, blood running down his neck, was rummaging in his desk drawer. When he heard us, he looked up. I saw the gun in his hand, a much bigger one than Mac had. "Drop it!" Mac yelled.

Jeff's hand jerked up.

I heard the booming noise of a shot. Jeff stared for a moment, then slumped forward.

"Mac—?" I said.

"Not Macrae, Ms. Covington, me," a voice drawled. And the long form of Sergeant Lowry appeared from behind Mac.

■ ▪ ■   "He got his money from drug dealing," I said to Mac, as the police were escorting us out of the house.

"Yes, I know."

"How on earth did you find out?"

"I talked to your friend Brett Cunningham, who, by the way, was doing intelligence work for the army when you and Jeff were trying to burn down the establishment. After we put a couple of things together and I got some help from people in the Bureau, it suddenly seemed obvious that it must be drugs that Jeff's extremely clean, well-washed money came from. And there was an awful lot of it. So I contacted the police here."

"You mean Jeff was operating in the spirit of 'If I can't bring down the capitalistic society one way, I'll try it another,'?" I said.

"Is that why he did it?" the sergeant asked.

"Maybe," Mac said, "along with enjoying the perks."

Suddenly I remembered Jeff counting some money that had come from a bank they'd held up. "Might as well enjoy the perks," he'd said.

"I remember," I said slowly.

"What do you remember?"

"I guess I remember most the contempt Jeff had for everybody, but mainly the ordinary people who did the country's work, paid its bills and fought its wars. Middle-class nerds and slobs, he used to call them. Which makes it even funnier about all his charitable work here."

"And anyway, can you think of a better smokescreen," Mac said.

There was a silence, then I said to the sergeant, "Well, are you going to arrest me?"

"What for?"

"For being a fugitive from the New York Police Department. Because I'm a fugitive, period, as I'm sure you know by now. And because I stole somebody's car."

"I don't think the NYPD are interested in you anymore. If they ever really were. They were pretty sure from the beginning that somebody else killed your—er—Paul Davenport. We know now it was one of Mr. Driscoll's henchmen. He accidentally left a fingerprint on the knife which the NYPD finally dug out of a garbage can on the next street. The blood matched and the fingerprint led us to who did it and was pointing the way up here when Mr. Macrae finally told us who did it and why."

"Then why did they make all that noise about arresting me?"

"Partly as a cover. But you notice that you weren't stopped at any of the places you could have been—various airports, the car rental agency, even the apartment of that crazy psychic."

I almost felt disappointment. "And I thought I was being clever. Did Mr. Wilson know any of this?"

"None," the sergeant said. "He was shocked and horrified after you left when we arrived and told him.

"And as for the older charges, of course I can't guarantee anything, but I've been led to believe that because of the help you're giving here, they might be dropped."

A huge weight was falling off me when the sergeant drawled, "Now about the theft of Mr. Higgins's car—"

To be jailed for that after having been let off all the rest was almost too much.

"Well?"

"We told him that since he'd ignored a whole bunch of tickets and been driving without a valid license, he'd be really silly to bring the matter up in court. The judge would probably excuse you as being under terrible pressure. But they'd have him. So he allowed as how he mightn't press the matter."

There was a silence. Insanely, I found myself thinking of Letty the psychic and my conviction when I was in the study that I shouldn't touch the French doors—rather like people who, without knowing why, canceled flights on planes that later crashed. "Was there something wrong with those French doors? The ones in the study. He offered to let me go out through them. In fact, he was trying to make me go out that way."

"Was he now? Well, something or somebody was watching over you. We have been told—we have reason to think—those doors are wired. If the switch in his desk was on, you'd be dead within fifteen seconds of touching the handle. If the switch was off you could go in and out. That garden of his, by the way, it's on top of a cellar the rest of the family doesn't know about, but we have reason to believe there are drugs there."

"How long have you known that?" Mac asked.

"A while. We have our sources of information. But to know is one thing and to do something about it, legally, is something else."

"So you knew that Jeff or James or whoever he was wasn't everything he seemed to be."

"We had our suspicions."

"But he was still going to run for office. What would you have done if he'd gotten that far?"

"Pray we had something we could use—legally."

There was a short silence. The sergeant said, "Seeing as how Mr. Macrae's car is in the garage being fixed after suddenly coming down with four flat tires when Matthews put it in the garage here, would you like us to drive you back to the motel?"

"I don't have a reservation," I said, almost crossly.

"We've made reservations for both you and Mr. Macrae. And we'll drive the car you rented there."

"You think of everything," I said. Relief was having a weird effect on me.

"Would you rather be arrested?" Mac asked.

"No. And what happened to you?"

"I'm ashamed of that. I went and bearded Driscoll and confronted him with some of the things I had learned. And I was in the middle of this when his butler, or whoever he was, knocked me out with a heavy cane. I didn't hear him come up behind. When I woke up I was as you found me. Not very heroic."

"Come on," the sergeant said. "We have a lot of work to do, and I daresay you wouldn't mind a good sleep."

"No," I said. "I wouldn't." I shouldn't have felt depressed, but I did. I had been let off a lot of hooks, but there was still a task in front of me which in some ways was more frightening than all the rest.

■ ■ ■ The police took us to the motel I'd been in before and the desk clerk handed us our keys looking as though butter wouldn't melt in his mouth.

The sergeant said, "Your car is outside when you want to go to the airport." He paused. "You might give a thought to talking to Mr. Wilson. He's in a state of shock, and is feeling conscience-stricken about letting himself get pushed by Driscoll into hurrying you out of town."

"I'd be curious to know what reason he gave Mr. Wilson."

"Apparently he hinted, more than hinted, that you weren't interested in finding your own child. That you were a reporter out to get a story, and a lot of his sources would dry up with the wrong publicity."

"He never missed a beat, did he?" I said wearily.

"Not until tonight."

"I wonder how come he didn't succeed in killing me."

"Overconfidence, I'd guess," the sergeant said. "If we turned up with a battalion, he'd probably have outsmarted us."

I remembered the scorn with which he treated my revolutionary efforts. "I'm sure you're right."

■ ■ ■ I thought the rooms would almost certainly turn out to be adjoining and was surprised when they were divided by a complete hall. I was ushered into mine, and my bag put on the rack.

I should, I thought, take a shower to ease some of the tension that seemed to focus on the muscles of my shoulders and back, to say nothing of my neglected ankle. And I spent some time sitting on my bed wondering why Jeff hadn't killed me when he had me in the car driving me home. Then I decided that it was too risky for him, out there in the countryside. Back in his castle he could arrange things more easily.

I should call Mr. Wilson, I thought. I should call Claire. I did none of this. I continued to sit on the bed and stare at the blank television screen.

After a while there was a knock on the door. I got up slowly and went to it. Mac was standing there. I stood back and he came in.

"I've come to thank you for saving my life, even though it does make me feel foolish."

"Why? Because in the best run adventures it's the hero who saves the heroine?"

"Something like that."

"It doesn't sound like you to let that jerk creep up behind you and hit you on the head."

"I was almost insane with worry so I wasn't minding things I knew perfectly well to mind."

"Worry about what?"

"About you. I thought he had you there in the house, and with all I'd learned about him, I didn't think he'd hesitate to cut your throat as well as Paul's."

His statement would have made me happier than I was if my task—of what I knew I had to do—weren't confronting me.

"Mac," I said. "There's something I have to tell you."

I stared up into his face and thought again how attractive it was.

"You don't have to tell me anything you don't want to," he said gently.

I closed my eyes. "I've always been afraid that my daughter was the . . . the result of my father's raping me." Having got that much out I raced on. "But although he did—assault—me, I did my best to make him. I mocked him and tantalized and enticed him. I always thought it was a final form of revenge. He was such a moralist. But what has made me feel sick all these years—in fact I buried it—I wanted him to." And I burst into tears. "I wanted him to," I repeated.

Then I was crying on Mac's chest as he held me and stroked my head. "I know."

"How the hell do you know?"

"Because your charming ex-boyfriend told or implied most of it. Apparently you told him once when you were drunk."

As in my dream, it was true. "Yes," I said, and sobbed some more. "I wanted him—my father—to love me. He never did. So it was, well, both getting what I wanted and revenge."

"I understand."

There was a long silence.

"You don't hate and despise me?"

"I love you. Didn't you know that?"

"I thought . . . I thought you didn't want me anymore."

"And I thought you didn't." His arms tightened around me. "Do you love me?"

"Yes, more than I ever have anybody. I couldn't love anybody because of what I just told you. Now I'm free to love. And I love you." The truth of what I'd just said swept over me. I tightened my arms around his neck. "I do," I said.

"Will you marry me?" he said.

"Yes. I will. Soon I hope."

He laughed and kissed me. Then he said, "And I have a wedding present for you."

"What?"

"This." He let go of me and put his hand in his inside pocket. What he brought out was a picture of a girl of about eighteen. Her hair was lighter than mine but in all other ways she looked like a strange cross of Jeff and me.

My eyes filled with tears. "Where did you get it?"

"Through that friend in Boston. Your father put her with a cousin of his former secretary. If she had lived, Sister Mary Joseph might have learned that from one of the nurses who remembered Martha. Anyway, this came after my apartment was ransacked, I'm sure at Driscoll's order. So he didn't get it. But I couldn't get hold of you, and I was very sure you didn't want me to try. So I was going to send it to you. By the way, my informant told me that the girl, your daughter, is well aware she was adopted, so you shouldn't have any problem in talking to her."

I stared at it and felt the tears coming down my cheeks, tears of relief, gratitude and affection. "How can I thank you," I said.

"I'll tell you a variety of ways, after we're married."

"Being so bent on marriage sounds so old-fashioned."

"Is that bad?"

"No. It's perfect."

About the Author

Isabelle Holland was born in Switzerland, the daughter of an American diplomatic officer. She was educated in England and the United States and spent a number of years in publishing before turning to writing as a career. She is the author of more than a dozen suspense novels, including five earlier novels set in St. Anselm's parish, and has written a number of books for young readers. She lives in New York.